Last Laugh in the Halls

By

Angela Chapman

"Last Laugh in the Halls" by Angela Jobe Chapman, ISBN 978-0-9845362-0-7

Published 2010 by Fire Pit Creek Publishing, 31208 E. Heidelberger Rd. Buckner Mo 64016 US. ©2010, Angela Jobe Chapman. All rights reserved. No part of this publication may be reproduced, stored in a retrieval system, or transmitted in any form or by any means, electronic, mechanical, recording or otherwise, without the prior written permission of Angela Jobe Chapman.

www.firepitcreek.com

Book cover designed by: Brady Jobe

Edited by: Candy Myers

Manufactured in United States of America

To my husband—David
Thanks to my loving husband for all his support and love.

CHAPTER ONE

Wednesday, April 21, 2001

David let the front screen door slam behind him as he hurried into the kitchen. He dropped his school bag on the cluttered table and darted straight to the cabinet. He stood on his tiptoes and grabbed a glass off the middle shelf. The glasses that usually set on the bottom shelf were dirty and heaped in a pile in the sink. His mother never had time to wash the dishes anymore, and there was no way he was going to do it. He didn't mind any of the other housework, but he loathed washing dishes. Luckily, his mother never pressured him to do them.

David snatched the ice tray out of the refrigerator and dropped a few cubes into the glass. He ran his tongue over his cracked lips, anticipating how good the cold tea would taste. The shuffling sound from his mother in the next room made him quicken his pace. He hurriedly filled the tray with water and set it back in the freezer.

He glanced toward the apple-shape clock on the wall. It was almost time for her second job. He was hoping to get down to his own room before she could start her usual every-day nagging.

It was too late—she'd heard him come in.

"David, is that you?" Ann stood in the doorway arch, jabbing at her ear with a pierced earring. "How was school today?"

"It was okay." David reached for the pitcher of tea in the refrigerator and poured it over the crackling ice. He gulped down half the glass in one swallow. "Ahhh—this hits the spot."

"Do you have a lot of homework?" She asked while fastening the back of her earring.

"Not too much." David avoided his mother's gaze as he grabbed his school bag off the table. He headed toward the stairs that led to his bedroom in the basement.

"Did you sign up for the Science club yet?"

"No." He moaned impatiently. "I decided I didn't want to belong in that after all." He stopped midway down the stairs, spun around, and glared at his mom as if to finalize the conversation.

"And why not? You need to get involved in some kind of activity. All you want to do is lie around in your room and play on the Internet. It's not good for you!"

David rolled his eyes. "Mom, don't start on me."

"Well, it's not good for a teenager to never want to do anything." Ann glanced toward the clock while pulling her lengthy dark hair into a ponytail and securing it by twisting a rubber band around it. "I have to go, or I'm going to be late for work. There're plenty of TV dinners and pot pies in the fridge."

"Are you coming home after work?" David was sure he knew the answer. She was never home anymore—she was always working or out with her idiot boyfriend.

"I doubt it. Roy wants to take me out for a little while. I won't be late, though." Ann reached for her purse on the kitchen table and trotted down the stairs to plant a quick kiss on David's forehead. "Don't wait up for me." She jogged back up the stairs and turned back. "Oh, make sure you keep the doors locked. Grace said there was another break in up the street last night. I swear this neighborhood is getting crappier every day." Ann glanced back toward the clock. "Got to run." She swung the purse strap over her shoulder and scurried toward the front of the house.

David tossed his bag on his bed and cranked up the stereo before settling into the swivel chair in front of the computer. He had been anxious all day for school to let out so he could log into

5

the chat room and talk to Eliza, a girl he had met a few months earlier. She had just recently emailed him a picture of herself, posing with her black poodle. She appeared to be a trouble-free girl with short-layered brown hair, dark eyes, and a few freckles sprinkled on each cheek. She was an attractive girl with a smile that was mesmerizing. Every time he admired her picture his eyes were drawn to her mouth. He had never seen such a flawless smile. Her rosy lips were full, and her teeth couldn't be straighter.

Eliza had been the one to introduce him to the coolest website ran by Professor Slate. He couldn't thank her enough for all that she had done for him.

David quickly located her online and pressed the private button so no one else could monitor his conversation.

Hello, Eliza. Did you have a good day?

Hi, David. I had a wonderful day! One of my teachers started chewing me out for no reason at all, so I told her to F---- ----. Fill in those blanks if you can. LOL. Anyway, I walked out of school and then I let the air out of one of her tires before coming home.

No way! David typed.

I did. I just got up, collected my books off the desk, and walked out. She started yelling at me to get back in the classroom, but I just kept walking. That will teach the bitch to mess with me.

Will you get in trouble from your mom? David knew from his past conversations with Eliza that she was always in the doghouse, and Professor Slate was always bailing her out.

Yeah, I'm sure I will be. I don't care, though. I'll just go live with Professor Slate again.

Does he really let you stay with him any time you want?

Of course he does. And when I stay at his pad, I have my own private maid and room service. He's the greatest! Don't you think he's wonderful?

Yeah, I do. I wish I could meet him, though. I'm so glad you told me about his website.

Has he given you any special assignments, yet?

6

David hesitated—he knew his assignment was supposed to be confidential. *Yeah, he has, but I can't talk about it.*

I understand. He has only had me to do one assignment, but it was so cool. After I was done, he took me on a cruise to the Bahamas.

No kidding! Your mom let you go? David couldn't believe the Professor was so hip.

Of course not—that was just another time I ran away. LOL. My mom says if I run away one more time, she's going to put me in a juvenile home.

Do you think she means it?

Maybe. Who cares, though? I won't go! I'll just stay with Professor Slate until she changes her mind and begs me to come home.

What does Professor Slate think about you running away so much? David was thrilled Professor Slate had picked him and Josh for the next assignment.

He's just fantastic about it. He said my mother shouldn't treat me like a child so much, now that I am almost an adult. He says I should be allowed to make my own decisions in life. The professor says my mom is too controlling and doesn't want her baby girl to grow up. He thinks she might be jealous of my youth and that is why she is so manipulating.

David reached for his Bon Jovi CD and positioned it in his CD player. *Wow, I bet you're glad you have him on your side.* He drummed his fingers against the desk while waiting for Eliza to write.

He is the best thing that has ever happened to me. I would do anything for him because I know he would for me, too.

I hope that one day he likes me as much as he does you.

David, believe me, he will. He loves all of his students. He has brought your name up several times. He thinks you're going to be a huge success.

Really?

Oh yeah! He said you're just what he has been looking for. Hey, I have to go. I might be back on later.

Okay, thanks Eliza, for everything.

You're welcome. Talk to you later.

David leaned back in the chair and smiled. Talking to Eliza warmed his insides. She always knew how to say the right words to lift his spirits unlike his mother, who was always complaining about everything he did. He would rather be talking on the Internet to his friends than sitting in some tedious Science club meeting.

He couldn't understand why his mother just didn't accept him for the way he was. School was for the bright students who planned on going to college. It wasn't for peons like himself, who'd never amount to anything anyway. Besides, there wasn't any way his mother would ever be able to afford to send him to college. He was certain he would end up with some lousy job picking up garbage or working in a backbreaking factory loading boxes.

David kicked his shoes off and finished the last of his tea. He sucked an ice cube into his mouth, rotating it back to his jaw teeth and chomping down. He loved the crunching sound and the feel of the freezing crushed ice across his tongue. It reminded him of a rare occasion when he was small, and his mother had bought him a snow cone at the school carnival. He'd been so impressed with the sound that the ice had made as he chomped that he'd shoveled it down way too fast which resulted in a sudden headache.

David propped his opposite foot upon his knee and leaned forward. He was anxious to check Professor Slate's website to see if he had any new messages.

***

Professor Slate tossed his head back and laughed callously. He had more fun pretending to be rebellious young teenage girls. He often wondered if he should have been an actor instead of a computer genius. He would have been superb at it, but it wouldn't be near as much fun as this was. It had been easy for him to portray Eliza and coax David right into his clever trap. He had David believing that him and Eliza lived in Fargo, Idaho, when he was actually in Shelby, Idaho, the same town as David.

8

The little black poodle barking at the basement door forced the professor's attention back to the present. The mutt had been barking ever since Professor Slate had run across him and his owner, and it was really starting to annoy the hell out of him. "Shut up." He waited a few seconds for the dog to quiet down, but it continued to yelp. "I said shut up." Professor Slate rose from his chair and came within reach of the dog—he gave the small creature a swift kick in his side. The dog whimpered and bowed his head before limping off to a corner to lie down.

Professor Slate didn't have much patience when it came to animals. He'd hated the repulsive little monsters as long as he could remember.

He only had one fond memory of ever liking an animal. It was when he was four years old—he wanted a puppy and told Santa Clause that was the only thing he wanted for Christmas. Santa delivered him a puppy that year and the professor was ecstatic. It was the cutest little beagle named Snoopy. For two weeks, the puppy was the highlight of the professor's days. He would wake up every morning anxious to crawl out of bed, so he could play with his new friend.

But his jubilation didn't last long. One morning after the professor was scolded for wetting the bed, he was sent to his room for the day without being allowed to play with Snoopy. The following morning he woke up extra early, eager to play with the pup, but his father told him Snoopy had ran away because puppies didn't like little boys who wet the bed. It was the last dog Professor Slate ever had or wanted.

As he grew up, he found other uses for small animals such as target practice with rocks or sticks. He liked to shoot his BB gun at birds, although he was never too good at it. Once he took his neighbor's cat and threw it in the refrigerator in his basement for a few hours. The cat went nuts when the professor finally opened the door. It pounced on him, scratching his face. The professor caught the ferocious creature, hit it in the head with a hammer, and tossed it in the middle of the road so his neighbors would think a car killed it.

9

When he was sent away to a private school, all the other boys would talk about their pets they had left behind. The professor never understood how they could miss the horrible beasts.

Professor Slate sighed as the images from his past diminished. He knew the reason why the mutt kept barking at the basement door. He glanced toward the digital clock on the desk before strolling into the kitchen. He was certain she would be hungry. The professor made a peanut butter sandwich, grabbed a glass, and filled it with water. He made his way to the basement door and slowly opened it. He peered down the stairs into the darkness; the silence from below troubled him. He quickly flipped on the light. The black mutt came running up behind him, and he hurriedly slipped through the door, pulling it shut before the dog could slither through. He slowly moved down the steep stairs, stepping carefully on each one. It was an older house and the worn wooden stairs squeaked with every step.

Professor Slate approached the bottom stair and immediately spotted her huddled in the dark corner. She hadn't moved any further than where he had left her. She had her knees drawn up to her chest in a fetal position. The rhythmic movement of her upper body confirmed she was breathing. She still had the blindfold around her eyes, and her hands and feet were still bound together with rope. Her short hair hung limply around her delicate freckled face.

Professor Slate grasped her shoulders and pulled her up into a sitting position. He yanked the tape off her mouth. Her tongue darted over her dry, cracked bleeding lips. He was certain that she wouldn't try screaming again. He had warned her earlier if she screamed anymore, he would kill her dog. That had gotten her attention—she begged him not to hurt Taffy.

Professor Slate lifted the glass to her lips, and she swallowed in big gulps, not caring that it was spilling down the front of her dirt-stained blouse. In a small, weak voice the girl asked, "Where's Taffy? You didn't hurt him, did you?"

"Not yet. If he doesn't stop barking—he might be your next meal."

The girl shivered. "Please, don't hurt him—please, let us go. I won't tell anyone anything. I promise."

10

"Shut up!" He untied the rope around her wrists.

She repeatedly massaged her hand over her bruised wrists.

He left the blindfold over her eyes and thrust the sandwich into her trembling hand. "Eat this, or you won't get any more food."

The girl hesitated and then raised the sandwich to her lips. She nibbled cautiously on the edge of the crust. After a few seconds, she shoved the rest of it in her mouth, chewing hungrily.

Professor Slate figured she should be famished—the last few times he'd brought food down to her, she'd refused to eat. He tried forcing her to eat, but she only spat it out on the floor. She never refused the water, though. She always acted as if she was dying of thirst, letting it dribble out of her mouth as she drank.

Professor Slate waited until she'd finished chewing the sandwich and then brought the glass back up to her lips. She guzzled the remaining water down in one gulp. He replaced the rope back around her wrists and tightened the ends into knots. She didn't try to fight him this time like she'd done previous times before. He tore some new duct tape off the roll and placed it over her mouth. Wet tears escaped from underneath the blindfold and slid down her cheeks. He knew she was getting weaker, and he was sure she wouldn't put up a fight much longer.

His mind drifted to the time his father had locked him in a closet down in a basement, similar to this one. It was on his tenth birthday. He'd started crying because his father promised him a birthday present but then didn't get him one. The professor knew that it wasn't because they hadn't any money—his folks were beyond wealthy. They lived in an up market house and feasted on fancy dinners every evening.

His mother was out at the Country Club with a friend that particular night, so he was home alone with his father. His father grew angry at the professor's temper tantrum. The professor could remember his father screaming and shaking his fist at the ceiling. He kept cursing and repeating, "Why me, God?"

His father had grabbed the professor's hair and yanked him toward the basement stairs. He'd drug him down the flight of

11

stairs, despite the professor's pleading. He had told the professor that when children reach the age of ten, the devil tries to conquer their soul and force kids to do sinful acts. He'd said that God intended children to be punished every time they cried because it was the only way to scare the devil out of the children.

He had shoved the professor into a dark closet, locked the door, and left him for over three hours.

Professor Slate had always remembered that birthday. It was the beginning of the worst three abusive years of his life. He never understood how his parents could be so caring while he was young, and so heartless as he grew older. His mother wasn't as bad, but she still always took his father's side—if she was even at home. It seemed like she was always at the Country Club.

The professor tried once telling his mother about his father's aggression. But instead of compassion like he'd expected, she scolded him and told his father which triggered another beating. After that, he was certain his mother didn't love him anymore than his father did. All she cared about was socializing with her friends and partying.

Professor Slate started to believe his father and wondered if he really was possessed by the devil.

He was shipped off to a private school at the early age of thirteen. At least there weren't any dark closets or leather belts there. But his father's words still hung over his head. The professor alleged he was past the age of eighteen before the devil finally left him alone and went on to torment another child.

Professor Slate suddenly snapped back to the present and peaked one last time at the girl huddled in the corner. He grasped the railing and slowly edged his way back up the aged stairs.

He knew he didn't have any use for the girl anymore. She'd served her purpose. He'd found her and her poodle at the City Park, and approached her disguised as a professional photographer. He convinced her that she was model material, and she'd been thrilled to come back to his house to take some photographs. It had been that simple. Professor Slate had used her to take digital pictures to convince David that Eliza existed. Now he didn't need her any more, but he couldn't just let her go.

She'd already seen his face and knew where he lived. Professor Slate couldn't afford any careless mistakes linking back to him.

He'd kept her in the basement for a few days while trying to decide what he should do with her. He finally decided he would have Slug dispose of her and her prized dog.

He hurriedly closed the door to the basement and crossed the room toward the phone near the computer. He called Slug to confirm he would be over tomorrow to pick them up.

Professor Slate glanced toward the yelping mutt. He was back at the basement door, barking like he'd seen a ghost. The professor inhaled a deep breath and released it slowly. He closed his eyes, threw his head back, and massaged his temples with his fingertips, trying to prevent the oncoming headache. He traced his fingers gently around his receding hairline as he rubbed. The professor slowly opened his eyes and studied the reflection in the mirror hanging over the computer. His hair was definitely thinning. He already had a bald strip down the center, and now the salt and pepper strands were starting to fall out on the sides, too. His eyes shifted to his protruding nose—it seemed as if the more hair he lost, the longer his nose grew.

The Professor knew he was ugly. He always had looked like some kind of creature from a lagoon. He had bulging eyes, a monstrous nose, and deep pits scattered across his face. No wonder children stared at him in the grocery stores.

When he was in school, the kids used to call him all sorts of names: Beetle Eyes, Pinocchio, and even Frankenstein. He had a new nickname almost every week. However, now it made sense—all those evil kids were possessed by the devil!

He turned away from the appalling image in the mirror and glared at the barking dog. Just the sight of the disgusting little critter made him ill. He was also getting tired of having to take him outside to potty. The professor decided he might not be able to wait another day until Slug arrived. If the mutt didn't shut up soon, he was going to put him in the bathtub and teach him how to swim. He smiled at the thought of the pleasure he would have—drowning the hideous beast.

13

CHAPTER TWO

Thursday, April 22, 2001

It was time for Cally's last and final stunt. She'd been worried all day about her performance. She took a deep breath and exhaled slowly as she tried to relax. She found her position on the floor and placed her feet a few inches apart. She gracefully slid her arms down to her sides and glanced toward the judges. "Judges ready?"

When the judges acknowledged they were ready by nodding, she turned her concentration back to the floor in front of her. She extended her hands above her head, returning them to her sides slowly. Suddenly, she sprinted at a fast pace, twisting her body around into a front flip, right into a round-off, and without any hesitation, she ended with a back flip, landing with both feet together facing the judges. The crowd went up in cheers. Cally couldn't have been more satisfied.

She gained her composure as the applauding ceased and walked toward the judges. "Thank you for judging."

The woman that was in charge spoke for the rest of them. "You're welcome. It was our pleasure. Good job on your back flip, great landing." The other judges nodded and murmured some kind of approval.

"Thank you." Cally was thrilled at their reaction. She'd been so nervous.

The cheerleading sponsor dismissed all the girls. "Don't forget to be back in one hour and no later!"

Cheerleading tryouts were finally over, and Cally couldn't have been more relieved. Although it was only April, they were already trying out for cheerleader for the following year.

She'd been working hard every evening for the last two weeks. She had mastered a variety of jumps, along with a dozen different cheers, memorized a dance routine, and had done numerous acrobatic stunts. She truly did enjoy cheerleading—she was just worn-out and needed a break from it. Her body could only take so much.

Now they would have an hour to wait while the judges tallied up the score sheets. She had desperately wanted to be a football cheerleader this past season, but last spring she'd caught the flu, missed a whole week of school, and wasn't able to try out. She'd been so disappointed. Her two best friends had made it and had an exciting time cheering for the varsity team. Cally had sat on the sidelines, enviously. She'd wanted so much to be a part of the squad.

Cally's parents were exceptionally strict about her grades so they limit her extracurricular activities. She wanted to try out for football and wrestling cheerleader—that way if she didn't make football, she could still make wrestling. However, her parents were worried she might make both and not have time to concentrate on her schoolwork. Despite all of her pleading, Cally lost out and had to choose just one. She knew that football cheerleader was much more difficult to make but that was what she wanted the most.

Liz slipped up behind Cally and swatted her across the back with a towel. "Hey, showoff, where did you learn to do a back flip?" She grinned and shoved the towel into her gym bag. "That was awesome! You have been holding out on us, and your jumps were perfect, especially the American Eagle!"

"I didn't decide to do the back flip until today. I was scared I would fall on my face, but I pulled it off somehow. Thanks for the compliment. You did a good job too," Cally tried to sound sincere, although she knew Liz had messed up on the dance routine. She sucked her lower lip in between her teeth and

15

chewed nervously—an annoying habit she had picked up at the beginning of the year.

"Yeah, well, I won't hold my breath on getting anything, not after watching how good everyone else was. Anyway, thanks and good luck. I'll see you in an hour." She disappeared down the hall.

For once, Cally was glad she attended a small school—it would help broaden her chances.

Shelby was a small, picturesque town with a population of twenty-one thousand in a rural area of Idaho. The high school had only 965 students. Cally knew all the other classmates moderately well or at least recognized most of them in the halls.

The school was newer, built only two years earlier. It had the more modern up-to-the-minute features. There were fifty-six different dimension sized rooms along with a huge octagon gym, a spacious library, and a five-hundred-seat auditorium. The restroom stools flushed by themselves, and the water turned on automatically when you stuck your hands under the faucet.

The school had three entrances to the building. The glass double doors on the side were the ones most all of the students used because the parking lot was on the side of the building along with the buses. The front door was only used for visitors and teachers. The opposite side entrance was used occasionally by students who were dropped off by their parents.

Cally's best friends, Jessie and Beth, were waiting by her locker.

Jessie was the first to speak, "Cally, you were amazing! I really think you have a good chance at making it."

Beth added playfully, "You'll probably make it, and we won't!"

"I don't look for that to happen. Remember you guys are the ones with the experience, not me. However, thanks all the same." Cally spun the combination on her locker and jerked it open. "Hey, I think I worked up an appetite for a chocolate shake. Anyone else?" Cally pulled the rubber band out of her hair and shook her head vigorously, letting the natural blond curls fall over her shoulders.

16

"That's a brainless question—I'm officially off my diet now. I'm starving. Let's go!" Beth flung her gym bag over her shoulder.

Cally grabbed her purse from her locker, kicked the door shut, and led the way down the hall. She was so busy discussing tryouts that she didn't see the kid coming around the corner until it was too late—she collided with him, knocking his gym bag out of his hand. "I'm so sorry—I didn't see you."

"Okay," the kid muttered as he snatched his bag from the floor. He lowered his blushing cheeks toward the floor and continued toward the glass doors.

Cally cursed silently at herself for her clumsiness. She reached for the car keys in her purse as she stared curiously ahead at the kid hurrying toward the double doors. She tried to recollect who he was but couldn't remember ever seeing him before. He was a petite, skinny kid with untamed reddish-brown hair, similar to the color of autumn leaves. An out-dated pair of silver wire-framed glasses fit snuggly over his pug nose. His jeans were faded and a tad bit short, and his solid blue t-shirt was wrinkled.

She assumed he was a freshman. With Cally being a junior now, she had a hard time keeping up with all the underclassmen.

The kid hadn't been a bit friendly—almost as if he was annoyed with her. It perturbed Cally at first. She wasn't used to underclassmen being so rude. Most of them respected the juniors and seniors. She shrugged. Maybe, he was just shy.

She grinned silently as she recalled Beth's teasing about how she was always trying to analyze everyone. Beth always bragged how fortunate she was to have her own private psychologist. Cally had to admit she did enjoy listening to her friends' problems and trying to solve them. Maybe Beth was right. Maybe she should go into psychology.

She suddenly forgot the kid as her mind raced back to the tryouts and the judge's scores. In an hour, she would either be extremely happy or very disappointed.

17

***

David rushed through the double doors just as his friend Josh was pulling up in his black 1992 Ford Escort.

"Hurry up—get in!" Josh yelled.

"Okay—okay." David dumped his bag in the back seat and jumped into the passenger seat.

"Did anyone see you?"

"Just some stupid bitch, who wasn't watching where she was going and her stupid-ass pom-pom friends." David pulled his glasses off and tossed them on top of his bag. He rubbed his nose where they had left a crease. He was glad he didn't have to wear them all the time.

"Super! Why didn't you check the halls first?" Josh smacked the steering wheel. "You could have waited until they left the building!"

David rolled down the window and spat. "Well, I sure didn't see you volunteering to go in, did I?" He rolled his eyes. "Let's just get the hell out of here."

The Escort accelerated as Josh pulled out of the parking lot.

Although they bickered like brothers, David Clemons and Josh Petty had been best friends since the beginning of the school year.

David wished he had his driver's license, but he was only a freshman, and probably would never have a car anyway. He was thankful that Josh was old enough to drive, even though Josh sometimes liked to throw his weight around since he was a sophomore. David was still glad he didn't have to ride the bus any longer and be tormented by hoodlums.

"Watch out!" David yelled as Josh pulled out in front of Dodge pickup.

The elderly man in the other vehicle shook his fist in anger.

"Fuck you too, Mister." Josh mouthed to the guy.

"You trying to kill me?" David wiped his brow. Josh had only been driving for a month and sometimes it was obvious. Josh's father had made a special trip down from Wisconsin to bring him the car for his birthday which was extremely unusual because Josh hadn't seen much of his dad since his parents had divorced.

18

After a few miles, Josh pulled the car up in David's driveway. "Is it okay to park here or will your mom be coming home soon?"

David grabbed his bag out of the back seat. "You're kidding me, right? You really think you will still be here when my mom gets home. Did you forget she took that other job at The Diner?"

"Oh yeah, that's right. Well, I guess she won't get to see your future father as much." Josh grinned.

"Whatever! That man will never be my daddy. I'll blast him away first." David pulled the key out of his bag and unlocked the front door. "Besides, my mom said she wasn't ever going to get married."

"Well, I hope for your sake she means it. I'd hate to see you get too distressed before our mission is completed."

"Oh, believe me, there's no way I'm screwing this up." David poured two glasses of tea and handed a glass to Josh. He grabbed the bag of potato chips from the counter and nodded toward the stairs for Josh to follow him.

David's small room was artistically decorated in black. He'd painted the top half of the walls black and left the remaining bottom half white. He'd spray-painted his entire garage sale furniture glossy black. Posters of Kid Rock and other rocks stars were plastered to his walls. His mother had let him decorate the room however he'd wanted. The only time she ever came downstairs was to look for something, and she was never concerned how it looked. He didn't even have to keep it clean. His laundry was piled high in the corner of the room while other clean shirts were scattered across the floor. He usually would go through two or three shirts in the morning, trying to decide which one was less wrinkled. He'd then discard the unwanted shirts on the floor, where they would remain until the next time he needed them. Potato chip crumbs were scattered on the discolored gray carpet around the computer, and the dust on the furniture was thick enough to write your name in it.

Ann Clemons had never married, and David never knew who his father was because his mother refused to talk about it. If David would ask about his father, his mom would get upset and change the subject.

19

His mom worked a forty-hour week in a large expanding factory, sewing sports coats. And recently, she'd taken on another job as a part-time waitress at The Diner. David knew he'd being seeing her even less now. He never saw her much anyway, so it really didn't matter to him. When she did have time off, she'd spend it with Roy—an asshole she'd met at a bar.

David couldn't stand him—he didn't know how to keep a job and was always mooching off his mother. David insisted on staying downstairs every time Roy came to the house to avoid looking at the creep.

David dropped his school bag and headed straight to the computer. He kicked his shoes off while pushing the power on and connecting to the Internet. Josh pulled up the only extra chair in the room and sat down beside him. David went straight to the address bar and entered the web page address he had been entering for the last few months.

"Don't forget to tell him about my computer," Josh said.

"I won't." David waited until the web page of the 'Hidden Undertakers' was fully loaded. He typed in his password and started typing.

Professor Slate:
I did as you said and checked the boys' room out today. There is a vent in the back stall that has four screws in it. Everything is going as planned. Let me know what to do next. Scooby blew up his hard drive and won't be able to email you for a while. I'll have to relay your messages to him.
Smurf

Smurf was David's secret code name. The professor selected the name because he said Smurf was an intelligent and smooth character that he felt David could relate to.

David flipped the TV on a news channel while waiting for his message to send. He read all his e-mails and then spun toward Josh, who was browsing through CD's. "All we can do now is wait."

David shifted his attention to the newscaster's pulsating voice. He hurriedly grabbed the remote and turned up the volume.

20

The newscaster repeated, *"Again, there has been another tragic school shooting. It happened this afternoon in the town of Monte, Illinois, a small town thirty miles north of Chicago. A sixteen-year-old boy opened fire at the public high school. He killed three people and injured eight more before he was apprehended. We do not know the motive at this time, but we will keep you posted."* The camera man suddenly zoomed in on a thin boy with long, scraggily dyed black hair, pierced earrings through his nose and eyebrows, dressed in baggy blue jeans and black t-shirt, being handcuffed and shoved into the back of a patrol car.

David's heart raced. "No way—look at him! He's not even sweating—that is one smooth hero. Kill the freaking enemies! You rule!" He held up a thumbs-up sign. He could easily relate to the kid—his classmates probably harassed him all the time like they do him. David knew how frustrating it was to be made fun of day after day. He wondered why the kid didn't have a good escape plan.

Josh high-fived David. "He should have smashed all of those ass-holes. Just think how much he would rule then." His face turned serious. "Do you think he is part of it?"

"I don't know, maybe." David wiped the sweat off his hands onto his jeans. "Hey, you still got my Korn CD?" David picked up his ACDC tape and shoved it into the CD player. He cranked the music and started jumping around like he was playing a guitar.

Josh shouted over the music, "Oh yeah, I have it. It's at home. I'll bring it by tomorrow. Speaking of home, I need to head that way." Josh stood and stretched. "Call me if you get an email from Professor Slate tonight." Josh started up the stairs.

"I will. Don't forget my CD!" He grinned. "You know I can't function without listening to my music before I fall asleep."

Josh spun around. "Okay, I won't. Don't forget to swear to secrecy—only to the mission—no matter what."

"To the mission," David made an X across his chest with his pinky finger. "See you later, Scooby." Scooby was Josh's secret code name. They all had code names of fictional characters. The

21

name was given to Josh because the professor thought he was responsible and had a good sense of humor.

Professor Slate was the head-honcho of the 'Hidden Undertakers'. David respected him highly, although he hadn't met him yet. He'd been the only person to express interest in David's future. At least he saw David with potential unlike his mom.

"Okay, Smurf—later. I'll lock the front door on the way out," Josh called back.

David settled back in front of the computer screen and logged back into the chat room to see if Eliza was online. After a few minutes, he located her.

Hello Eliza. Are you chatting with someone else right now?

Hi, David. I was, but I can always chat with him later. I would rather chat with you anyway.

David's stomach tightened. *Did you get in trouble for leaving school yesterday?*

Yeah, I did. My mom can be a real bitch sometimes. I hate her. Is your mom nice?

If you can call her a mom at all! She could care less about me. She's always with her idiot boyfriend. David crammed a hand full of chips in his mouth.

Oh, yuck! You got one of those kind of moms—they act like you don't exist! Well, if you ever need to get away, let me know.

Really? Where would we go? We have so many miles between us. David knew Eliza was from Fargo, a town over an hour away from him.

Don't worry. We can always meet up and go stay with Professor Slate.

David's smile widened. *That would be fun! I'll keep that in mind.*

Any time you want, just let me know. I can run away any day and skip school whenever I like. I'm as free as a bird. LOL

I'm fed up with school and my mom. David's enthusiasm increased with every key he punched.

Well, soon, we'll have to do this! Hey, a friend just came over, and we're going to go get high. So, I'll chat with you later.

Okay. Talk to you later. He punched his hand through the air. "Yes!" he said aloud.

He shut the TV off and cranked the volume on the stereo—he didn't want to miss any of the chords from the lead guitar. He leaned back in the chair so he could prop his feet upon the desk and drum his thumbs to the rhythm against his thighs.

He thought Eliza was one of the wildest girls he'd ever met, but that's what he liked about her. She was different from any girl he knew, even though he really didn't know many girls. He couldn't believe that she actually wanted him to hang out with her and the professor. David wondered what life would be like to live with Professor Slate. He figured it would be awesome. He'd already heard so many positive things about him. The times David had spent with him on the Internet had already proved what a good guy he was.

***

Cally agreed to drive her car to The Diner since her back seat was already cleaned out. Her parents had agreed to buy her a good quality car as long as she helped pay for the gas. She'd selected a 1996 red Nissan with bucket seats and took on a part-time job at The Diner to make the extra money.

The Diner originally was named The Palace Café. However, some high school kids thought that it was a corny name and nicknamed it The Diner. Before long everyone was referring to it as The Diner. Just recently, the owners caved in and officially changed the name. It was different in many ways from the usual café. Not only did it have the biggest tenderloins ever made and the creamiest milk shakes, but it also had all the necessities needed for social gatherings: pool tables, pinball machines, and a jukebox that played all the latest hits.

Usually Cally only worked weekends. However, lately they had been short on help so she'd agreed to help some after school. The owners were more than understanding when it came to Cally needing off for school events or personal matters.

23

The best thing about working at The Diner was that all the high school kids hung out there after school, plus the tips were fairly good.

Cally pulled up to The Diner and parked the car. The parking lot was already crowded. She hoped there would be an empty table, so they wouldn't have to wait. She didn't want to miss the announcement of the new cheerleaders, especially if one of the names called was her own.

"Hey, Cally, isn't that Brad's car?" Jessie pointed to a black camaro across the parking lot.

"Ha ha, like you didn't know that." Cally grinned. "Don't you guys dare embarrass me in here, pretty please." She held her hands in a praying position.

"It depends if I get to pick out the movie on Saturday." Beth giggled and opened the café door.

They quickly spotted an empty table in the back corner of the room where they could watch the boys play pool while they were eating. Jessie volunteered to place their order at the counter to speed up the service.

"Hey, Mark," Beth shouted, "I bet you're losing."

Cally grinned and slid into the booth. It didn't surprise her that Beth was already harassing the guys. She was the comical one, always bantering with her friends. If Beth weren't picking on someone, you'd think she was sick. She was known for her outspoken personality.

Her nickname was Sweet Potato because of her lustrous red hair. A name she'd carried since she was in the seventh grade. Marty Lewis had called her Carrot Top in school one day, and she'd replied with sarcasm, *'Oh boy, that's funny—like I've never heard that before.'* Tony Wilkerson just happened to be standing behind her and commented, *'Yeah, her real name is Sweet Potato.'* Everyone laughed, and the name stuck with her ever since.

Mark strutted toward Beth, twirling the pool stick between his fingers. He stopped a few inches from her and shoved the pool stick in her hand. "I just won, Sweet Potato. Would you like to challenge me?" He asked tauntingly.

Brad and Jeff crept up behind Mark to eavesdrop on the conversation.

"Well, you know, Mark, I'd love to, but I've got to get back to the school shortly to see if I will be cheering on the side lines for your *winning* football team next year." Beth smirked.

Everyone laughed—Shelby High had only won two games during the past season.

"Any other time I would be glad to show you how to play pool." Beth tossed the pool stick in Mark's direction, and Mark quickly reached for it before it hit the floor.

Cally and Jessie applauded.

Brad slapped Mark on the back. "Whoa, I guess she told you."

"Yeah, and who did you just lose to?" Mark's eyes narrowed. "That's what I thought."

"Actually I let you win that last game so you wouldn't throw one of your temper tantrums," Brad said.

Jeff spun toward the girls and threw his hands up in the air. "See what I have to put up with."

The waitress hurriedly brought the girls' order to the table. The lady was attempting to set one of the shakes down but it slid out of her hand. Cally quickly caught it before it dumped in her lap.

"I'm so sorry!" The waitress set down the other shake. "You have great reflexes. Thanks for catching it. I'm sort of new here and that might not have set well with the boss."

"That's okay." Cally smiled. "I know how you feel because I work here part time also. I've actually dumped a plate of eggs and bacon into a guy's lap before, and he was wearing an expensive suit. He wasn't too happy with me." Cally pulled the paper off her straw and stuck it into the shake. "He didn't even leave me a tip. I don't know why." She pretended to be serious for a brief second and then laughter filled the air.

"Well, I bet you're going to be fun to work with. My name is Ann Clemons. I'll be working here in the evenings and on weekends."

"Nice to meet you. My name is Cally Reeves." She reached out to shake Ann's hand. "I'm sure I'll enjoy working with you, too."

25

The bell dinged several times by the impatient cook.

"That's another order. I better get busy. Thanks again." Ann turned and hurried toward the kitchen.

Cally took a long slurp of the shake, letting the sweet cold ice cream slide down her throat. It tasted heavenly. Tryouts had left her dry.

Brad's eyes remained on Cally, although he addressed everyone. "Did you guys hear about Mike's party tomorrow night?"

"Yeah—we were just talking about it." Cally wiped at her mouth with the back of her hand. She hoped she didn't have chocolate all over her face. She'd been patiently waiting for Brad to ask her out. They had been flirting with each other for a few weeks now, but he still hadn't asked her out. He hadn't dated anyone that she knew of since him and Cindy broke up over two months ago. And Cally didn't think Cindy was exactly anything to get upset about. She had the personality of a snake. Besides, they'd only dated a month, so how could he be heartbroken?

Maybe he just wasn't interested in her. She hoped that wasn't the scenario because she thought Brad would be the ideal date. He stood close to six foot tall with wavy brown hair and dark narrow eyes that slanted in a strange and sexy way. His braces had recently been removed, and Cally melted every time he smiled at her, especially since he had the cutest dimple in his left cheek. He had a powerful build and was one of the star senior football players. Cally had first met him in art class last year. He was an extremely creative artist. He'd shared many interesting tips on sketching.

Cally picked up a french fry, dipped it in the ketchup, and bit into it. She remained silent while waiting to see if anyone else had anything to add.

Jessie glanced cautiously toward the older couple in the next booth and whispered, "I heard his mom was going to let him have a keg."

"I'll be there!" exclaimed Mark.

"No way! You're not drinking! You're driving tomorrow night—I drove last weekend," Jeff reminded him.

26

Brad shifted his attention back to Cally and spoke softly, "You need a ride tomorrow night to the party?"

Beth overheard the question. She grinned and patted Brad's arm. "Hey Brad, is that how you ask girls out on a date?"

Cally could feel her face glowing. "Sure Brad. I was hoping I wouldn't have to drive." She instantly regretted her words—she must have sounded so stupid. She didn't know what it was about this guy that made her act so corny.

Brad swallowed and continued, "How about I pick you up at eight? Is that okay?"

"That would be fine. Do you know where I live?"

"Across from the city park, right?"

"Yeah, that's right, the middle house. It's the blue one with the white shutters." Cally hesitated and turned toward her friends. "Well, you guys about done—we should be heading back."

She had to get out of there before she exploded. She took one last sip of the shake and stood to wait for Beth and Jessie.

"See you guys later." Cally's eyes locked with Brad's.

"Good luck with cheerleading. I hope you make it," he said.

"Thanks."

"Hey, what about me?" Beth asked.

"You too, Sweet Potato, and you too, Jessie."

"Hey, Sweet Potato, if you need me to show you how to cheer—just let me know." Mark snickered.

"I'll try to remember that," Beth called over her shoulder.

***

They stepped outside the café, and Jessie wrapped her arm around Cally's shoulders. "Well, I bet you're on cloud nine right now." She knew how long Cally had been waiting for Brad to ask her out.

Jessie wished she could be more like Beth and Cally. Cally was the gorgeous one with all the brains. She was perfect in almost every way—five-foot five inches, one hundred thirty pounds, shoulder length curly blond hair, and laughing blue eyes. Who wouldn't want to go out with her?

27

Beth, on the other hand, was just as pretty as Cally, just in a different way. She was on the short side, five-foot three inches, average built, medium length red hair, and hazel eyes. She used to wear glasses, but had recently started wearing contact lens. She had an incredible personality—so witty, always making everyone laugh.

Nothing like herself—she was excessively shy. Jessie had never had a lot of confidence in herself. She didn't consider herself ugly nor did she consider herself attractive. But she was certain that she was too tall—five-foot ten inches and on the thin side at one hundred twenty-five pounds. She wore her flimsy dark hair short and flipped up on the ends. Her eyes were a dull brown and too small for her round face. And she still had her gaudy braces on! She'd worn them so long it seemed like she was born with them on. However, only three more months, and finally, she'd be getting them off. Maybe she'd feel better about the way she looked then.

She wasn't asked out on dates much either. However, there was one guy from her English class, Austin Kramer, whom she liked, and he acted like he liked her too. He was extremely smart and made straight A's. One day after school, he came over to Jessie's house to help her with her homework. She popped popcorn, and he stayed to watch a movie after they finished their studies. He thought all of Jessie's stuffed animals hanging on the walls were a riot. He laughed even more when she'd told him they all had names too. She'd had so much fun that day. She thought he would ask her out after that, but so far, he hadn't. He still flirted with her at school, so she was still hopeful.

Jessie was thrilled for Cally, though—they had been best friends since second grade. She was like a sister. Jessie appreciated the fact that Cally was always complementing her and trying to build up her self-esteem. Beth had become their friend in junior high. Now, all three of them were inseparable and the best of friends.

Cally pushed the button on her key chain and unlocked the car doors. "Can you believe it? He finally asked me out. I was so nervous. I hope he didn't notice."

28

"Now if you make cheerleader—you will really be having one hell of a day." Jessie knew how much Cally wanted to be a cheerleader—what fun it would be for all three of them to cheer together.

***

"Okay, ladies—I want to thank all of you for trying out today." Patsy Allen picked up a glass of water, swallowed, and gestured with her hands for everyone to sit down. She set the glass down on the podium and continued, "I know all of you have worked very hard the last few weeks. I wish there were more spots open. If you don't make it this year, don't get discouraged—come back and try again next year. Again, I applaud your effort and hard work, and I wish you the best of luck. As you know, I didn't do any of the judging; they were all qualified judges, pre-selected, and interviewed. They didn't know any of you, and they selected by the numbers you were wearing. I've matched your numbers with your names and will be reading the names. If I call your name, please stick around so I can go over a few things. The rest of you will be dismissed. Again, thank you and good luck."

Cally grabbed Jessie's hand. "I'm so nervous." She watched as her cheerleading sponsor crossed the room and flipped on a different light switch. You couldn't help but notice Patsy's muscular legs as she walked; they were easily visible in her Nike shorts and tennis shoes. For a petite woman, she was built as sturdy as an ox. Everyone seemed to like her, and many of them called her Patsy rather than Miss Allen when they weren't in school. She didn't seem to mind. She was mostly pleasant, but she didn't take any crap from the smart mouth students either. Cally always wondered why she never married; she had to be close to thirty.

Patsy unfolded the piece of paper and started reading, "Wrestling cheerleaders are—Terry Ragsdale, Carla Means, Taylor Lawson, Debbie Ryan, Tiffany Evans, Janelle Hall, and Daylea White. Congratulations ladies." She paused until the applauding ceased. "Okay, now for the basketball cheerleaders—

29

Brittney Lawrence, Sherie Jo Curtis, Desi Hayes, Meg Braden, Jonna Waterworth, and Shelly Naylor. Congratulations girls! Now for the football cheerleaders." She hesitated and grinned. "Maybe I should wait until tomorrow to announce them?"

A chorus of '*No's*' shot through the anxious crowd.

Patsy laughed. "Okay—okay. The football cheerleaders are— Holly Bryant, Jessie Duffett, Desi Hayes, Liz Sturgis, Beth Fisher, Fallon Jenkins, Brittney Lawrence, Penny Long, and Cally Reeves. Congratulations girls." She glanced up from the sheet of paper. "Thank you all for trying out and drive safely home."

The crowd of girls stood as chatter flowed throughout the gymnasium. A lot of '*congratulations*' and '*I'm sorry*' murmurs could be heard.

Cally was baffled. "I don't believe it." She gave Jessie a bear hug, and then grabbed Beth and did the same.

"I thought you were going to break my hand while she was reading the names." Jessie massaged her hand.

"I never had any doubt you would make it," Beth said. "We're going to have so much fun this year. You know we get to initiate you, don't you." She winked as a slow mischievous grin spread across her face. She nudged Jessie. "Right, Jessie?"

"That's right. You're going to wish you'd never made cheerleader."

Cally knew they were just giving her a hard time. She was used to it and didn't mind at all. She was just thrilled that she'd made football cheerleader. Now she was a cheerleader and going on a date with the sexiest guy in school. She'd have to say that this was one of the best days she'd had in a long time.

Cally told her friends goodbye and hurried toward her car. She couldn't wait to tell her mother the news. She wanted to jump up down, scream, and tell the world how happy she was. This was the first day of her new, exciting life, and it was going to get even better. Her senior year was going to be the best yet. She cranked up the volume on her radio and drove the rest of the way home, singing aloud to the blaring radio.

She pulled down the street that she lived on just as the new man on the block was stepping out of his house. He'd purchased the Jones's house a few months earlier, but Cally hadn't met him yet. His bulging eyes met Cally's as she passed. She waved and smiled but the peculiar man didn't bother to lift his hand. Instead, he stopped, shoved his hands in his overalls, and stared after the car.

Cally shivered—he was the homeliest man she'd ever seen. She quickly shifted her eyes back on the road.

She quickly disregarded the stranger as she pulled into her driveway and the events of the day came rushing back.

CHAPTER THREE

Mary Reeves compared herself to Mrs. Cleaver on the 'Leave it to Beaver' show. Her days were filled with vacuuming, cleaning, and browsing through cookbooks trying to find something different for dinner. She grew tired of the meat and potato routine that her husband usually preferred. Every now and again she would stir up a fun casserole and that was about as crazy as her life ever got.

She'd just turned fifty in November, but she didn't feel a day over forty. She knew her husband, Bob, was especially fond of her looks. She was petite, barely five-foot two inches. At one hundred ten pounds, her curves seemed to be all in the right places. Although her skin was pale, it aided in keeping her face youthful looking. But she refused to leave the house without a little blush on her cheeks. Her blond curly permed hair was cut into a fashionable, shoulder-length style. A few weeks ago, she noticed a few gray strands. She'd been debating whether to color it. She really didn't want to until she absolutely needed to. She was proud of her natural color.

Mary considered herself a good mother and a loving and devoted wife. She was fortunate that she didn't have to go to work every day like other wives. Bob made enough money as an insurance sales representative to provide for the family. She enjoyed staying home, being a housewife and mother to her two children. She adored her kids. Cally was seventeen years old, and Corey was fifteen. She was granted exactly what she wanted—one girl and one boy. They were exceptional kids, both were honor roll students, involved in school activities, and well liked by the other students and faculty. Cally was a junior this year, and Corey had just started high school. She couldn't have asked for two better kids.

Of course, she felt the same way about her adoring husband, too. There couldn't be a more perfect man than Bob. He was the complete opposite of her. He was six-foot one, one hundred ninety pounds, and in perfect physical shape. He worked out faithfully every evening. No one would guess that he'd be fifty-three years old on his next birthday. He had dark wavy brown hair like Corey, a handsome little black mustache, and his dark eyes twinkled when he flashed that perfect smile of his.

Cally darted into the kitchen as Mary carried a bowl of corn to the table. "Mom, guess what happened today?" she asked. "I made football cheerleader and guess what else?" Cally wrung her hands together in excitement. "Brad asked me out for tomorrow night. Can you believe it?"

Mary understood how important this was to her daughter. She knew how desperately she'd wanted to be a football cheerleader, and Brad was a boy who she'd had a crush on for some time now.

It made Mary sad to see how fast her little girl was growing up. She wished she could persuade Cally not to date guys until she was out of high school, but she knew all of the other girls were already doing it. She didn't think it was fair to tell Cally she couldn't date. She knew she had to trust her daughter to make the right choices. And Brad was a good kid; he came from a decent family. She sat the potholder on the table and wrapped her frail arms around Cally shoulders. "Congratulations, honey. I'm so proud of you." She gave Cally a tight squeeze and kissed her forehead.

"I'm going to have a great senior year. Beth said we'd probably go to camp at Dakota University this summer." Cally chanted, "I'm a varsity cheerleader." She added cheerleading gestures. "Hey rah, hey rah…."

33

Corey galloped down the stairs. "Is it time to eat yet?" He glared at Cally. "What is your problem? You think you could keep it down a little bit."

"Shut up, dork! It's none of you're...."

Mary interrupted, "Okay you two—don't start fighting. Corey, your sister just received some exciting news. She's going to be a football cheerleader next year."

"We might as well have some loser cheerleaders cheering for the losing team." Corey cackled at his own joke.

"Shut up, jerk," Cally snapped.

"That's enough! Both of you go wash up for dinner. Your father will be here any second, and I don't want any feuding going on." Mary hurried toward the stove to finish preparing the dinner. She wished they would at least try to get along. That was her only regret with her family. But that was a small dilemma compared to what she'd heard about other families. She still found herself considerably blessed, and she was very content with her life.

***

David finished his shower, wrapped the towel around his waist, and tied it in a knot. He grabbed the comb in the drawer and ran it hurriedly through his hair. He decided to skip brushing his teeth because he knew his mom would be coming home soon, and he didn't feel like arguing with her.

David stopped in the kitchen, grabbed a glass, filled it with water, and took a long swallow.

He tried to avoid as much conversation with his mom as he possibly could. It was always the same sermon anyway. She'd want to know if he'd eaten, done his homework, and took his shower. Then she'd start talking about her day and mention Roy's name, which would always trigger an argument and end in a big fight. David decided it was much easier to pretend to be asleep. Lately, Roy was with her most the time anyway.

David ran down the stairs, skipping every other one. He threw the wet towel down on the pile of dirty clothes and threw on his pajama bottoms. He pushed his computer on and set the time on

34

his alarm clock while waiting for the computer to boot up. He flipped the light switch off so his mom would think he was asleep. He scanned his e-mail looking for one from the Professor. He'd been waiting for a couple of hours and still hadn't received anything from him yet. He was beginning to wonder if the professor had even received the email that he'd sent him earlier.

David was considering resending it but suddenly located what he was looking for and anxiously clicked on it.

Smurf
Ah my son, you have done remarkably well. I am proud of you. I can always depend on you and Scooby to do a good job. If you keep doing so well, I'll have to transfer you here for jobs that are more difficult and need more seniority. I praise you and Scooby for all your hard work. You both will be rewarded when the mission is complete.

Now for your next task—go to the 2000 block of Maple Street tomorrow night at 12:00 A.M. Be sure that no one follows you. Do not drive a car. Take a gym bag with clothes in it. You should be the one carrying the gym bag over there, and you should be the one carrying it when you leave.

You will see a big warehouse on the left side of the street. There will be no other buildings on that side. You are to go to the north side of the building. You will then see Slug standing by the entrance of the building—he will be wearing a purple bandana around his head. He will say to you 'my brothers, long time since I have seen you two.' You are to say back to him 'you're looking tight my friend. How is the east side?' If anything other than what I just told you is said, or if anyone else is with him, you must disregard this task and leave at once.

Once you have established contact with Slug, he will take you into the building and down to the basement. He then will give you two Rugged KP95 Center fire pistols with ten-round magazines. He will show you how to work and load the magazines. When you feel confident enough about loading and firing the gun—you will unload them and hide them in your gym

35

bag. Be sure to wrap the clothes around the guns and magazines. You are to go straight home to your room. Hide them under your mattress in the middle of the bed. Let me know as soon as this is done and then I will get back with you for your next task. Good job, boys! Keep up the good work!

Professor Slate

David could feel the pulse in his neck throbbing against his skin. He couldn't believe the Professor had complimented him. He'd said he was proud of him and that he'd done a good job. David didn't remember anyone ever telling him that before. Maybe once, when he was younger—he recalled giving his toy to a crying kid at the park, and his mom had told him she was proud of him. That seemed like years ago. She didn't even seem to notice him anymore. As long as she had Roy, David hardly felt visible at all.

He picked up the phone to call Josh, but quickly changed his mind—the front door upstairs opened. He placed the phone softly back in the cradle and crept over to the bed. He pulled back the covers and quietly climbed into it. He could hear his mother's familiar heels clicking over his head as she walked to the top of the stairs.

"David, are you still awake?"

He didn't answer and she called again.

"What is it, Mom?" David pretended to be half-asleep.

"Are you asleep already?"

"I was," he lied.

"What did you eat for dinner?"

"Just one of your famous pot pies," he said sarcastically. He didn't know when he'd eaten a home cooked meal last.

"I'm sorry about that, but I do have to make money for us to live, you know." Changing her tone she added, "Did you finish your homework?"

"Yes, mom. I'm going back to sleep now. Okay?"

"Okay. I have to work tomorrow night at the café, so come by there and let me know what you have planned. I'll leave you some money on the table. If you want, you can eat at The Diner. It's good and inexpensive." Ann paused. "Good night."

36

"Night." David listened as the patter of her heels clicked against the linoleum floor and then silence. He could tell by the pause and the distant feather-like footsteps that she had slipped out of her heels and gone into the living room. He thought he heard laughing and assumed Roy was with her. He pulled the cover up over his shoulders and turned toward the wall to shut out any annoying sounds. David was sure Roy would probably still be there when he woke in the morning.

He cleared his mind as he tried to concentrate on the assignment for tomorrow night. He sure didn't want to mess anything up.

David's mind raced back to earlier today, to the girl whom he'd run into in the hall. He knew who she was—Cally Reeves, one of the most popular girls in the school. She was pretty, but no doubt, a snob like the rest of the girls. They all thought they were better than everyone else. They would snicker at the unpopular boys and whisper little jokes to each other, and then pretend to giggle uncontrollably.

David wasn't an idiot. He knew when they were making fun of him. However, he thought, that's okay for now. Their time will come, and then we'll see who is left standing up—laughing. That goes for you too, Miss Cally Reeves.

***

Professor Slate held the black mutt up over the tub while the remaining water dripped off the motionless dog. He wasn't able to wait for Slug—the constant yelping had penetrated his nerves. He laid the lifeless creature down on a towel, relieved that it wasn't barking any longer. The professor wrapped the towel around the dog, stuck him into a garbage sack, and set it in the garage.

It was after midnight when Slug showed up. The professor had told him to park his car in the garage, so the nosey neighbors wouldn't suspect anything.

Professor Slate shook Slug's hand. "You're as good as gold to me. You always come through with flying colors." The professor

37

reached across his desk, picked up a bundle of money, and tossed it to Slug. "This should hold you over for a while."

Slug flipped through the bills with his thumb. "Thanks. Maybe I'll get some new threads this time." He grinned. "And maybe an eight ball." He slipped the bundle of money under his jacket. "Anything special you want done with her?"

"Whatever your pleasure. Just make sure her body can never be found." Professor Slate knew Slug was referring to buying cocaine, but he didn't care what he did with the damn money as long as he continued to do what was expected.

"You know that's not a problem," Slug said.

"She shouldn't give you too much trouble; she's getting weaker." Professor Slate trudged over toward the basement door. "I'll bring her up. You can lock her in the trunk along with that precious dog of hers. You won't have to worry about him biting you. I already took care of the little monster. He's in a trash sack in the garage."

"Okay. You want me to go drag her ass up here?"

"No—I'll be right back."

Professor Slate flipped on the light switch. He briefly listened to the stillness and climbed slowly down the stairs. She was still in the same spot he'd left her in. As he drew closer to her, her body jolted toward the sound of his footsteps. He reached down and jerked her up with one swift movement. She didn't try to pull away. He yanked the blindfold off, so he could observe the fear in her eyes. That was something the professor had always enjoyed, the terrified look in the eyes of his victims.

She blinked and then squinted her red, swollen eyes toward the bright light as she tried to focus them.

The professor's eyes traveled slowly across her face, absorbing every detail. Her cheeks were blotched with red streaks, and her eyelids were crimson and puffy. His eyes locked with hers as the muscles in his stomach tightened. His lips parted as he watched the anguished in her frightened eyes. He stared for several minutes until his adrenaline skyrocketed. He quickly wiped at the saliva trickling out of the corner of his mouth.

He bent forward to untie the rope around her bonded ankles so she could walk. He grabbed her arm and shoved her up the

38

narrow stairs. Once they were upstairs, the girl's horrified eyes darted from Slug to her surroundings, searching every corner of the room. Professor Slate was sure she was looking for that repugnant mutt.

"Looking for something?" Professor Slate grinned deviously. He turned toward Slug. "C'mon, let's get her in your trunk."

"I'll get it ready." Slug slipped out the door leading to the garage.

Professor Slate pushed the girl forward in the same direction. She hesitated. For a brief second, the professor thought she might try to resist. But he quickly dismissed the notion and shoved her again.

Suddenly, the girl spun around and kicked him powerfully in the knee, sending him stumbling backwards against the wall. She ran toward the front door. She had her bonded hands on the doorknob and was fumbling with the lock as the professor regained his balance and rushed after her.

He barely reached her in time. She'd managed to get the door unlocked and was just about to pull on the doorknob. He roughly grabbed her by the shoulder and threw her up against the wall as the pain shot up his own leg. On impulse his hands slipped around her slender neck. He sunk his neatly filed fingernails into her smooth skin. Her eyes enlarged with fear, rousing the situation even more. His grip tightened as he choked her. She tried to pull away, but she was too weak. The more she fought for air, the tighter his hands squeezed her throat. "You, bitch. How dare you kick me!"

The professor exulted as the girl's frantic eyes rolled up inside her head like a porcelain doll turned upside down. She squirmed helplessly as she struggled to breathe. He shuddered as sweat beads formed across his forehead. He was enjoying every minute, watching her die.

"Boss, what are you doing?" Slug stood in the doorway. "I thought that's what you were paying me for."

Professor Slate immediately released his hands from her throat, and the girl fell forward on her knees, wheezing madly through the duct tape. "Oh yes, of course." The professor inhaled deeply as he tried to come down from his high. "Sorry about

39

that! She tried to escape, and I guess I got carried away. Go ahead and get her out of my sight.

"Don't you try anything funny with me, missy, or you'll regret it." Slug pulled the panting girl up from her knees. He shoved her toward the door.

Professor Slate's head rush slowly ceased as he followed Slug out the door, limping.

Slug forced the girl into the trunk, grabbed a nearby rope, and tied it around her ankles. "There! Are you comfortable, missy?" He snickered.

Professor Slate picked up the garbage sack and wobbled toward the open trunk. He searched the girl's dazed eyes, enjoying the bewildered, pleading look. He held up the garbage bag for her to witness. "Is this what you've been looking for?" The professor flung the bag on top of her stomach. A muffled sob escaped from under the duct tape. He laughed as desperate tears slid down her freckled cheeks. He stared for a few seconds longer, relishing the look in her eyes and then he slammed the trunk shut.

Professor Slate smiled and glanced at Slug. "Well, she's all yours. I hope you have as much fun as I've had today. I'll be getting back with you soon on the other matter."

The professor turned and went back into the house whistling a tune.

***

Friday, April 23, 2001

The next day Cally's enthusiasm was still going strong and being Friday made it all the better. She actually looked forward to going to school.

Even the unfriendly, unsightly neighbor didn't damper her spirits as she drove by. He was setting a metal trashcan on the side of the curb. She waved—thinking he didn't see her yesterday. But again, his chilling eyes seemed to stare a hole right through her. He straightened, shoved his hands into his

40

pockets, and rocked on his heels. He didn't show any sign of friendliness. She'd never met anyone so rude.

She wondered why he'd moved into the neighborhood in the first place. The vicinity was too upscale and sociable for his type. No one even seemed to know his name. She'd heard he didn't have a wife or children. Cally couldn't imagine why he would want such a spacious house. Most of the people in the area had large families with children. The City Park drew most of the families to the neighborhood. She quickly adjusted her eyes back on the road—that was the last time she was going to try to be nice to the ill-mannered man.

She wasn't surprised to learn that most of the kids at school had already heard that Cally had made cheerleader.

Brad's locker was right across from Cally's. "Hey, congratulations, big football cheerleader. Maybe we will win a few more games now."

Cally stopped spinning the combination on her locker and spun toward Brad. "Thanks, but I don't think I'm going to help you win any more games. Now if they'd let me play, I might."

"Then I wouldn't be able to concentrate on the game."

Cally blushed. "I'm sure you'd do fine."

Mark marched up behind Brad and whacked him on the arm. "Let's go. We're going to be late."

Brad glanced back at Cally. "See you later."

Mark spun on his toes and called out to Cally, "Oh, I forgot, congratulations."

"Thanks—see you later." Cally jerked the locker open and scanned the stack of books, searching for her Spanish book. A group of rowdy students were shouting at the end of the hall, the same direction Brad and Mark had gone. She spotted her Spanish book, grabbed it, and slammed her locker shut.

She sucked in on her lower lip and chewed as she headed toward the chaos, even though it was the longer way to her class. At the end of the hall, a group of seniors stood circling a student. As she neared, she recognized the boy who she'd run into yesterday after tryouts.

The tall, arrogant guy, J.D. Smith, thumped the kid on his head. "Well, are you going to answer me? What the hell are you

41

doing in our halls? There isn't supposed to be any scrawny freshmen in this hallway! Is there, guys?"

A string of '*no's*' echoed through the crowd.

A guy named Jack added, "Yeah, the last freshman that went through this hallway ended up missing. I don't think they ever have found him."

The guys laughed.

Cally knew that they were just tormenting the kid. Freshmen had to go through the hallway all the time to get to their English class. She hated to see the upper classmen picking on the freshman. They seem to forget that they were once freshman. She scanned the crowd and spotted Brad and Mark standing nearby, laughing, as if they were enjoying the show. Cally was disappointed.

The poor kid didn't say a word nor did he look up. Cally felt sorry for him. What a bunch of jerks, she thought. Somebody needed to speak up. She was just about to defend the kid when the bell rung. The students quickly scattered and rushed toward their classes.

The kid waited for the guys to leave the area and then with his head bowed he turned down the hall.

Cally rushed ahead and tapped the kid on the back. He quickly spun around defensively.

"I'm sorry, I didn't mean to scare you," Cally said. "I just wanted to tell you to ignore those guys! They're just a bunch of losers." She smiled and turned down the opposite hallway.

CHAPTER FOUR

Cally hummed quietly as she wiped off the table. She positioned the salt and pepper shakers in the center. She finished by setting the wrapped silverware in their appropriate places.

She'd told her boss that she could only work a couple hours after school because of her date. Cally assumed that would give her enough time to get ready before Brad picked her up. Her stomach felt like a bowl of jittery jello. She was so nervous. She normally wouldn't get shook up over a date, but this time it was different. It was special because she'd longed for it for so long.

She slung the wet washcloth over her shoulder and strolled toward the sink. She was glad that Ann Clemons was working today. Not only because she was fun to work with, but because they'd been extremely busy, too. She'd already waited on six different tables, and she had only been there an hour. And to top it off, the dishwasher had called in sick, so they also had to keep the tables bussed off too. The boss had a replacement coming, but he wouldn't be there until six. Ann and Cally were doing their best to keep the dishes washed up along with waiting on the customers and clearing the tables off.

Ann rinsed the soap off a plate and attempted to pass it on to Cally to dry, but her fingers slipped, and Cally caught the plate before it smashed onto the floor. "That's twice you've had to save me from a near disaster. I owe you," Ann said with a relieved laugh. "Thanks a million."

43

"You're welcome. Don't worry about it." Cally scanned the half-full diner.

"How long have you been working here?" Ann handed Cally another plate.

"Not very long—I started this past fall."

"What grade are you in?"

"I'm a junior this year."

"Oh, really? I have a son that started high school this year. His name is David—David Clemons. Do you know him?"

"No, I don't think so. I've probably seen him, though. I'm just not too familiar with the freshman class yet." Cally dried her hands. "I'll be back; I need to see if my tables need any refills." She dropped the towel and picked up the pitcher of tea.

Ann snatched the towel and dried her hands. "Okay. I guess I better check mine, too."

As Cally refilled tea in a glass, the bell on the front door chimed. She glanced up to see the same kid that had been harassed in the hall earlier. He hesitantly eased up to the counter and sat down on one of the spinning stools.

Ann eagerly rushed toward him. "Hi, David. I wasn't expecting you by this early. Do you want something to eat?"

He glanced uneasily around the cafe, finally resting his eyes on Cally. "I'm not hungry. I just wanted to see if Josh could stay the night."

"That would be fine. I probably won't be home until late anyway. Roy and I are going out dancing after I get off."

Cally didn't mean to eavesdrop, but Ann's loud voice easily traveled across the small room.

Ann gestured to her. "Cally, I want you to meet my son."

Cally glanced toward the boy and decided it was best to pretend nothing had happened earlier.

"David, this is Cally Reeves. She goes to your school. She's a junior this year." Ann turned toward Cally. "And this is my son, David."

Cally smiled. "Hi, David. You have a really swell mom."

"Thanks," David said softly. He bowed his head.

"How are your classes this year? Do you have any hard ones?" Cally asked.

44

"No, not really." David didn't lift his eyes from the counter.

"Did you get Mrs. Rivers for Algebra?"

"Yeah."

"Watch out, she's big on pop quizzes, and she don't give you any breaks whatsoever."

"Okay." He casually glanced up at Cally and then turned toward his mom. "I got to go now. Josh will be waiting for me to call."

"Okay, honey. Have fun tonight and don't stay out too late," Ann called as he hurried toward the door.

"I won't." David waved impatiently and slipped out the door.

Ann stared after her son for the longest moment and then spun back toward Cally. "I'm sorry he wasn't more polite. He's just a bit shy around girls." She pulled a long thin cigarette from her apron, lit it, and turned toward the window.

"Oh, I didn't think anything about it," Cally said.

Ann stared silently out the window.

Cally tried to visualize what Ann looked like when she was her age. She was an attractive woman, probably not over forty. She wore her black hair slicked back in ponytail which emphasized her cheek bones on her perfect oval-shaped face. Her partially parted lips were colored with a soft pink shade, and the shimmering brown eye shadow made her eyes look more green than hazel. The black eyeliner smudged underneath her eyes added to her dramatic features. She looked stunning in the tight fitting black skirt and white button up blouse. If it weren't for the few wrinkles around her eyes, she could have easily passed for years younger. Cally concluded that she must have been beautiful as a teenager.

Cally turned toward the door's bell as Liz and Jenae entered. They marched toward the back where the rest of the high school students were playing pool. Liz waved at Cally.

Jenae shouted across the room, "Hey, you going to Mike's tonight?"

Cally nodded. "Yeah, I think so—if everything goes as planned." She bent over a table to clear the dishes off, and hopefully, silence Jenae. She liked her, but sometimes she could

45

be annoying with all of her questions. She didn't feel like going into detail about her date with Brad.

"See you tonight then. It should be an awesome time." Jenae continued toward the back of the cafe.

Cally collected the change off the table, shoved it into her pocket, and picked up the empty glasses. She glanced toward the clock on the wall; it wouldn't be much longer before she clocked out. She placed her hand over her stomach—the turmoil hadn't ceased.

Cally glanced toward Ann—she was stubbing her cigarette out in the ashtray. She thought briefly of David and wondered what kind of life he and Ann had. He sure was a peculiar boy. She figured the way the kids teased him—he probably had a lot more problems than she could ever imagine. Her mind abruptly changed back to Brad, and David's image subsided.

***

David threw his gym bag on the bed and skimmed through his CD case until he found the one he was searching for. He turned the TV on, switching the volume to mute. He stuck the CD in and cranked it up.

David's mind raced back to the girl at The Diner—the scumbag blond bimbo named Cally. It seemed like she was behind every corner he turned anymore. He didn't know why she kept trying to be nice to him. Whatever the reason, he wasn't fooled by her phony kindness.

He sure didn't need her to defend him this morning. Does she think that she can act like Mother Teresa during the day and a slut in the evenings with her skimpy pompom dress? David laughed aloud at his clever interpretation of her. He was certain that she'd probably slept with every guy on the football team.

He sure didn't need anyone feeling sorry for him. Those jerks hadn't bothered him in the least this morning. The harassment was nothing new to him, same old daily shit.

David kicked off his shoes, booted his computer, and picked up the phone to call Josh. Earlier at school, he'd told Josh about

46

the letter the Professor had sent. He turned the volume down on his CD player while waiting for Josh to answer.

Josh finally picked up the phone after the fourth ring. "Hello."

"Hey, it's me. I didn't think you were ever going to answer."

"Sorry, I was busy," he whispered softly. "My ma's drunk again, and I just got done sweeping up a vase she broke." Josh paused and continued in a low tone, "I just talked her into lying down. Boy, I sure hope she passes out soon."

"Is there going to be a problem with you coming tonight?" David asked.

"Are you for real?" Josh asked. "Hell, no! She won't even know I'm gone. She'll be in bed until morning. I'll probably be back home before she ever wakes up."

"Good!"

"Hey, I have to go—I can hear her moaning. I'll be over soon as I get her drunken ass asleep."

"Okay—see you later."

David knew from a personal experience what Josh's mom was like when she was drunk. He'd stayed at Josh's house once before when his mother had come home drunk. At first, she was all giggly like a schoolgirl, but she suddenly switched—like a crazy woman. She started arguing with Josh over something petty and then she grabbed a whiskey bottle and swung it at his head, missing it by inches. Josh struggled with her until he finally wrestled the bottle away. She picked up the toaster and flung it toward Josh, and then she grabbed a glass out of the sink and smashed it against the wall. Josh screamed at David to run. They ran to Josh's room and locked the door. His mom was furious. She kept beating on the door screaming, '*I'm going to kill you, you damn brat'*.

After that incident, David didn't sleep over at Josh's house anymore. Josh always swore his mother was a completely different person when she was sober, but according to Josh, those days were getting less frequent.

Josh's mother lived on a minimum amount of income from welfare and child support. And the money she did get she spent mostly at the corner bar on Frost Street. The only money Josh ever received came directly from his father.

47

David didn't feel too fortunate with his own family life, but he did feel luckier than Josh. He was glad that he and Josh had become friends. In a way, they both needed each other, and the mission needed them. David was also glad he had befriended the professor, and that Professor Slate had accepted him into his exclusive club.

David stretched his arms above his head, yawned, and bent back over the keys on the computer. He went straight to the chat room and scanned the names in the room. He immediately found her.

Hi, Eliza. How's life treating you today? David typed.

Hey, David. I'm pretty mellow right now. I just got done smoking a joint with some friends. What's up with you?

Not too much. School was boring as usual.

Have you heard anything from Professor Slate?

Yeah, he's keeping in touch. I can't talk about it, though. David wished he could talk to Eliza in person.

Hey, I understand. You just do as he tells you, and he will treat you good forever. At least he has everyone else that I know.

Yeah, he seems so cool. I'll be glad to meet him.

Well, David, I hate to cut this short, but I have the munchies. I need to find something to eat. I may be on later.

Okay. See you later.

David wondered if Eliza smoked dope all the time. It seemed like she was always getting high. He didn't find fault in it because he liked to smoke pot every once in awhile, too. But he knew it could be an expensive habit because Josh had a bad habit of doing it. Josh had to steal often to get his money for it. Eliza must have a lot of money, David thought. Or maybe she gets it from the professor.

David stared blankly at the advertisement on the computer screen while thinking about how one day soon his life would change, and he too would be living the high life.

***

Josh sighed as his ma called his name for the third time. He remained silent, hoping she would give up and pass out. After

48

realizing that wasn't going to be the case, he crept into the room to check on her. "What is it, ma?"

"Get me a drink. I think I left my bottle on the cabinet in the kitchen."

"Ma, please go to sleep. The bottle's empty." Josh lied.

"You better get me a drink now if you know what's good for your skinny ass." Elaine Petty pulled herself into a sitting position on the bed. Her shoulders remained slumped. One of the straps from her slip had slipped off her shoulder. She left it and awkwardly reached for the empty glass on the nightstand, knocking a book onto the floor. Suddenly, she flung the empty glass toward Josh. It smashed against the bedroom door, and glass shattered all over the floor.

"Okay, Ma. I'll get it! I'll be right back." Josh knew better than to argue with his ma once she had her mind made up. He'd had enough bruises and cuts from her drunken rages in the past—he sure didn't want anymore.

Josh didn't know when his ma's drinking had gotten so out of control. It seemed like only yesterday that his ma and pa had been happily married, and they were a normal family. A typical Sunday would consist of going to church, out for pizza, and ending the day playing baseball at the park. There use to always be big meals of meat and potatoes for dinner and bedtime stories every night. They would rent Disney movies on the weekends and pop popcorn. Josh vaguely remembered his pa wrestling around with him on the living room floor. His ma would try to break it up and then his pa would tackle her, too, and they would all end up laughing.

He was almost seven years old when his parents started fighting. At first, it had been little petty fights and then his pa started coming home late from work. The fights got worse, and his pa sometimes wouldn't come home for days.

His ma started drinking. Josh wasn't aware at the time how much she was drinking, but he seemed to recall her holding a drink in her hand a lot. The fighting got worse, his pa was gone a lot more, and his ma was drunk almost every night. The big meals stopped along with the bedtime stories; the movies and popcorn all ended.

49

At eight years old, Josh's life came crashing down on him. His pa came home one night and told his ma he wanted a divorce because he was in love with another woman.

His father moved away to Wisconsin to marry the other woman. At first his pa had come back to visit him frequently, but as the years went by, and him and his new wife had other babies, the visits became less frequent. Although his pa continued to provide him with money and gifts, he didn't know how to give Josh the love he needed.

After his pa left, his mother was never the same again. The drinking continued nightly, and she hung out at bars more often. Many nights Josh could recall waking up in the middle of the night to find he was alone in the house. He was sure she had waited until he'd fallen asleep and then she'd sneaked off to the bar. He could still recall those lonely nights that he'd been so scared. He'd been certain that there were vampires hanging upside down in his closet, waiting for him to go to sleep so they could suck all the blood out of him. Josh would circle his stuffed animals around him, hoping they would protect him. He recalled crying himself to sleep many of nights.

He couldn't remember what age he was when his ma had started beating him. The whiskey made her crazy—he'd been cut with broken glass, bruised from kicking and hitting, had a dozen black eyes, and several bloody noses. She was a totally different person when she was drunk. Any little thing could trigger her temper, and she would go into a rage throwing anything she could get her hands on or beating him with anything from belts to broom handles. Once when he had taken out the trash and accidentally spilled some on the floor, she'd grabbed a rolling pin and hit him in the center of the back with it. Josh cringed at the memory. It had left a massive red whelp that didn't disappear for days.

Josh didn't have any other relatives besides his pa, and he felt like his father didn't love him any more than his ma did. And his stepmother didn't like him at all. When Josh would visit she would act as if he was invisible. She tended to her other kids and kept her distance from him. It was as though she thought Josh would corrupt her sweet, innocent children. He knew life wouldn't be any better if he lived with his pa.

Josh learned to cook his own meals at a young age. He also learned how to do the laundry and clean the house. By the time he was ten years old Josh was practically taking care of himself and his ma.

His ma never cared where he went or what he did as long as he kept the house cleaned. He eventually started hanging out late on the block. He got involved with a rough crowd when he was twelve—he popped pills, smoked doped, and even snorted some crack once. His grades were usually never higher than a D if he showed up for class at all.

When Josh turned fourteen he found a part-time job as a busboy. He saved his money until he had enough to buy a computer. Slowly, he started spending more time on the computer and less time in the streets. That is how he had come to meet Eliza, Professor Slate, and David.

He soon realized that he didn't have to settle for being a drunk's son for the rest of his life. He knew now that there were other people out there who did actually care about him, like Professor Slate. Josh didn't care what happened to his ma or pa any more. He didn't feel any compassion for either one of them. He was just biding his time until he could leave home.

Josh picked up the whiskey bottle off the counter and grabbed another glass out of the cabinet. He hurried back to his ma's room. She was on her stomach, spread out sideways across the bed, her arm dangling off the side. Her eyes were shut and loud snores were escaping from her opened mouth. He returned to the kitchen and dumped the whiskey out into the sink. Josh knew by the time she woke up she wouldn't remember anything, and she would just assume she drunk it.

He picked up his ma's purse on the counter and rummaged through it. Spotting a five-dollar bill, he pulled it out and tucked it in his jeans pocket. It had become easy to steal from his ma since she could never remember anything.

He went back to his room, locked the door, and pulled the bag of pot out from under his mattress. He rolled a joint and lit it.

51

He ran his hand through his spiked hair as he wondered how much longer he could go on living this way. If Professor Slate didn't get him out of this hellhole soon, he was going to explode or do something to his ma that he might regret later.

***

Cally yanked the curlers out of her hair. Brad would be there in ten minutes, and she wasn't ready yet. She pulled on her favorite faded Lee jeans and slipped into a white and green cotton flowered shirt. She threw on a lightweight green button up sweater. She figured if it got too warm at the party she could just remove it. Either way she'd still looked nice.

She wondered what she'd talk about on the way to the party. Usually she didn't have trouble making conversation. But with Brad—she was sure she'd be speechless most of the night.

She bit down on her lower lip as she brushed and sprayed her curls. She grabbed the Abercrombie perfume and dabbed a little on each wrist. She stepped back and studied the reflection in the mirror. She turned sideways and sucked in her stomach until she was satisfied with the image of her protruding breasts. Her eyes traveled the length of the mirror. Her blond curls had turned out perfectly, neatly lying across her shoulders with a few wisps from her bangs falling loosely on her forehead. Her makeup was light, a smudge of green eye shadow, and a hint of blush on each cheek. She tilted her head sideways as if that would change the image in the mirror. She flashed a smile and was satisfied with her straight teeth. She was fortunate enough to had braces a few years earlier to straighten the few crooked teeth that she'd had.

She quickly spun to inspect the backside of her jeans and her petite rear. She hoped Brad was satisfied with the way she looked. The doorbell rang, interrupting her thoughts. "Okay here we go," she whispered and took one last glance toward the mirror.

Mary paused at the bottom of the stairs just as Cally approached the top. "Brad's here."

"Okay, I'm ready." Cally paraded slowly down the stairs. "Hi, Brad." She thought he looked incredibly sharp in his tight fitting bootleg jeans, tucked-in plaid western shirt, and glossy black cowboy boots. She recognized the scent of Maui because it was her father's favorite cologne.

"Hi, Cally. You look nice."

"Thanks. My mom wasn't giving you a hard time, was she?" Cally grinned.

"Not at all." Brad hesitated and glanced toward Mary. "What time do I need to have her home?"

"Twelve-thirty, please. That's her curfew."

"No problem. I'll have her back by then." Brad's eyes shifted back to Cally. "Are you ready to go?"

"Sure. Bye, Mom." Cally leaned over to kiss her mother on the cheek before following Brad silently out to the car.

He opened the door of his black camaro and waited for her to climb in.

"Thank you." She was amazed at what a gentleman he was. "I love your car." Cally scanned the immaculate interior of the car. Everything was neatly in its place. His sunglasses clipped to his visor, his CD case was opened, and his CD's were visible and neatly arranged.

"Thanks, it was a gift from my parents." He paused. "Your mom is really nice." Brad pulled into the traffic. He momentarily glanced toward Cally. "I'm glad you agreed to go tonight."

"I am, too." Cally shifted her eyes nervously out the window as she racked her brain trying to think of what to say next. She couldn't think of a thing, so they drove most the way in silence. She was glad when they finally reached the party.

Beth and Jessie had already arrived and were huddled in a circle with a group of girls.

Jessie glanced up and excused herself from the other girls. She hugged Cally. "You made it!" She bent over to whisper in her ear, "You look hot."

"I'll be back. Do you want something to drink?" Brad asked Cally.

"Yeah, I guess." Cally leaned forwarded to peak in Jessie's cup. "Are you drinking beer?"

"Guilty as hell!" Jessie giggled.

53

"I'll have the same." She really didn't care for the taste of beer but that was usually the only kind of alcohol they served at high school parties.

"Okay. I'll be back shortly." Brad disappeared into the crowd.

Beth moseyed up next to Cally and Jessie. "What's going on over here?"

"I wondered when you were going to be social." Cally took a step back to inspect Beth's outfit. "You look spectacular tonight. Who are you trying to impress?" She was surprised to see Beth in a jean skirt—she usually didn't like to dress up. She had piled her hair on top of head and a few spit curls hung loosely on each side.

"I don't know, yet. Mark isn't too bad looking—but if Jeremiah comes—I'm grabbing him." Beth fanned her face.

"I don't think so, Sweet Potato." Jessie snarled her nose. "That hunk is mine."

The trio burst into laughter.

Brad returned carrying two cups of beer. He handed one to Cally. "What am I missing over here?"

The girls exchanged secretive glances and giggled.

Cally sipped her beer. "My friends are just being goofy as usual."

Brad nervously shifted his weight from one foot to the other. "Should we dance?"

"Yeah sure." She glanced at Beth and Jessie—they were grinning. "Here, do something useful." Cally winked and handed Beth her beer. She followed Brad unto the dance floor.

She glanced toward Cindy who was standing alone on the far side of the room, glaring at her. Cally felt a little guilty, but it had been two months since her and Brad broke up, and it wasn't like she was stabbing a best friend in the back. She barely knew the girl, and what she did know of her she didn't like.

Brad pulled Cally to the center of the room among the other couples. He placed his hands gently on her waist, and she draped her arms around his masculine neck. The feel of him so near stirred her senses as they moved closer together. She wanted to embrace the moment as they swayed slowly to the music. He

54

bent down and gently brushed her lips with his own. She thought her stomach was going to burst—the sensation was magical.

He leaned forward and whispered softly, "I've wanted to ask you out for a long time. I'm glad I finally did."

"I'm glad you did, too," Cally replied in a raspy voice. She cleared her throat, embarrassed by her hoarse words—now she understood what it meant to have your heart stuck in your throat.

She leaned her head on his shoulder and closed her eyes. She tried to imagine that they were the only two people in the room. She was relishing every moment of the dance. She never knew a slow dance could feel so wonderful, and she hoped they continued to play slow songs all night long.

CHAPTER FIVE

Chief Jordan Brady was ready to call it quits for the day. He'd been working a twelve-hour shift because they were short on men. It seemed like when one of the officers got the flu, they all passed it around. It had been a long, drawn out week. He was looking forward to a weekend off and spending some quality time with his wife and three kids.

He flipped the coffeepot switch off and dumped the remaining coffee into the sink. He gathered up the empty candy wrappers scattered across his desk and tossed them into the trashcan. He patted his full-size belly and shook his head—he was glad that his wife hadn't seen all the wrappers. Every day he said he was going to change his eating habits, but he always found a reason why it was bad timing.

Officer Williams tapped lightly on the Chief's door. "Sir, are you in there?"

"Come on in, Williams." Chief gathered up the clutter of pens on his desk and threw them in the drawer.

"Are you on your way home, sir?"

"Yeah, I think so. Anything going on?" Chief Brady ran the back of his hand over his bristly chin. He hated going without shaving. He liked setting a good example for the other men, but he had overslept and didn't have a chance to shave this morning.

"Not too much. We just got a disturbance call on loud music. I think it's a teenager party over on Walnut Street. Andrew is going by to check it out."

"Call Andrew and tell him not to worry about it. It's on my way home—I'll stop by and break it up."

"Do you want him to meet you there?"

"No—I'll be fine. I'll call for back up if I think it's necessary. It's probably just a bunch of rowdy kids drinking beer and listening to loud music. You remember those days, don't you, Williams?" He grinned and smacked Williams lightly on the back.

"Yes, sir." Williams chuckled.

The chief grabbed his jacket off the back of the chair and took a quick look around the office, double-checking that everything was turned off. "See you later, Williams. I hope you have a good evening."

"Okay, sir. Good night." Williams hurried out the door.

Chief grabbed his car keys and turned off the lights. He was glad the day had finally ended. He hoped his wife wasn't waiting up for him; it was almost midnight. More than likely, she would be, though—she usually did. Chief had been married to Sheila twenty-two wonderful years. She'd given him three great children, Julie, fifteen, Jeff, eleven, and Justin, eight.

Chief Brady pulled down Walnut Street. He knew if he'd been at home, Julie would have told him about the party. She didn't like high school parties too well. He didn't know if it was because he wouldn't let her go, or if she just didn't like them, because of the alcohol. However, she always kept him posted on any parties happening on the weekends. He would then have his men monitor them early in the evening. The kids never had a clue how the police always seemed to locate their parties, and that's just the way the chief wanted to keep it.

The chief imagined he was partially guilty for turning his daughter into a teenage nark. He smiled—he knew she would make a great cop. But she had other plans and a policewoman wasn't one of them. She wanted to be a veterinarian. As much as the chief would like to see her follow in his footsteps, he knew she would be a lot safer if she didn't.

57

He pulled up in front of the reported house and pulled into the only empty parking space. Either someone just left the party or they knew I was coming and saved me a space, he thought. He laughed silently and glanced at his reflection in the rearview mirror. For a fifty-year old he wasn't too shabby looking besides the graying hair and the potbelly. He could remember the days when he would refuse to go to sleep without a good workout. Now he couldn't imagine going to sleep without a piece of homemade pie. Sheila didn't seem to mind the way he looked, but he knew he needed to get in shape because of his job. If he had to chase a criminal down, he would probably lose the foot race.

He strolled through the iron gate and glanced around at the parked cars as he made his way to the front door. There were at least twenty-five cars, mostly sporty cars, which confirmed his assumption that it was a teenager's party. He wasn't sure whose house it was, but more than likely, the parents were probably not be aware of the gathering. The chief glanced at the mailbox and pushed the doorbell—Sam and Krystal Grover. He couldn't recall hearing the name before.

Someone shouted loudly from inside the house, "Come in. It's unlocked."

He turned the doorknob. It opened easily so he stepped inside. They're sure going to be surprised when they realize who they just invited in, he thought.

The chief scanned the massive room as the teenagers continued to talk and dance. Most of them were holding cups of beer. He caught sight of the keg in the corner of the room. Chief Brady silently looked around the room, wondering how long it would take the kids to notice him.

Slowly, heads spun toward him and the talking subsided. Someone turned off the music. The people on the dance floor protested at first and then looked in the direction everyone else was staring. Suddenly, the whole room grew quiet.

"What's going on here?" Chief growled. When no one answered, he shouted again, "I said what's going on here?" Still no one volunteered to speak up. "Okay, whose house is this?"

Mike hesitantly stepped forward. "It's mine."

"Where are your parents, son?"

Mike glanced around the room as if he was waiting for someone to jump in and defend him. Hesitantly, he mumbled, "They're not home. They'll be home after while."

"What is your name?"

"Mike Grover," he said softly.

"Mike, do you know how much trouble you could get in for this? Especially if you're serving beer to underage minors." He glanced at the remaining kids that were still holding the cups. The others had set their cups down as soon as they spotted the chief.

"Yes, sir, I do. I'm sorry."

"Well, Mike, I don't do this often, but since you haven't been in any trouble in the past that I am aware of anyway." He paused to make sure he had Mike's full attention. "I'm going to let you off the hook this one time, but you better have all these people out of this house in five minutes."

The kids were already grabbing their jackets.

He raised his voice and warned loudly, "If I drive back here and see any cars outside, I'm dragging your ass down to the jail, and I'll keep you there all night. Do you understand me, Mike?"

"Yes, sir."

Chief spoke in a thunderous voice, "All of you, out of here, now! If you've been drinking, you better not be driving! You can call your parents to come and get you if you don't have a driver."

The kids trampled out the door like a herd of elephants.

"Every one of you better get your butts home and stay there the rest of the night." Chief looked back at Mike. "You better not let this happen again."

"I promise I won't. Thank you, sir."

"Okay. I'm taking your word for it."

Chief turned and exited out the door. He smiled silently; he knew he wouldn't have any more trouble with these guys the rest of the evening—probably the rest of the weekend. Hell, they'd probably behave the rest of the year. Chief really wasn't a dreadful guy as he liked to portray in front of the kids. It certainly worked to his advantage to have the bluff over them, though. He pulled away from the curb and headed home to his patient wife.

***

"Hurry up," David called over his shoulder to Josh.

"I'm going as fast as I can," Josh snapped.

David was furious because he'd lost track of time. Now they didn't have much time left to get to the warehouse to meet Slug. They'd been listening to CD's, and David had glanced at the clock on the wall—it said 11:00 p.m. He figured it would only take them around fifteen minutes to get to the warehouse. Little did he know that the battery had quit on the clock. He decided to check his email one last time and that's when he noticed the time on the computer—it was 11:50. They immediately grabbed the gym bag and rushed out of the house.

They were just about to hit Walnut Street and from there the warehouse was three blocks. David figured it had to be close to 11:55. He hoped they could make it there in five minutes. He wished he'd received the watch for Christmas like he'd asked for. It would have come in handy now.

As they approached Walnut Street, David noticed a police car pulling away from an upscale house. There were a bunch of teenagers standing around the driveway.

"I wonder what's going on there," Josh said.

"Who cares? Let's run or we're going to be late. Let's cross over to the other side."

David broke into a jog. He glanced over his shoulder to see if Josh was keeping up.

Suddenly, Josh screamed, "David, watch out!"

A black camaro came to a screeching halt inches from David.

Startled, David froze. The blood rushed to his face as his heart throbbed irregularly against his ribcage. He couldn't see anything—the headlights were blinding him. This can't be happening, he thought.

Brad and Cally jumped out of the car and ran around to the front of the car.

60

Brad yelled loudly, "You stupid jerk! Why don't you watch where the hell you're going?"

Cally gently touched David's shoulder. "Are you okay, David?"

"I'm fine," he whispered.

"Isn't it a little past your bedtime, low-life? Maybe this wouldn't have happened if you were home where you should be," Brad shouted.

David glanced toward Josh who was silently staring, wide-eyed. He imagined he was in as much shock, too. David suddenly remembered the warehouse. He gestured to Josh to follow. They broke into a jog and then a hard run.

"Are you sure you're okay?" Cally called after him.

David didn't respond. He just kept running. Why did this have to happen tonight, he thought. Now they were going to be late for sure!

"Wow, you sure did scare me. I thought you were going to get smashed for sure." Josh increased his speed until he caught up with David.

"The way the night is going so far, I'm surprised he didn't run over me." David spat on the sidewalk. "Did you hear that bastard? I should have punched the creep." He slowed to catch his breath and then continued to mock Brad, *"Way past your bedtime."* He glanced over at Josh "Who does he think he is? What—does he think he is out of high school or something?"

"Don't worry about him. His day will come." Josh snickered.

David swore one day he would make Brad pay for his smart-ass remarks, but right now, he had to concentrate on more important matters. He hoped they weren't too late; he didn't want to disappoint the professor.

As they approached Maple Street, David spotted the warehouse. His speed increased as he ran toward the north side of the building. They rounded the corner, and David saw Slug standing at the entrance of the building. As they drew closer, he could see that Slug was wearing a purple bandana just like the professor had said he would be. He was a thin, balding white guy with a scrawny black beard. He wore a pair of holey blue jeans and a double pocket black shirt with the sleeves cut off. A gold

61

hoop dangled from one of his ears and a chipped diamond earring was inserted into one of his nostrils.

David came within a foot from Slug and stared curiously at him.

Slug's eyes traveled the length of the street behind the boys—he eyed both the boys cautiously. "My brothers, long time since I have seen you two."

David had memorized his own line. "You're looking tight my friend. How is the east Side?"

As David finished his sentence, Slug opened the entrance door and motioned them both to enter. Once inside, Slug glanced up and down the street again before pulling the door shut. He switched on a flashlight and nodded to the boys to follow.

David followed closely behind Slug as he led them through the dark halls. He squinted to see what was on each side of him, but it was hard to make out anything. He reached his hand out to the side of him until he touched metal. As his eyes grew accustomed to the dark, he realized that it was lockers surrounding him. He glanced above him; the ceilings were high and arched at the top. There were cobwebs across the ceilings, and mounds of dirt scattered across the floor. He suddenly ducked to avoid a spider web hitting him in the face. After a few minutes, down the long hallway, they came to steep concrete stairs leading to a basement. So far, Slug still hadn't spoken a word. David strained to see the stairs—he was glad there was a handrail. He sure didn't want to fall down the stairs in front of Slug.

David proceeded to follow Slug down the stairs with Josh right behind them. As they reached the bottom, he noticed a dim light shining at the end of the hall. He followed Slug down the narrow hallway toward the light. The ray was coming from a single room.

Slug led the boys into the brightly lit room. He pulled the door shut behind them and locked it. He pulled a cigarette package out of his shirt pocket. He tapped a cigarette out of it and lit it. He then held the pack out to the boys. "Want one?"

David shook his head. "We don't smoke." He smiled and nervously glanced toward Josh. "But thanks anyway." His voice shook as he spoke. He didn't realize how nervous he actually was until now.

Slug winked. "Sorry, all I have is cigarettes to offer you. I don't have any of the good stuff left." He walked over to a long, oblong wooden table where a large metal trunk set. He reached for the key in his pocket and unlocked the padlock. He opened the trunk slowly and then reached in the trunk to pull out two pistols. He laid them easily down on the table. He glanced from David to Josh. "Do either of you know anything about these sweet babies?" He picked up one of the pistols, blew the dust off, and twirled it around on his finger. He took a long drag off his cigarette, blowing the smoke out in smoke rings.

"Not really," Josh mumbled.

"What time do you dudes have to be home tonight?" Slug rubbed his hand over his baldhead.

"It doesn't matter. I'll sneak back into my house. My mom will already think I'm in bed when she gets home from work," David said.

Slug nodded toward Josh. "And you?"

Josh pointed his thumb toward David. "Oh, I'm staying the night with him."

Slug flipped his cigarette onto the ground and smashed it with his shoe. "You dudes can loosen up because you're going to be here for awhile."

"That's okay." David glanced at Josh, who was nodding his head in agreement. This was going to be a blast, David thought. He was actually going to learn how to handle a gun. The thought of using a pistol was stimulating. He thought of the power he would soon have. He could already feel his confidence growing as the image of him blowing off the head of the cocky bastard that almost ran over him flashed through his head. He smiled silently—life is finally getting better!

***

Professor Slate swallowed the end of the whiskey from the shot glass and slammed it down on the table. He glanced at the clock on the wall. It was time for Slug to be meeting with David and Josh. He was sure everything would go as planned. Slug had never failed him yet. He glanced toward the basement door, resenting the fact that the girl was no longer down there. He would have enjoyed toying with her a few more days. He couldn't quit thinking about his hands around her slender neck, or how her eyes filled with terror before they rolled up in their sockets. He could still hear her gasping for air from under the duct tape. He didn't understand why he hadn't just finished her off like he had yearned to. If only Slug hadn't walked into the room. "Damn," he said aloud.

He opened the whiskey bottle and poured more in the glass. He leaned forward, propped his elbow on the desk, and rested his chin on his hand. He grunted—he knew he needed to get back to work.

He tried to focus on the computer screen, but his mind kept drifting. He couldn't quit thinking about the mind-blowing sensations he'd experienced in the past while killing his victims. Once he got the notion in his head, he usually couldn't shake it until he acted upon it. Sometimes the missions alone weren't enough—he had to have more. He craved the exhilaration that crept through his groins as he watched a beautiful girl suffer, especially if it was one of the devil's children. His adrenaline was at its peak when his victim was taking her last breath—it was far better than an orgasm could ever be.

He strolled over to the TV and flipped through the channels, pausing on a horror flick. He watched a few moments while the woman on TV murdered her husband with a butcher knife. Professor Slate shuddered; he couldn't take it anymore. He glanced up at the clock; it was just after midnight. The professor grabbed his jacket off the back of the chair. He tucked a ski mask into his back pocket and his prize switchblade into his front pocket. He knew he wouldn't be able to rest until he satisfied his craving.

***

64

Brad hadn't spoken a word to Cally since the near accident. She assumed he was still fuming; he'd been so angry. She stared out the passenger's window as he drove silently down her street.

He parked the camaro in front of Cally's house, reached across the seat, and grabbed Cally's hand. "I'm sorry for the way the evening turned out. I sure didn't want to have to bring you home before your curfew, but I don't need any trouble from the police."

"Don't worry about it. I had a good time. I'm just glad we didn't get into more trouble from the chief." She hesitated. "You better get going."

"I'll walk you to the door."

"That's not necessary. You need to get home. I hear the chief can get pretty ugly if he's tested." She smiled at him. "Besides, I'll be fine."

Brad leaned forward and clasped Cally's shoulders with his hands. He bent forward and kissed her tenderly on the lips. "Thanks for going tonight."

"Thank you for taking me." Cally's stomach tightened as she dug out her keys. She wondered if Brad could hear her heart pounding.

"Good night," Brad said softly.

Cally climbed out of the car and stood on the sidewalk. She waved as he pulled away from the curb. Something about that guy gave her the warmest fuzzies.

She glanced down at her key ring, searching for the right key—her mind drifted toward the earlier slow dance. She spun slowly around toward her house as she tried to single out her house key from her collection on the ring. Suddenly, her keys hit the ground as her body slammed into a dark figure. She screamed as her eyes lifted toward the stranger. She struggled to see his face, but he was already bending down to retrieve the keys. "Oh my God, you scared me to death," she shrieked.

"You dropped these." The man stood, lifting his head to meet her gaze.

She froze—goose bumps emerged on the back of her neck and traveled down her spine as her eyes rested on the repulsive

65

neighbor. Her hand trembled as she reached out to grab the keys. Her heart nearly stopped as he clasped his hand firmly over hers.

The front porch light flickered on, and the front door opened. "Cally, is that you?" Mary called out.

"It was nice meeting you." The man released Cally's hand and smiled, flashing his crooked yellow teeth. He quickly turned and walked across the street toward the park.

Cally trembled. She could have sworn his grasp to mean something more than a mere introduction. She didn't think it was just a figment of her imagination playing tricks on her, either, and the way he stared at her as if he could see right through her. She rubbed her hands up and down her arms, trying to shake the chill. She jogged up to the door where her mother stood waiting.

"What was that about?" Who was that guy?" Mary looked up and down the street. "And where is Brad?"

Cally hurried into the house, pushed the door shut, and locked it. She sighed and leaned back against the door. "That is our new neighbor that bought the Jones's old house. And he's one weirdo! I have no clue why he's out walking this late, but he gives me the creeps."

"Oh yeah, the new guy. I've seen him out working in his yard. Poor guy, he's not too attractive." Mary shook her head sadly. "Although he's a homely man, that doesn't mean he's weird. Besides, many people like to walk at night." Mary rested her hands firmly on her hips. "Now, where is Brad? And how come he didn't walk you to the door?"

"I told him he didn't need to because he needed to get home. The police chief came by Mike's house and broke the party up because there was beer there. He told everyone to go straight home."

"They were drinking at the party?" Mary's eyes widen.

"I wasn't," Cally lied. "But yes, there was beer."

"Oh goodness! It wasn't Chief Brady, was it?" Mary covered her mouth with her hand.

"Yes. Don't worry, Mom, he didn't even know I was there." Cally knew her mom would be disturbed about the news. Her mother was a good acquaintance of the chief's wife, Sheila Brady.

"Cally, I can't let you go to parties where there is alcohol. Even if you're not drinking, you shouldn't be at those kinds of parties. Do you understand me?"

"Yes, Mom." Cally was too tired to argue with her. "Where's Dad?" She peeked in the living room to see if he was in his big easy chair. It was empty. He always waited up for her to come home on the weekends. Sometimes they would even watch a late movie together.

"He wanted me to tell you that he's sorry he didn't wait up, but he had a busting headache."

"That's okay—I'm going to bed myself. Good night." Cally trudged up the stairs. She paused in front of Corey's room and tapped lightly on the door. "Corey, are you still awake?"

Corey opened the door and stared blankly at Cally. "Yeah, what do you want?"

"Do you know a kid in your grade named David Clemons?"

"Yeah, why?"

"What's he like?"

"He's just a strange kid that no one likes. Why?"

"I was just curious. I work with his mom at The Diner. Tonight Brad almost hit him with his camaro while he was jogging across the street."

"So? Why do you want to know about him? Do you think he's cute or something?" Corey giggled.

"No! Why do you have to be such a brat?" Cally spun on her heels and marched toward her own room. Sometimes she'd like to sock him right in the jaw. He was the worst brother a person could have. He didn't know how to utter a kind word; it always had to be something sarcastic.

She quickly changed into her pajamas, switched on the bedside lamp, and crawled into her bed, tucking the covers under her feet.

She pulled her yearbook out of her nightstand drawer and immediately flipped to the beginning of the book. She'd looked through it already a dozen times, but every time she'd noticed something she hadn't seen before. She turned to the second page and spotted a picture of herself, wearing a football helmet when she was goofing off. She decided to count how many pictures

67

she was in. She knew there should be twenty-three of them because she'd already counted them at least five times before. But just in case she missed a picture, she recounted them.

After counting twenty-three, she flipped to a picture of Brad. She stared at the handsome guy as she summoned up the entire evening in her head. She laid the yearbook down, flipped off the light, and scooted down into the covers. She lingered over every detail of the evening. Cally was confused how she felt about Brad. She thought he was cute, and she did get butterflies in her stomach every time she thought about him. However, something about him was disturbing.

Cally didn't care for his temper flaring up when he'd almost run over David. She didn't understand why he'd acted so irrationally. She also remembered how he'd laughed earlier in school when the older guys were picking on David.

Nevertheless, when he kissed her, it was so sensuous. It was different from past boyfriends who had kissed her. He made her feel warm all over—so why were his recent actions bothering her? It really wasn't that big of deal, was it?

There were so many unanswered questions spinning though her head. Her mother always told her being a teenager was tough, and she definitely agreed. Cally's eyelids grew heavy, and she slowly drifted into a restless sleep.

***

It was three in the morning by the time David and Josh got home. They quietly slipped down the stairs without waking David's mom. David assumed his mother stayed out late with Roy and went right to sleep when she'd gotten home.

"These are so cool," David whispered as he removed the pistols out of the gym bag.

"Hurry up, in case your mom wakes up." Josh kept his eyes fixed on the stairs.

"Hold the mattress up for me." David waited for Josh to lift the mattress and then he placed the pistols underneath it.

"I'm so tired. I didn't think Slug was ever going to let us go." Josh kicked his shoes off. "He had to go over everything way too many times." He pulled his pierced earring out of his ear and laid it on David's dresser, and grabbed a pair of pajama bottoms out of his bag and slid them on.

"We can't go to bed yet—we've got to write the professor."

"I'm going to bed. We can write him in the morning." Josh scrambled up into the bed and climbed under the covers.

"You go ahead. I'm just going to write him and let him know everything went okay." David slipped his glasses on over his nose and fired up the computer.

"Whatever, Smurf. Good night." Josh turned his back toward David.

David navigated to his email and started typing.

Professor Slate,

We just got back from meeting with Slug. Everything went as planned, and we got the pistols. They are super-sharp looking. He showed us how to load them and fire them. We are very excited and thrilled that you chose us for this special mission. Let us know what to do next.

Smurf and Scooby

David threw on a pair of shorts and crawled into bed next to Josh. He closed his eyes and tried to sleep, but he couldn't seem to clear his head—he kept seeing her face. As much as he tried to get her out of his mind, he couldn't shake the images. Cally was asking him if he was okay. She was smiling at him in the diner. She was being nice to him at school in the hallway. Why is she doing this to me? He flipped over restlessly. She's supposed to be the enemy. And she has to be so damn pretty on top of everything else.

David briefly wondered what it would have been like to have been Brad tonight—out on a date with Cally. He quickly dismissed the crazy notion. He had to forget about her! He wouldn't let her ruin the mission for him. He wasn't allowed any friends in school except Josh; he'd made a pact with the professor before he took the assignment. He wasn't going to allow her or anyone else to mess up this big opportunity for him. One day soon, everyone would recognize and respect him.

69

CHAPTER SIX

Professor Slate's real name was Charles Hains. People that knew him called him Charlie. Not many people knew him, though. The little waitress, Kandi, at The Prize Café, and Dale, his barber, knew him as Charlie. Mrs. Perkins, the inquisitive neighbor, across the street also called him Charlie. He often wondered if she purposely spied on him because she always managed to come out at the same time to get her daily newspaper, each time calling out, *'Good morning, Charlie.'* He'd also caught her a few times peeking through her blinds as he pulled into his driveway. The curiosity of what he did for a living was probably driving the nosey bitch insane.

Charlie's parents had both been killed in a car wreck twenty-one years ago. He'd been only nineteen years old at the time and still in college. His parent's wealth had kept him in private schools most of his childhood. He usually just visited home on holidays and summer vacations. His father eventually stopped beating him, but the verbal abuse continued. The professor usually preferred not to go home at all. When his parents died, it was more of a blessing than a loss. Besides, their deaths had left him loaded with money. He finished his schooling, majoring in computer programming. Charlie decided not to go into the work field immediately because he didn't need the money. He spent most of his time reading educational material and surfing the Internet.

It was right after his parents died that he had the pleasure of killing his first victim. He hadn't planned on it happening—it just did. It was a young female student who had parked outside the local library. Her car wouldn't start because of a dead battery. Charlie had offered to run home, get his jumper cables, and jumpstart the car. She asked if she could ride along and use his phone since she was running late for a meeting. She rode with him back to his house, and the rest just fell into place.

She had her back toward Charlie and was dialing the number when the urge to strangle her overwhelmed him. It was the best impulsive decision he'd ever made. There wasn't a feeling like it in the world! He couldn't eat or sleep for three days afterwards because he couldn't shake the sensation. Discarding the body had been a piece of cake also. He knew right where a well was located. He knew his dad would have been proud. His dad always said that it was best to control the devil before the devil controlled you.

Charlie found out a few years earlier how much power and control the Internet could produce. His victims were mostly young teenaged students; they were so vulnerable. Young adults were the perfect targets because there were so many lost souls. He could easily convince teens to do anything he said and carry out any mission he planned. It was definitely a high to have such strong power over people. Charlie might have once been possessed with the devil, but now he was the one conquering the devil's children.

He built his own web page and named it the 'Hidden Undertakers'. Only certain members could tap into the links on the web page by secret passwords. His pupils were increasing more and more every day. One day he hoped to control a sizeable group of students. He smiled proudly—all of his pupils respected him highly.

Charley would find students by entering chat rooms, disguised as someone else and chatting with teenagers. He never gave out his identity. Charlie would pretend to be another teenager or a pretty girl, such as Eliza. He'd talked with his victims until he became their best friend. He'd learned everything about them

71

before they ever became potential targets. Once he learned their identity, he could investigate their backgrounds.

While disguised he'd chat with potential pupils for months before he selected one of them for his program. After he made his decision and while he was still in disguise, he'd tell the student the address of the 'Hidden Undertakers.' He'd tell him that it was a cool webpage to view. When the kid became eager to join, Charlie would tell him he would have to have Professor Slate email him. From there Charlie would capture the kid's innocence. Slowly, he would brainwash the kid and teach him to think the way he wanted him to think. The professor always praised them; they loved that the most. They all learned to appreciate and respect everything about Professor Slate.

The professor would convince them to believe that they were in charge of the world and that they were the only ones who were important. Charlie taught them that there were only two types of people in the world—the Hidden Undertakers and the enemies. He taught them to feel nothing but hatred toward the enemies.

Charlie slowly turned his pupils against their parents, friends, teachers, and anyone else who he thought might be a threat to his mission. He tried to prey on lonely kids, ones from broken homes, and those whose parents neglected them.

A few months before the actual mission date, he'd move to the town where the mission was to be performed. It was such a rush to be near the excitement and witness some of the devil's children being executed. He never strayed too far away from the mission, and he never let his pupils know he was in the same town as they were.

Charlie leaned back in his chair and grinned. He reread the note Smurf had sent him one last time. Perfect, he thought, everything was going as planned. He'd needed two high school students from Shelby, Idaho, and he was glad he had settled on David and Josh. They had both been loners without any friends except for the ones they'd met in chat rooms. He'd brought them together through Eliza.

He was sure that the mission would go successfully. No one would ever listen to Charlie as he was growing up—he was

72

going to make sure Professor Slate had everyone's attention now.

He picked up his pocketknife and walked over to the rusty metal container across the room. Charlie watched the little mice scampering around in the box. He eyed the smallest one darting from side to side. They were such innocent, helpless little creatures. He plunged the knife abruptly into the back of the tiniest mouse. Blood gushed out of it and splattered on his hand. The mouse fell on its side. Its stomach ceased movement as its breath diminished. Charlie smiled as he watched the little creature gradually die.

***

Saturday, April 24, 2001

"David, are you boys up yet?" Ann called downstairs. "It's after noon."

"What do you want, mom?" David yelled. He stretched his arms over his head and yawned.

"What time do you boys plan to get up? I have to go to work shortly."

"We're getting up in a minute. Do you have any money?"

"I'll leave some on the table. I went to the store earlier and got some donuts for breakfast. Why are you boys so tired?" Ann paused. "The lights were off down there last night when I came home. I yelled at you and assumed you were asleep. You boys weren't drinking last night, were you?"

"No mom, it's just been a long week, and we were tired. We're getting up," he grumbled. "Hey, what time did you say it was? The battery on my clock has stopped down here." David glanced over at Josh. He was rubbing the sleep out of his eyes.

"It's 12:30. I'll try to remember to pick you up a battery next time I go to the store. What have you got planned today?"

"We're not sure," David replied.

"Hello, Ann," Josh called up the stairs as he stumbled out of the bed.

73

"Hello, Josh. Sorry I don't have time to stick around, boys. I have to get ready to go to work. David, come by The Diner and let me know what you are doing."

"Okay, Mom. Bye." David fell face first on the bed with his arms stretched out on each side of him. "I'm so tired."

Josh was already getting dressed. "Me too. I don't think your mom has a clue about anything, do you?"

"No. She wouldn't care anyway. All she has on her mind is handsome, strong Roy," David said in a high-squeaky voice. He flipped over on his back, flexed his muscle, and fluttered his eyes.

"Oh, you love him and you know it!" Josh grinned. "Hey, did you email the professor last night? I think I fell asleep as soon as my head hit the pillow.

"Yeah, I did." The memory of the night before suddenly came rushing back. He immediately jumped up and headed toward the computer. "Let's see if he has written us back."

"Did you tell him we got the guns and all?"

"Yeah, I told him everything except about me almost getting ran over on the way there." David snickered. "I don't want him to know how stupid I actually am."

Josh laughed. "At least it was you for a change. Usually it's me that does the brainless things."

"That's true," David mocked.

"Hey, watch it." Josh punched David in the arm.

David found the email he was looking for and read it out loud.

Smurf & Scooby,

You boys are amazing! I couldn't have picked two better students for this mission. I'm so glad I found you two. I've already talked to Slug, and he said you both did a great job. Everything is going as planned. Your next task is to rent a digital camera and take pictures of the school. Also, I want one of you to draw me a layout of the school and all the rooms. You will have to do this when school is out and the building is empty. The custodian might be around, so you need to find out when he does his cleaning. It is very important that no one sees you doing this.

I will get back with you and let you know how to get the disk and sketches to me.

If you look in the bottom of the ammunition pouch, you will find a hundred-dollar bill. That should cover renting a digital camera if you don't already have one, some sketchpads, and pencils. If there is any money left, you boys take the afternoon to do whatever you want. Maybe you can go see a movie or go out to eat. If you have any questions about anything let me know. You two have a good day, and I will talk to you soon. You're doing super!

Professor Slate

David stared at Josh. "A hundred-dollar bill? Wow!" He ran toward his bed and lifted up the mattress.

"Shouldn't we wait until your mom leaves?" Josh asked nervously.

David was already pulling out the hundred-dollar bill. "She won't come down here." He fanned his face with the bill. "Can you believe this? What are we going to do today?" He handed Josh the bill.

"I don't know." Josh turned the hundred-dollar bill over to examine the back of it. "Hey, guess what, my dad has a digital camera. I could ask him if we could use it and then we wouldn't have to rent one.

"Do you think he would let us?"

"I'm sure he will. He was planning to come down anyway. I'll call him today to make sure." Josh handed the bill back to David. "I'll let you be responsible for this."

"Just call him from our phone after my mom leaves."

"Okay." Josh rubbed his hands together. "So what do you want to do with the money?"

"I'm not sure. I still can't believe Professor Slate gave us a hundred dollars. He's just too cool! I guess, first we need to go to the mall and get the sketchpads and other things we need. Then with the money left we'll decide what to do next. Maybe go eat or buy some cool clothing to wear the day of the mission."

"That sounds cool! Today is going to be a blast." Josh held up his hands for David to high-five.

"Yeah, we're so lucky." David cranked the volume to his stereo. "I'm going to jump in the shower and then you can." He gathered some clothes out of his drawers and hurried up the stairs. He was in an extremely good mood. He couldn't remember the last time he'd went shopping usually his mother picked up his school clothes at garage sales and thrift shops. This was going to be a grand day.

***

Cally stretched and rolled over to glance at the alarm clock; it was 8:10 a.m. She'd set the alarm clock for 8:30 a.m., so she still had twenty more minutes to sleep. She flipped back over and closed her eyes. The aroma of fresh brewed coffee stirred her senses. Her mind drifted ahead to the plans she had for the day. Jessie and Beth were supposed to go to the mall with her this morning and then she had to go to work for a few hours this afternoon. They would all probably end up at the movies this evening, and hopefully, Brad would be there, too. She lingered on the events from the night before and realized she was never going to fall back to sleep. Besides, she had things to do and wanted to get a head start on the day. She pushed the alarm clock off, pulled back the covers, and slowly crawled out of bed.

She chewed on her lip as she searched through her closet, trying to decide what to wear. She placed the back of her hand over her bottom lip to see if it was bleeding, and sure enough, it was. Her lips were going to be all chewed up before she ever went to college if she didn't stop the nasty habit. She grabbed a tissue and dabbed at it while rummaging through the clothes. She finally decided on a lightweight brown and green striped shirt with a pair of blue jeans. The April weather was still slightly chilly, so she grabbed a brown sweater to bring along just in case she needed it.

Cally jumped into the shower and then quickly dressed. She did a fast blow-drying job on her hair and brushed on some eye shadow with one hand as she dialed Jessie's phone number with the other.

After a couple of rings, Jessie picked up the phone. "Hello."

76

"Hi, Jessie. It's me, Cally. Are you ready yet?"

"It's only 840; the mall's not even open yet. I thought you said to be ready by 9:30?"

"I know—I just got up earlier. I'll grab some breakfast and give Beth a call before I come pick you up."

"Okay. That should give me enough time to take a shower. Talk to you later."

Cally called Beth next.

Beth's mom answered on the first ring. "Hello."

"Good morning, Edith. This is Cally. Is Beth awake, yet?"

"Oh, hello, Cally. Yeah, she's up. Hang on. I think she just got out of the shower."

"Okay. Thanks." Cally heard a thud and then Edith yelling at Beth.

A few minutes later Beth picked up the phone on the upstairs line. "Hello."

"Hey, Sweet Potato, are you ready to do some shopping?"

"You bet. I couldn't sleep this morning and woke up at 7:30."

"You beat me. I got up around eight."

"So tell me, how did everything go last night with you and Brad? Did you go on home after the party broke up?"

"Yeah, we did. Brad didn't want to get in any more trouble with the police. What did you do?"

"I can't tell." Beth giggled.

"C'mon, fess up."

"I'm kidding. Actually, I did have a good time. Mark came by after the party broke up, and we just sat outside and gave each other a hard time. It was fun," Beth said. "What about you? Are you engaged yet?"

"Ha ha, you're so funny. I'll fill in all the blanks for you when I pick you up."

"How much longer will you be?" Beth asked.

"I'll try to be there in the next half hour. Can you handle that, miss goofy?"

"I shall be ready. See you then."

Cally grabbed her purse and headed down the stairs toward the smell of fresh coffee, bacon, and eggs. Her mother always

77

made a big country breakfast on Saturdays. She thought her mom was the best cook in town.

Her dad and brother were already sitting at the table, and her mom was just sitting the bacon down.

Mary looked surprised to see Cally. "I thought you would sleep in this morning."

"Not today." Cally sipped the orange juice that her Dad handed her. "I've got things to do. I wanted to get going early since I have to go to work later." Cally bent down and kissed her father on the cheek. "Good morning, Pops."

Bob laid down his newspaper and smiled up at his daughter. "Good morning, honey. I'm sorry I didn't wait up for you last night."

"That's okay. Did mom tell you about me making football cheerleader?"

"Yes, she did. That's wonderful. I'm very proud of you. How did your date with Brad go?"

Cally glanced toward her mother as she sat down to join them at the table. She didn't know how much her mom had told him about the party. "It was fine. We had a good time."

"Yeah, but she really has a crush on a dork in my class." Corey snickered.

"I do not."

"Oh?" Bob's eyebrows furrowed.

"No, Dad, I don't." Cally glared at Corey. "I asked Corey last night about a kid in his class only because some older kids were picking on him in the halls yesterday. Then last night he darted out in front of Brad's car. I was just curious about him." Cally snarled her nose up at her brother. "You're always trying to start trouble. You're such a pain!"

Before Corey could respond Mary interrupted, "Let's eat in peace this morning, please. Don't you two start fighting! Corey, you need to keep your opinions to yourself."

"Sure." Corey shrugged his shoulders and shoved a fork full of hash browns into his mouth. He smiled deviously at Cally as he chewed.

Mary turned toward Cally. "So, what all do you have planned today?"

78

Cally finished chewing and patted her lips with the napkin. "I'm going to the mall with Jessie and Beth and then to work, and maybe a movie tonight."

Mary glanced toward her husband, who had picked his newspaper back up. "Honey, did you have anything planned for Cally to do today?"

Bob glanced from Mary to Cally. "Not a thing. You guys can all do what you want. I'm going to try to get the garage cleaned out."

"Do you want the kids to help you?" Mary asked.

Cally's mouth dropped opened as she stared helplessly at her dad.

Bob glanced toward his wife. "No, honey. I think I would prefer to work by myself today. I'm just going to try to organize it a little better." He winked at Cally. "They would probably just get in the way anyway."

Cally smiled at her dad. She loved him so much. He'd always been the one to spoil her, and her mother was the one who did the disciplining. If Cally ever wanted something, she always knew she would get a lot further with her father than her mother. Her dad was always sneaking her money to help her with gas for her car—just last week he'd given her forty dollars to go shopping. Cally hadn't even asked for the money.

Cally finished her breakfast and kissed her dad on the forehead. "I'll probably be home before we go to the movies."

"Okay, honey, be careful." Bob went back to reading his newspaper.

Corey spoke up before Cally could get out the door, "Mom, can Cally give me and Travis a ride to the mall?"

"Oh, Mom, no," Cally whined.

Mary gathered the plates off the table. "No, Corey. I'll take you boys as soon as I do the dishes."

Before Corey had time to protest Cally called out, "Bye, Mom and Dad." The screen door slammed before she could hear Corey's huffed response.

79

***

By the time Cally picked up Jessie and Beth, it was time for the mall to open. The girls all agreed that their first stop would be Mindy's Casual Clothing.

Cally was looking for a new shirt to wear to the movies. She browsed through the racks, studying the variety of sweaters and blouses.

"Did Brad ask you out for another date?" Jessie asked.

"Not yet," Cally replied.

"That doesn't sound good." Beth frowned briefly before laughing.

"Oh, well, that's his loss." Cally tossed her head back and batted her eyes.

Jessie grinned. "I guess he doesn't know what he's missing out on."

"Or how grateful he should be." Beth rolled her eyes.

Cally popped Beth on the arm. "Hey, be nice." She spotted a pink top with navy flowers on it and held it up to her chest. "What do you gals think about this one?"

"I like it." Jessie nodded.

"I think it's cute. It would look so cool with jeans." Cally glanced at the price tag. "Hey, it's on sale, too. I think I'm going to get it."

"If you gals are done in here, can we go get a pretzel and juicy juice?" Beth smacked her lips together.

"Sounds good to me," Jessie said.

"I couldn't eat a thing. I just ate a big breakfast." Cally pulled her money out of her wallet and paid the clerk. "I might get one of the juices, though. Let's go," she said as she tucked the change into her purse.

Cally gasped as she stepped on the escalator. Right across from her, going up the other side, was Brad and Mark.

Beth spun around. "Look."

"I can see." Cally grinned and waved. Brad looks hotter today than he did last night, she thought.

Beth yelled, "You guys want to get a juice with us?"

"Sure, we'll meet you back down," Mark called out.

80

Beth glanced at Cally as they climbed off the escalator. "You don't mind, do you?"

Cally rested her hands on her hips. "What do you think?"

"She doesn't mind." Jessie smiled.

"It'll be fun. Mark is always a riot to hang out with." Beth motioned for the guys to hurry up as they climbed back on the escalator at the top.

Cally's eyes narrowed as she poked fun at Beth. "I think you have a crush on Mark. You're always talking about him."

"Get out of here!" Beth rolled her eyes.

"What do you think, Jessie? Do you think Beth has a crush on him?"

"I think…" Jessie didn't finish her sentence because the boys were climbing off the escalator. "Hi, guys," she said instead.

"What's going on? Hey, Sweet Potato, long time, no see." Mark smirked.

"Yeah, it's your lucky day," Beth teased.

"I'm surprised you girls are out and about this early," Brad said.

Beth smiled deviously. "Maybe if you wouldn't have taken Cally home so early, she'd still be sleeping."

Cally blushed—she could have killed her!

Beth smiled apologetic at Cally and turned toward Brad. She held her hands up in defense. "Sorry, I was just kidding. She didn't say a word."

"C'mon, let's go get that pretzel." Jessie led the way.

Cally pointed to a table against the wall. She forgave Beth and shoved her into the booth next to Mark. She then climbed into the seat across from Beth, and Brad scooted in next to her. She could feel the warmth of his leg, and her insides tingled slightly.

Every one chatted about the party from the night before, and Cally couldn't help but feel a whirl of emotions rousing inside every time Brad smiled at her. Her stomach was in twisted knots again. She couldn't understand why she'd had any doubts the night before. She was certain there wasn't a cuter or sweeter guy anywhere in the world.

81

CHAPTER SEVEN

David counted the money before tucking it into his wallet. "We still have eighty-two dollars. What else do you want to do?"

David and Josh had picked up the supplies they needed for the mission as soon as they arrived at the mall. They purchased disks for the camera, a sketchpad, pencils, pens, and some mailing envelopes. Josh had already called his dad, and he'd agreed that they could use the camera.

"Let's go to The Zone and see if they have any gloves that we could wear for the mission."

"That sounds awesome. We ought to get some black leather ones."

"Okay," Josh agreed. "That would look tough."

As they neared The Zone, David glanced into Leo's, a fast food place that students occasionally hung out at. David spotted Cally sitting with Brad and some other friends. What a jerk, David thought, as he glared at Brad.

Suddenly, Cally glanced up and waved. David quickly shifted his eyes in a different direction, pretending not to see her. He hoped Josh hadn't seen her waving. He didn't want him to think he had a friend, or he might feel obligated to tell Professor Slate.

The Zone was a men's clothing store that carried an assortment of stylish men's clothing and accessories. The prices were reasonable.

David instantly spotted a table full of gloves that were on sale and started browsing through them.

Josh picked up a pair of black leather gloves and held them up. "Hey, these are pretty neat. They are marked down, too."

"I like those." David grabbed the gloves from Josh and examined both sides of them before sliding his left hand into one. "Perfect. Is there another pair?"

Josh skimmed through the remaining pairs of gloves on the table until he found another pair. "Here's some." He slipped his hand into one of them. "Dude, I think these have my name on them!"

"I can't believe they are marked half price. They were originally twenty dollars."

"They're marked down because winter's over." Josh noticed some bandanas hanging on a rack nearby. "Hey look." He pointed toward the rack. "We could wear black bandanas, too."

"Awesome!" David picked up one of the bandanas and tied it around his head. He looked in the mirror that was hanging nearby. A few strands of his untamed hair hung loosely on his forehead. He thought the bandana made his protruding forehead smaller, and his eyes appear slightly larger. If it weren't for his pug nose, he would be a halfway-decent looking guy. He turned toward Josh. "Well, what do you think?"

"I like it. You look like an insane soldier! Awesome! Let me try one." Josh grabbed a bandana and tied it carefully over his spiked hair. He glanced into the mirror. "Now, all we need is some dark shades."

"You're right, that would look bad." David glanced around the store until he located them. "There they are." He pointed to the wall in the back of the store where rows of fashionable sunglasses were hanging.

They both tried on several different pairs and took turns admiring themselves in the mirror. Finally, ten minutes later, David asked, "How about these?" It was a black wire frame pair.

Josh found another pair just like the ones David had. They both tried to squeeze together in front of the little mirror to see how they looked together.

"I think we look hot. We'll look so awesome the day of the mission." Josh held his thumbs up.

"These aren't on sale—they're twelve bucks. We'll still have plenty left to eat, though." David calculated the figures with his finger on the palm of his hand. "It totals to fifty-four dollars plus tax. We'll still have over twenty bucks left."

"We can both eat on ten and that would still give us ten left to go to the movies or something." Josh paused. "Do you think we ought to save a little bit just in case we forgot something?"

"Yeah, you're probably right. We could skip the movie and just get something to eat." David pulled his wallet out to pay for all their new assets. "There aren't any good movies out right now, anyway."

Josh pointed toward Leo's. "Do you want to grab something to eat?"

"No. Let's go somewhere else." David didn't want to take a chance on seeing Cally again if she was still in there. He tried not to look in as he passed but couldn't help but glance toward the booth where they'd been sitting. He didn't see anyone, but they could be close by somewhere. "Are you ready to go? I'm getting hungry." He wanted to get out of the mall fast.

"I am too. I can't think of anything else we need," Josh said.

David kept his head bowed until they reached outside.

They were attempting to cross the street to the parking lot, but a car full of guys sped by in a blue mustang, causing them to jump back on the curb.

One of the stout guys in the back seat flung his head out the window and screamed, "Watch where you're going, losers!"

"Just ignore them!" Josh rolled his eyes. "That one guy is Nate Meyers. He's always trying to start trouble with someone."

David and Josh continued onward across the street toward Josh's car. They'd parked in the back of the parking lot due to the congested parking earlier.

David glimpsed toward the end of the block in the direction the blue mustang had gone. He watched as the car skidded to a stop, spun around, and headed back toward them. He had a sinking feeling that the guys were coming back to harass them some more. He thought they could probably run and make it to the car before the mustang reached them but that would make them look like chickens and then the bullies would probably never leave them alone. He nodded his head toward the blue car. "Looks like our friends are coming back. Here take these bags." David shoved the bags into Josh's hands. "If they start trouble, I'll distract them, and you go throw the bags in the car."

"I'm not leaving you alone with those creeps."

"I'll be fine. C'mon, please." David wiped his brow with the back of his hand. "We don't need to take any chances. Those punks might take all our new stuff, and we don't want to disappoint the Professor."

Josh ran his fingers through his spiked hair. "You're right. I'll get back here as soon as I can."

The metallic blue mustang pulled up right alongside of David and Josh. The same guy who had yelled earlier hung the top half of his body out the window. "You boys wouldn't need a ride, would you?"

"No, we don't." David shifted his gaze toward the ground.

The mustang came to a screeching halt. The boys hooted and hollered rudely as they crawled out of the windows.

There were four of them. David didn't recognize any of them, but he knew they meant trouble. He looked toward Josh's car; it was about fifty more feet away. David glanced awkwardly toward Josh and then toward the car. He was hoping Josh would get the hint and run. David slowed his pace down, and Josh picked upon the cue and broke into a jog toward his car.

The big boy that Josh had referred to as Nate seemed to hesitate as if he didn't know whether to run after Josh or stay close to David.

David cringed as Nate's malicious eyes met his. His body shivered as he glanced from one hoodlum to the next. They were dressed in baggy black jeans and sleeveless cut off black tee shirts. They had tattoos up and down their arms, earring piercings all through their ears, and their greasy hair was long and limp. A couple of them grinned fearlessly as cigarettes dangled from their lips.

Nate marched around the front of the Mustang, so he was directly in front of David. He flipped his cigarette on the ground,

85

shoved his hands in his pockets, and rocked on the back of his heels. "What was it that you called me back there when I drove by?"

"I didn't call you anything." David glanced to see if Josh was close to his car—he'd just reached the car and was fiddling with the keys.

"Oh, I think you did." Nate glanced toward Josh unlocking the car. "It looks like your friend isn't much of a friend." His eyes darted back to David. "Now, I think you owe me an apology for calling me that name."

The other three boys snickered.

"I didn't call you anything," David repeated.

"Do you know how mad I get when people call me names?" Nate pulled his hands out of his pocket, doubled up his fist, and repeatedly tapped his fist into the palm of his other hand.

David didn't respond. His stomach rumbled loudly—he wasn't sure if it was from hunger or from fear. His adrenaline was rapidly increasing. He'd been in a few fights before, but it was never his choice. And he'd never won a fight. He glanced toward the entrance door to see if a security guard was nearby, but there wasn't a sole around. He glanced toward Josh jogging back toward him. Oh great, now we're both going to be killed, David thought. Why didn't Josh blare on the horn or something?

"I'm talking to you, boy." Nate shifted his weight to his other foot and rested his hands on his hips.

David grimaced and shifted his eyes toward the ground.

Without any warning, Nate clinched his fist, pulled it back, and punched David in the nose, sending him stumbling backwards.

David's eyes widen—he hadn't seen the blow coming. He lifted his palm up to his nose and discovered dark scarlet blood oozing out. Before he could think what to do next, Nate's fist caught him in the eye. This time David fell completely backwards and hit the ground with a thud. The other boys were yelling and encouraging Nate to hit him again.

The boy with the longest hair teased, "Is that all you got in you, Nate?"

The other boys whistled and cheered more.

Josh yelled as he ran toward the group, "Hey, leave him alone. He didn't do anything to you."

David was trying to get to his feet. He could feel his eye swelling and blood running down his face. He had just regained his balance when Nate, ignoring Josh's pleads, doubled his fist up and socked David in the stomach.

David thought he was going to puke—he doubled over in pain. He didn't want to cry, but a small whimper escaped his lips. The blood from his nose was dripping all over his shirt.

"Stop it!" Josh screamed.

***

Cally locked hands with Brad and flirted as she followed Jessie, Beth and Mark out of the mall.

Beth was the first to notice the commotion going on across the parking lot. "Hey, look, a fight!"

Cally glanced in the direction Beth was pointing. There were a few people gathered around the fight. The stocky guy was Nate Meyers—she didn't know him personally, but she'd heard he liked to fight. She glanced toward the guy with blood on his face and immediately looked away—blood made her queasy. She knew who the other three guys were that were cheering for Nate because she had classes with them. That is…if they showed up. There was Rodney Davis, a total scumbag, Jake Welch, a pothead, and Randy Mills, another dope head. Cally knew that they were all known for causing trouble.

Cally's friends walked toward the fight. She reluctantly followed them. She glanced toward the guy with the bloody face as the poor boy took another jab to the jaw. He was still clutching his stomach with one hand and trying to stay balanced. He could barely stand on his feet.

The boy slowly lifted his head, and Cally almost collapsed. Her knees grew weak while her stomach rolled with nausea. She instantly recognized the boy—it was David. She hadn't recognized him before because he didn't have his glasses on. She now recalled his mom saying he didn't have to wear them all the time.

87

Cally's mind raced. She cringed as Nate hit David again. She was terrified that Nate was going to kill him. She shook Brad's arm frantically. "Tell them to stop! I work with his mom." Brad either didn't hear her or was ignoring her. She again repeated, "Tell them to stop! Please, Brad, do something! He's hurt. We need to get him to the hospital!"

"Oh, he's not hurt that bad," Brad said coolly.

She looked toward David just as Nate sent another blow to his stomach. This time David screamed in pain. He doubled over and fell to his knees. His hair was crimson from all the blood, and his shirt was covered with streaks of red. She spotted another kid, who she didn't recognize, trying to get to David. But Randy and Jake were holding him back, so he couldn't move. She assumed he was a friend of David's.

Cally was furious at Brad for not doing anything. She grabbed Jessie's shirt. "Help me stop this."

Jessie stared at Cally, puzzled. "How?"

Beth spun around. "That poor boy!"

Cally didn't have time to respond. She pushed her way through the crowd that had gathered. "Stop this right now, Nate Meyers!"

Nate casually glanced up at Cally. "What are you going to do, hit me with your pom pom?" Nate gave David a swift kick in the back while he was still on his knees. David fell over on his side, moaning.

Cally warned, "I just called the police, and they are on their way. And then your ass is going to jail." Cally swallowed—she couldn't believe her own words. She'd never been a very courageous person....until now.

Nate nervously glanced up and down the street. His friend, Rodney, was even more shaken up. He released the other boy's arms and jumped into his mustang. "C'mon, guys, let's get out of here!" Rodney fired up his car while the others crawled through the windows. The tires spun, and smoke clouded the area as he peeled out.

The crowd quickly thinned out, and everyone seemed to forget about David. Cally shook her head in disbelief. She assumed they didn't want to be a witness if the police really did show up.

She raced over to where David was lying on his side. His friend was already beside him. David's eyes were closed, and he was moaning in pain.

"We need to get him to the hospital," Cally said to the other boy.

The boy looked at Cally suspiciously. "That's okay. We don't need your help. I'll take care of him."

Beth and Jessie approached Cally.

"We're here to help," Jessie said.

Cally turned and nodded to acknowledge their presence. She spun back toward David's friend. "You do need our help. You can't get him to the car by yourself. I'm Cally Reeves. I work with David's mom at The Diner."

"He'll be okay." The boy bent down and tried to coax David into getting on his feet. But David couldn't get up—he continued to groan loudly.

Cally decided to take charge of the situation. She knew David needed to see a doctor. He'd already lost a lot of blood. She reached in her purse, grabbed her car keys, and tossed them to Jessie. "Go drive my car over here, so we can lift him into it."

Jessie, speechless and wide-eyed, clutched the keys tightly and dashed toward Cally's car.

Cally glanced at Beth. "Call The Diner and ask for Ann Clemons. Tell her to meet us at the hospital." She glanced around the parking lot. "Where are Mark and Brad? We could use their help lifting him into the car."

"Brad said he needed to get home, and Mark rode with him, so they left," Beth said.

Cally placed her hands on her hips. "He makes me so mad," she mumbled. She couldn't believe just minutes ago she'd had strong feelings toward him, and now she'd love to tell him to go to hell.

She sighed and turned toward David's moans. Jessie pulled up with the car, and Cally leaned forward and whispered to David, "You're going to be okay. We're going to take you to the hospital. Your mom is going to meet us there."

89

David's speech was slurred, but he clearly muttered, "No."

"See, he doesn't want to go to the hospital." The other boy nervously fiddled with the hoop earring dangling from his ear.

Cally ignored the boy's cocky remark and turned toward Jessie. "Open the back door, please." She glanced at David's friend, "Excuse me, what is your name?"

The boy hesitated and then grumbled, "Josh."

"Josh, will you please help me lift him into the back seat of the car?"

Josh shuffled his feet against the pavement—his eyes narrowed as he stared callously at Cally.

Cally thought he might protest.

He glanced toward David and then at Cally. He finally bent down and wrapped David's arm around his neck. He carefully lifted him onto his feet.

David gasped in pain.

They lowered him easily into the back seat of the car.

David's hand traveled slowly up toward his face. He touched his jaw and groaned.

By the time David was loaded into the car Beth had returned. "His mom is going to meet us there." She jumped into the passenger seat.

"Do you want to ride in back with David?" Cally asked Josh. "I can ride up front."

"No, I have my car here," he snapped. "I'll just go on to the hospital."

"Are you sure?"

"I'm sure." Josh rolled his eyes.

"Okay. We'll see you there." Cally crawled in beside David. "Let's go!"

Jessie checked the rearview mirror and pulled away from the curb.

Cally scooted up to the edge of the seat. "Beth, could you hand me all the napkins out of the glove compartment, please.

She snatched the handful of napkins from Beth and turned back toward David. She struggled to keep the food in her stomach intact; the blood was almost intolerable. "David, can you hear me? I have some napkins to help soak up some of the

90

blood." She noticed his eyes were continuously blinking as he tried to focus on her. "Here, I am just going to rub lightly on your face." She gently dabbed at his cheek.

"Ouch!" he winced.

"I'm sorry." Cally stopped. "Does that hurt?"

"Yeah." He tilted his head sideways." But that's okay," he mumbled. "Does it look really bad?"

"Well, it will look better when they get you stitched up." Cally tried to sound sincere, although she had her doubts. She continued to wipe at the blood running down his face. "Why did those guys do this to you?"

"It's just their nature, I guess." David's eyes locked with Cally's, and he immediately looked away. "Thanks for your help." He moaned as she touched the area around his eye. "I thought he was going to kill me."

"Yeah, I did, too. Well, you're going to be all right now. We're almost there."

David leaned his head back against the seat and closed his eyes.

A sense of relief flooded Cally as she spotted the hospital emergency sign. She was certain she wouldn't be able to eat for days after witnessing so much blood. She'd never been so frightened in her life. Fortunately, she'd never been in a fight before, and it wasn't something that she wanted to witness ever again, either. She blinked back tears and bit down on her lower lip. She refused to cry. She couldn't believe that Nate and his friends could be so cruel or that Brad could be so heartless!

91

CHAPTER EIGHT

The doctor pulled the needle out of David's arm, patted the injected spot with a cotton ball, and placed a band-aid over it.

David's pain eventually subsided. The emergency room hadn't been busy, and fortunately, he had got right in to see the doctor.

Dr. Nolker was a young doctor in his mid-forties with neatly cut curly black hair and gold wired-rimmed glasses that suggested he had elegant taste. The wrinkles in his forehead deepened as he examined David's face; he seemed to be in deep concentration. He bent forward to stitch up the cut above David's eye. "I sure hope whoever did this to you is sitting in jail."

"Probably not." David winced as the doctor touched his cheek.

"Is it sore there, too?"

"Yeah."

A middle-age redheaded lady knocked on the door before opening it slightly. "Dr. Nolker, the boy's mother is here and would like to come in."

"Sure, Alice, send her on in. Please inform her of David's condition and tell her not to be alarmed when she sees him."

"Yes, sir." Alice closed the door softly.

A few minutes later Ann rushed into the room. She took one look at her son and covered her mouth with her hand. "Oh,

David, what happened? Are you okay?" She gently placed her hand over his.

"I'm fine, Mom." David was aware of how bad he looked because he had stolen a glimpse in the mirror above the sink. His eye was swollen shut, and his hair was matted with blood. His clothes were stained and beyond cleaning. David glanced past her toward the door. "Where's Josh?"

Ignoring him, Ann repeated, "What happened?"

"Some jerk decided to practice his boxing on me."

"Is he going to be okay?" Ann asked Dr. Nolker.

"He'll be fine. I need to stitch him up in a few places and do some x-rays to make sure he doesn't have any fractured bones. He's going to be exceptionally sore for a while, but in a few days, he'll be back to normal. I'll give him a prescription for the pain." He sighed. "Someone should be reprimanded for doing this."

Ann stared at David. "I can't believe someone could be this cruel. Please, do whatever you think is necessary, Doctor." Ann shook her head in disbelieve. "David, did you do anything to provoke this guy?"

"No, Mom. This was just his idea of fun." David should have known his mom would suggest that it was his fault and that he had started the fight.

"Where did it happen?" Ann asked as the doctor stitched David's cheek.

"At the mall. Josh and I were just leaving to go get something to eat." He paused while the doctor finished stitching. "Now, I probably won't be able to open my mouth to eat."

"Sure, you will." Dr. Nolker smiled.

"Well, I'm glad Cally was nearby. I'm so thankful that she got you here." Ann squeezed David's hand lightly. "And bless her; she rushed right down to The Diner to finish my shift."

"Yeah," David mumbled. "Where's Josh?" He wished she would just go into the lobby and wait. All her jabber was making him nauseous.

Ann quickly let go of David's hand, so the doctor could slide up closer to David's other side. "He is still in the waiting room.

He's pretty shook up." She folded her arms across her chest. "Where was he while this was going on?"

"I'm not sure. I didn't have much time to look around for him," David snapped.

Dr. Nolker picked up a towel and wiped his hands. "Well, David, I think that's all the stitches you're going to need." He inspected David's face closely. "Yes, I think that'll do it. If you'll come with me, I'll take you down to the x-ray room."

The doctor strolled over to the sink to wash his hands while David eased off the hospital table.

David moaned softly as he attempted to walk.

The doctor dried his hands and turned toward Ann. "He'll need to stay home from school for a few days. I'll have Alice give you a doctor's excuse."

"Thank you."

The doctor held the door open for David while turning back toward Ann. "We'll be right back—you're welcome to wait here for us?" He pointed to the vacant chair in the room. "Have a seat."

"Okay, thanks."

"I'll send Alice in to do the paper work for insurance and ask you a few questions before I write out his prescription."

"Alright."

Dr. Nolker smiled sympathetically as he closed the door behind him.

***

A few minutes later, Alice opened the door and smiled warmly. "Are you doing okay?"

"Yes, I'm fine. I'm just worried about my son and how I'm going to pay for all of this." Ann threw her hands up in the air. "My insurance isn't the best." She already had to struggle day by day to keep her bills paid. She couldn't imagine another bill on top of the ones she had. She massaged her temples as she visualized the junk in the storage room at home and wondered what she could possibly sell.

94

"We'll be glad to work out payment arrangements." Alice paused before handing Ann some papers. "I need to know if David is allergic to anything."

Ann shook her head. "No, nothing."

"Okay. Fill out these papers, and I need to make a copy of your insurance card."

Ann's hand trembled as she reached into her purse to retrieve the card. "Here it is."

"Thanks. Here's his doctor's excuse. I'll be back shortly." Alice disappeared quietly out the door.

Ann finished the necessary paper work and then swore under her breath at David's father for being the bastard that he was. How could she have been such a fool to fall for such a loser, leaving her all alone to raise David? She had wanted so badly to give David a better life than what she'd had, but she just wasn't able to do it alone.

She tapped her pen impatiently on the clipboard as she waited silently for the return of her son. She prayed there wouldn't be any more bad news. All she needed was more medical expenses. She figured if the bills didn't let up soon, she'd have to get a third job. And then she wondered when she would sleep.

Ann stood. She figured she should let Josh know the outcome of David's injuries. But she suddenly changed her mind and sat back down. She was scared that the doctor would return while she was gone.

The door suddenly opened, and David entered with the doctor following close behind. "Well, it looks like he's a lucky boy." Dr. Nolker scribbled a prescription. "He doesn't have any broken bones."

"Oh, thank God." Ann sighed.

"I'm going to prescribe him some pain medicine. They will make him drowsy, so he might be sleeping a lot the next 48 hours, so don't be alarmed. You're pharmacy will give you additional information that will explain more in detail. If after a few days, he feels like he can return to school then go ahead and send him. He might want to take a couple of Tylenol before he leaves the house, though." He handed Ann the prescription and patted David on the back. "You're a fortunate boy; it could have

95

been a whole lot worse. You should be fine in a few days. Just take it easy and get some rest."

"I will. Thanks."

"Thank you so much, Doctor." Ann extended her hand to shake his.

"You're welcome. Take care of yourself, David." Dr. Nolker held the door open for them.

***

Josh jumped up to greet David as they entered the waiting room. "Are you okay?" He asked as he examined David's face. He wasn't a bit surprised at how swollen his eye was.

"I think so. I'm just in pain." David tried to grin but moaned instead.

"I'm sorry, man!" Josh shook his head. "I couldn't get to you. Those psychos wouldn't let go of me."

"That's okay. It's not your fault."

Ann dug her keys out of her purse. "You boys wait here. I'm going to go get the car."

The boys nodded as she exited the building.

"I shouldn't have left you alone with those thugs." Josh bowed his head—he was drowning in guilt. He couldn't believe he'd actually left his best friend behind.

"This is not your fault. I'm just glad you saved our merchandise."

"I feel really bad about this."

"I'm fine. The doctor says I'll be better in a few days."

Josh examined David's face again. "How many stitches did you get?"

"Doctor Nolker said there was sixteen total. Hey, how come that Cally girl drove me here?"

"She insisted." Josh rolled his eyes. "That bitch thought she was hot shit! She pissed me off." He'd never hit a girl before, but he'd come close today.

Ann pulled the car up to the front door and hurried around to open the door for David. "Did you want to come by the house, Josh?"

96

Josh couldn't help but stare at David—he looked horrible. "Do you feel like hanging?"

"Yeah, for awhile. I'll probably sleep soon, though. I'm really beat!" David tried to grin. "Okay, wrong choice of words. I am really tired."

"I bet you are! Hey, I'll just meet you at your house."

David slowly eased his body into the front seat of his mom's car. "See you shortly."

"I have to stop and get his prescription filled before we go home," Ann told Josh as she shut the passenger door.

"That's cool. I need to get something to eat first anyway." Josh waved and jogged across the parking lot to his car. He couldn't quit thinking about how the recent incidents were going to affect the mission. As awful as he felt about David, he was far more concerned what Professor Slate would say. Josh slammed his fist against the steering wheel—he would be devastated if the mission was delayed. He couldn't take living with his mother much longer.

***

Cally finished wiping off the counter and sighed. It was finally time for a break. The last customer from the rush hour lunch had just walked out the door. She rinsed her washrag, wrung it out, and draped it over the back of the sink to dry. It had been a busy hour, and the excitement of the fight earlier today had left her drained.

She fixed a glass of coke, grabbed a magazine, and sat down at the end of the counter. She skimmed through the pages but couldn't seem to concentrate on the pictures. Her mind jumped back to the earlier incident. She hoped David was okay. He'd been in a lot of pain when she'd taken him to the hospital.

She hadn't care for his friend Josh. He was extremely rude and acted like he didn't like her or want her to help David.

She flipped the page and stared at the picture of an attractive boy and girl holding hands, sitting on a bench in a park. She immediately thought of Brad. Suddenly her nostrils flared as her anger increased. She couldn't believe he wouldn't help David.

97

He'd left without even making sure the kid was all right. He didn't even say goodbye or tell her that he had to leave. "Bastard," she said aloud. She never wanted to talk to him again. How could he have been so shallow today and so sweet last night? Cally couldn't believe it had been only last night that they'd had their first date. She'd liked him for so long—now he'd totally disappointed her. Cally tried to fight back the tears but caught one tear with the back of her hand.

She jumped as the bell from the front door chimed. She spun around just as Beth and Jessie entered. She'd forgotten they'd taken her car to see if they could clean the blood off the back seat. Cally swallowed and cleared her throat, "Hi, gals. Did the blood come out?"

Beth laid a five-dollar bill on the counter. "We got most of it up—there's still a light spot that we couldn't get up." She tapped her finger on the five. "We're dying of thirst! Could we get a couple of cokes?"

"Put your money away. It's on me...for cleaning my car."

The cook stuck his head out behind the swinging door to see if he had customers.

"Don't worry, Don, they aren't ordering food," Cally said.

Don nodded his head toward Jessie and Beth. "Hello." He glanced back at Cally, "If you need me, I'll be out back smoking."

"Take your time; the rush should be over for a bit."

Don disappeared behind the swinging doors. Cally fixed the girls a coke.

Jessie took a long sip and stared at Cally. "Are you okay? You don't look so hot."

"I think I'm emotionally drained. That was a horrible experience today."

"And Brad probably didn't help matters any, either. He shouldn't have left until we knew that the kid was all right. That poor kid." Jessie shook her head as she sat down at the counter.

Beth nodded. "Yeah, that was pretty shitty of Brad. Mark had to leave because he rode with Brad. I don't blame Mark; he couldn't help it."

Jessie grinned at Beth. "Sure, defend Mark. I swear you have the biggest crush on him."

"Maybe I do." She smiled.

"Well, I don't blame Mark, but I'll never speak to Brad again." Cally was on the verge of tears again.

"Oh, don't be that hard on him, Cal—I'm sure he had a good reason," Beth said.

Cally's eyebrows furrowed as she glared at Beth. "Surely, you don't believe that, do you?"

"Well, maybe not." She shrugged. "Okay I'm just trying to cheer you up."

"Thanks. I know you mean well." Tears sprung to Cally's eyes before she could stop them. She didn't care anymore; she let them slide freely down her cheeks.

"Come here, you poor thing." Beth wrapped her arms around her. "It'll be okay."

Jessie dug a Kleenex out of her purse and handed it to Cally. She rubbed her arm. "I'm so sorry all of this happened."

"You need to take the rest of the day off," Beth said.

"I can't. There's no one else to work for me. My boss won't even be back until this evening." Cally quickly moved toward the sink. "Which reminds me, I better get back to work. I need to get this place cleaned up and ready for the dinner hour."

"Here are your keys." Jessie laid the keys on the counter.

"How will you guys get home?" Cally picked the dishrag up. "If you want, go ahead and keep my car. Just pick me up at six."

"Are you sure?" Jessie asked.

"Sure. Why don't you two go see a movie? I'll be too tired to go this evening anyway. By the time the movie is over, it should be time for me to get off."

Jessie glanced at Beth. "Well, Sweet Potato, what do you think? Do you want to?

"Sounds good to me." Beth gave Cally a brief hug. "Okay, we will be back later then."

"That's fine," Cally said.

Jessie snatched the keys up and hugged Cally. "I promise I'll be careful with your car."

99

"I know you will. See you gals later." Cally closed the door behind them. She closed her eyes as her mind drifted to her date with Brad. She could still feel his muscular arms around her waist as they danced. Her nose tingled as she recalled the sweet smelling cologne that he was wearing. She recalled how tickled he'd got earlier today when she'd told him about the prank she'd pulled on Corey when he was younger—feeding him burnt popcorn and telling him it was blueberry popcorn.

Cally's eyes fluttered back opened. She pressed her forehead against the clammy window and stared out into the lively street. "Well, Cindy, you can have him," she mumbled under her breath.

Suddenly, the muscles in her jaw tightened as she stared at the figure walking directly in front of her. His head jerked toward her, and she could feel his eyes swallowing every inch of her. He didn't wave nor did he smile. He just stared with those huge bulging eyes and then he shifted his eyes back in front of him and continued up the sidewalk...almost like nothing ever happened.

Cally shivered as she shrunk back away from the window. Every time that man got near her, she got chills. She knew it wasn't just because of his appalling looks either—there was something very disturbing about the man—and it frightened her terribly.

100

CHAPTER NINE

Josh flipped on the TV, quickly turned it down, and spun around to see if he'd woken David, but David was already awake and adjusting the pillows. He'd had a hard time getting down the stairs, but had insisted on being in his own bed since he had his own toilet downstairs. Josh had hung around and played on the computer while David dozed.

Josh felt like he might have prevented the incident had he stuck around and not gone to the car. He cringed as the horrible images tugged at him—but David had insisted that he put the bags in the car.

He'd suggested to David that they call the police and press charges against Nate and his colleagues, but David hadn't want to—in fear that Professor Slate would find out.

Josh could hardly wait for the day to come when he'd stand back and laugh, while Nate and his buddies were in pain. That day would come soon, too!

Josh studied the reflection in the mirror. His eyes were puffy and bloodshot from lack of sleep. He ran his hands through his hair, trying to tousle the limp spikes. He needed more gel to restyle it. He licked his fingers and slicked the sides of his hair back. A nasty habit he wouldn't dare do in public. He glanced toward David. He was starting to drift off again. "Hey, Smurf, what should we do about the pictures we were supposed to sketch and the photographs? This is going to delay the mission."

David's eyes flew open. "No, it won't! We can't let the professor find out anything. We'll just go ahead as planned." He tried to sit up but moaned instead and lay back down. "When is your dad bringing you the camera?"

Josh had already told David earlier, but he must have already forgotten, probably due to the medication he was taking. "He's coming down tomorrow at noon. I'm supposed to spend the day with him." Josh made a face. He didn't look forward to spending any time with his father. "Anyway, I won't get to come by here."

"That's okay. I'll probably sleep most of the day, anyway. You're going to have to take the pictures yourself on Monday. I'll work on some sketches of the school while I'm at home. After school you should come by, and we'll decide what to do next."

"What do I do if someone catches me and rats me out?" Josh patted his pocket where he had stashed his weed. He wished Ann wasn't home so he could light up.

"Hopefully, no one will see you, but if they do, just make up something. Tell them you're doing some kind of report on the architecture of the building or something."

"That's cool. I'll think of something. I sure don't want to drop the ball—it seems like I have a tendency to screw up every other situation!" He glanced toward the TV. "I guess I should take pictures of all the rooms and the vent in the boys' room."

"Yeah, you better. And then we'll decide what else we need to send."

"Do you think we should contact him and let him know we got everything to proceed to the next level?"

"No, let's wait until after Monday." David yawned. "I don't know if I can stay awake any longer—I'm getting really tired."

"That's okay. You go ahead and crash. I need to be getting home anyway. Ma might be sober and looking for me." Josh rolled his eyes. It was late, and he knew she would be drunk on her ass. He figured he'd swing by the lake and smoke a joint before going home to face the bitch.

David smiled faintly. "Okay, see you later. Call me sometime tomorrow."

102

"Okay. I don't know what time it will be..." Josh didn't finish because David's eyes were already closed. He probably wouldn't remember anything they had discussed anyway.

Josh gathered his CD's. This was the worst time for all of this to happen. They were so close to finishing the mission. It was just yesterday that he had been on cloud nine because they were getting closer to the end. He'd been patiently waiting for that special day—and now this had to happen. If the mission were delayed any longer—that would be so fucked up! If it was the last thing he ever did, he was going to make sure Nate Meyers paid for what he done.

***

By the time Jessie and Beth picked up Cally from The Diner, it was close to seven. Cally's boss had asked her if she would stay longer because they were swamped during the dinner hour. Virgil and Betty Raker had been so good to her since she'd started working there, she didn't have the heart to tell them no. She'd agreed to stay, although she was mentally exhausted.

Cally climbed in the driver's seat of her car and pulled away from the curb. "What a day. I just want to go home, soak in a hot tub, and go to bed."

"What a way to spend your Saturday night," Beth teased.

"I bet you are tired," Jessie added.

"I am. Have either of you heard anything about David?"

"No. I heard Sandi Lynn and Dee Bunner talking about it at the movies. All they heard is what had happened today. Of course, their story was totally stretched." Jessie said.

"Yeah," Beth added from the backseat. "They heard that Nate Meyers had already been arrested and was sitting in jail." She snorted. "Yeah right. He has probably already forgotten about David. He's probably high on dope and beating up some other kid by now."

Cally nodded. "Would you gals mind if I stop by and see how David's doing before I take you home? I won't be but a minute. I got his address from my boss."

"I don't have anything else to do anyway." Jessie cracked the window and tossed her chewed gum out.

"I do. It's Saturday night, I have to bathe." Beth giggled.

Cally glanced over her shoulder. "You do? I thought you did that last Monday."

"You're right, I did. Okay, I guess I can go then." Beth smiled.

Cally drove toward the opposite end of town. She came to a four way stop on Lexington Street and turned left onto Delaware Street. She straightened and flipped the visor back to its normal position, so it didn't obstruct her view. She'd never been on this side of town.

She drove down the narrow street slowly, looking for the number 815. She glanced around uneasily, noticing the run down and poorly maintained houses. Most of the homes were undersized and cramped too closed together, and they all desperately needed painted. A few of them had shattered windows and shutters that were barely hanging on their hinges The grass had grown knee-length in many of the yards, and wild weeds were sprouting up everywhere.

One faded gray house looked like a dumpster. There were old sinks, tin cans, beer cans, and even an old toilet stool sitting in the middle of the yard.

Cally momentary glanced up toward the loud racket coming from a red brick house with a shabby wraparound porch. Some scruffy looking men with scrubby beards and cigarette's dangling from their mouths were sitting on rusted lawn chairs, laughing and cursing loudly. Cally snarled up her nose and quickly shifted her eyes back to the street.

Jessie nervously glanced up and down the street. "I think we better lock our doors."

"No kidding," Beth quickly rolled her window up.

"I promise I won't be gone long." Cally slowed down as she approached some kids playing baseball in the street. Most of them were wearing ragged clothes, and a few of them were barefooted. They seemed annoyed because they had to move out of her way. They stared rudely, and one kid even flipped Cally off. "I don't think I like this neighborhood." She chewed nervously on her bottom lip.

A few blocks further, she spotted the number 815 on a tan house on the right side of the road. Parked in the driveway was Ann's old blue Citation. Cally quickly pulled up to the curb. The house was nicer than some of the other houses she'd just witnessed, but it still needed attention. The tan paint was flaking off, revealing several white spots. A few of the tiles from the roof were missing. One of the wooden stairs leading up to the front door was cracked and uneven. The dull green curtains in the window were drawn tightly closed.

Cally shuddered—she couldn't believe people actually lived like this. There was no way she could function in a place like this. Her mind raced to her own comfortable home, and she instantly wished she were there. She didn't know what possessed her to drive to Ann's house. Why didn't she just call her and ask how David was? Too late now!

Her eyes remained on the house as she slid the gear in park. She couldn't help but feel sorry for Ann and David. "I'll leave the car running." Cally looked up and down the street before climbing out of the car. "Lock my door when I get out."

"Don't worry, we will," Jessie said.

"I'll hurry." Cally slammed the car door and walked swiftly up the worn out stairs, taking extra caution as she stepped on the cracked one. It made a tiny squeak and she continued on. She paused briefly at the door and tapped lightly. She waited a few seconds and then knocked again. After a few more seconds, she heard feather-like footsteps.

Ann cracked the door slightly without removing the chain. She peeked out and then immediately unlatched the chain. She pulled the door open, "Cally, hi. Is everything okay?"

"Yeah, everything's fine. I just finished up at The Diner, and I was on my way home. I was just concerned how David was doing. Virgil didn't think you'd mind if he gave me your address?"

"Oh no, not at all. Come on in." Ann held open the door for Cally to enter.

105

Cally stepped into the living room. Although the room had very little furniture, it was still spotlessly clean. An older couch with a flowered throw cover was scooted against the wall; another brown chair that didn't match was in the corner of the room. A rectangle coffee table with a candle on it set in front of the couch. There was a nineteen-inch TV setting on a discolored TV stand with a rerun of 'I Love Lucy' playing. "I can't stay but a minute. I have friends in the car waiting for me. I just wanted to make sure David was okay."

Ann peered out the front door at Jessie and Beth sitting in the car. When they looked her way, she waved at them and turned back toward Cally. "He's fine. He didn't have any broken bones. Thank God! The doctor stitched up the cuts on his face and gave him some medicine for the pain. He's been sleeping most of the day."

"I'm so glad he's okay. I've been worried about him all day."

"Cally, thank you so much for what you did for him today. I'm so glad you were there." She embraced Cally and then held her at arm's length. "You're a real life saver. And then you covered for me and worked my shift, too. I bet you're beat! I owe you, whatever favor you need...anything! Just let me know."

"Don't worry about it. I know you would have done the same for me."

Ann glanced toward the basement stairs. "David's awake now if you want to go say hi. I just took him some soup down."

"Well, if you don't think he'd mind." Cally would rather not. She felt foolish enough for stopping by.

"No, not at all. Follow me." Ann walked through the narrow kitchen to the top of the stairs and yelled down, "David, Cally's here to see you. Are you feeling up to some company?"

After a few seconds of silence David called back up the stairs, "Yeah, sure."

Ann pointed to the stairs. "Go on down."

"Thanks." Cally walked awkwardly down the stairs and into David's secluded room. "Hello, David."

David was sitting up in bed with the covers pulled over his lap and a bowl of soup sitting on a tray in front of him. "Hi."

106

"You sure do look a lot better. Are you feeling okay?" Cally tried to keep her eyes focused on David and not his messy room. Although she could see all the scattered clothes, out of the corner of her eyes.

"Yeah, better than what I was." David hesitated and shifted his eyes toward Cally's feet. "Thanks for your help today."

"Oh, you're welcome. I'm just glad you're okay." Cally folded her arms across her chest. "I can't stay. My friends are waiting out in the car. Is there anything you need?"

"No. Thanks for stopping by." He briefly glanced up and then immediately lowered his eyes toward his bowl.

"You're welcome. See you later." Cally spun around and jogged back up the stairs where Ann was waiting.

"Well, what did you think?" Ann asked.

"He looks a lot better than the last time I saw him."

"I hope he won't have scars." Ann frowned and followed Cally to the front door.

"I bet he won't. I think doctors now days do a great job. Well, I better go—I need to take my friends home."

"Okay. Thanks for stopping by."

"You're welcome." Cally shivered as she walked back to her car. She didn't know if it was from the cool breeze or from witnessing such an unusual lifestyle.

***

Ann waited for Cally to pull away from the curb before she shut the door and latched the chain. She glanced uneasily around her tiny house, embarrassed that Cally had seen it. She ran her hand across the coffee table to see if any dust collected to her fingers. She didn't see any but blew on her fingers anyway to make sure. She was sure David's room was a mess, though. He never cleaned it, and she didn't have the time to do it either. Not with all the other housework she had to keep up.

She didn't have nice furniture because money was too hard to come by. By the time she paid her bills and bought food, there was never much left. When she did have leftover money, she saved to buy David the things he needed, although there were

107

still many things that he had to go without. He didn't have nice clothes like the other kids in school. Most of his clothes came from garage sales. However, she'd been fortunate enough to find him a computer and stereo at an auction for very little. She'd also found him a nice thirteen-inch color TV for twenty dollars at a flea market. He'd been so thrilled and appreciative of them. He never complained about the way they lived.

The only thing that really seemed to disturb David was not knowing where his father was. He was always asking questions. His dad hadn't been in his life since he was born. When Ann was seventeen she'd fallen in love with Darrel and became pregnant shortly after her eighteenth birthday. Darrel had promised her that they would marry and raise the baby together. But they never did marry. Instead they lived together in a poorly maintained one-bedroom apartment.

As the pregnancy advanced, Darrel's behavior changed drastically. He started staying out late with his buddies and drinking more. It wasn't long before he started physically abusing her. Two weeks before the baby's due date, they got into a huge fight. Darrel had been seeing another woman, and Ann had found out. It was late that night when Darrel arrived home, and he was drunk again. She confronted him about the other woman. He became so angry and beat her so badly—she thought she was going to die. He cursed and yelled things like, '*you fat bitch. I don't want any crying baby around this house. I'm going to kill the fucking baby if you have it.*'

Ann believed he meant every word, too. She was surprised she hadn't lost the baby from all the beatings already. When he passed out, she packed what little she had and left him. That was the last time she ever seen Darrel.

She stayed with her cousin until she got back on her feet. Her parents were both deceased, and she hadn't any other relatives. Her aunt, who had raised her while she was growing up, had recently past away. Ann asked Family Services for help and they helped her until she could get back to work.

Darrel never did try to contact her to see his child. She later heard he'd gone to jail for robbery. Ann didn't know if he was still in jail or not—nor did she care. She just knew she didn't want David to ever know who his father was. Ann knew it'd be painful for him to learn what kind of person his father had become. But at the same time, she didn't want to lie to him either. So far, she'd been able to avoid the issue when David asked about him. She knew the day would come when she would have to tell David the truth.

Ann had started seeing Roy nine months ago. Roy was everything Darrel wasn't. He was kind, intelligent, and extremely good-looking. Although he'd asked her to marry him, she hadn't accepted yet. She knew David didn't get along with him too well, and she didn't want to complicate the situation. She also wanted to wait until Roy had a reliable, steady job. She was hoping to only have to work one job. Ann was tired of trying to juggle two jobs and be a mother, too. It was a good thing that David was a decent kid, and she didn't have to spend a lot of time worrying about him getting in trouble. Maybe in time, David and Roy would start to like each other and then they could all become one big happy family. Until then she would just live day by day and hope for the best.

CHAPTER TEN

Sunday, April 25, 2001

Sunday wasn't usually a restful day for Cally. Most of the time, it was hectic with church, working at the café and doing homework and laundry. But earlier in the day Ann had called and offered to work for Cally to return the favor. Cally eagerly accepted. She was still worn out from the chaos the day before.

She took advantage of the time off from work and relaxed some. She didn't even get out of bed until after noon. Her mother had let her skip church, so she had the whole house to herself. Her family usually went shopping or to a movie after church, so she knew they wouldn't be home until later in the day. She'd missed breakfast, so she grabbed a cold sandwich and some chips for lunch. Cally watched a movie and soaked her aching muscles in a hot bubble bath.

She decided to curl her hair with soft sponge curlers for some extra bounce. As she gathered the curlers, the phone rang. With her free hand, she picked up the receiver. "Hello." She half expected it to be Beth and was shocked to hear the voice on the other end.

"Hello, Cally. It's me, Brad. Are you busy?"

Cally silently gasped. He'd caught her off guard, and she wasn't sure whether to slam the phone down or tell him off first.

But she was curious why he'd called—she'd give him a chance to speak first. "No, I'm not."

"Cally, about yesterday, I'm sorry I didn't stick around. I guess I was scared to get involved. I thought the police would be coming, and I just wanted to get away from the situation."

"Brad, the boy was badly hurt. He needed help." Cally paused letting her words sink in. "You didn't even tell me you were leaving."

"I'm sorry. I just didn't think about it at the time. When I thought the police might be coming, I just panicked and told Mark if he wanted a ride, we needed to go."

"But you knew I hadn't really called the police." Cally twisted the phone cord around her finger.

"Yeah, but I didn't know if someone else had. I'm sorry, Cally. I just got scared. My parents have threatened to take my car away if I get involved with the police in any way."

"Did you know that we had to take him to the hospital? I really could have used your help."

"I know. Beth told Mark about it this morning, and he called and told me. I was going to call you last night, but I had to help my grandpa move some furniture, and it was late when I got home. I wish I could take back the childish way I acted."

Although Cally was upset with him, something was tugging at her heart to forgive him. She never could stay mad at anyone very long, especially if they were remorseful. She sighed. "Well, let's just forget about it."

"Does that mean you forgive me?"

"I'm thinking about it." She grinned. "Give me some time."

"Do you think you might still want to go out with me next weekend?"

"I'll have to let you know later in the week."

"You mean you don't know if you'll still be mad?"

"No, silly." Cally's anger quickly diminished. "I don't know what my work schedule is yet."

"Oh, okay. Well, I'll see you tomorrow at school then."

"Okay." Cally listened for the click on the other end.

She couldn't believe she'd just talked to Brad and forgave him—after she'd cried herself to sleep last night. She'd thought

111

everything was over between them. It hadn't even been 24 hours since she'd been so mad.

Her insides suddenly warmed. She was glad he'd called and apologized. Cally knew it still didn't excuse the way he'd acted. However, she'd give him another chance. But next time, she wasn't going to hesitate to break it off with him!

***

David's body had never ached so badly in his life. He'd slept almost the whole day. He couldn't believe it was already Sunday night. His mom had gone to work earlier, but she'd brought his food, medicine, and a cooler of tea down to him before she'd left. The painkillers worked for a while but once they started wearing off, the pain was unreal. The only thing he'd accomplished for the day was a few trips to the restroom and even that took a lot of effort.

David never would have imagined a person could endure so much pain. Just the name Nate Meyers made his blood curl. He wanted revenge so bad; he didn't know if he could wait until the mission. He didn't have much of a choice, though; he could barely walk now. He sure hoped the soreness ceased within the next day or two, or they would have to postpone the mission. He talked to Josh earlier, and he'd gotten the digital camera from his dad. He was planning to take the pictures tomorrow after school.

David could vaguely remember discussing the mission with Josh last night, but he did remember telling him that they should wait and write the professor tomorrow after school. However, after he thought about it all day, he'd almost convinced himself that it would probably be best if he wrote the professor and thanked him for the money. He sure didn't want the professor to think something was wrong. He might decide to delay the mission. He let the thought stumble a few times in his head, and then decided to go ahead and write him. He'd explain to Josh later.

David moaned as he sat up. Just trying to get to the computer was going to be a task. He slowly eased off the bed and staggered slowly to the computer. He waited for the computer to boot up and then typed:

Professor Slate,
We wanted to thank you for the money you gave us. We got all the supplies necessary for the mission. We will take pictures of the school and draw sketches tomorrow. We should be ready to mail them to you by Tuesday. Everything is going smoothly. Thanks so much for choosing us to do this mission. We promise you won't be sorry.
Smurf & Scooby

David sent the message and then scanned his emails. After deleting all of the spam emails, he hobbled back to his bed. His jaw was aching—he reached for the pain medicine bottle on the floor with the arm that didn't hurt. He poured himself some tea out of the cooler and popped a pill in his mouth.

David wished he had something soft to eat. His mother had brought him a couple of sandwiches and some chips before she'd left. He'd devoured that earlier and was getting hungry again. He eyed the stairs and wondered if he should attempt to climb them. He would have to try it eventually. He kicked his feet over the side of the bed but was too weak to go any further. He decided not to push his luck.

He secretly wished his mom hadn't gone back to work. He'd enjoyed the extra attention he'd received from her yesterday. It was very rare to have his mom around without Roy hanging at her heels. David knew she'd lost money yesterday, staying at home with him, but he still wished she'd taken one more day off.

A single tear rolled down David's cheek. He flicked it off with the back of his hand. He thought of the professor and wondered what he would say. He recalled Professor Slate once quoting, *'the people in our lives who pretend that they care about us only care about themselves.'* David thought about it for a long moment. He suddenly changed his mind, he was glad his mom hadn't stayed home with him. If she really loved him, she wouldn't be seeing Roy. She knew how much he hated him.

He didn't need his mom; he'd get well all by himself. He didn't need anyone except Josh and Professor Slate. He would get even with Nate Meyers for what he'd done. He'd get even with J.D. for bullying him in the hallways. He'd show that punk, Brad Taylor, what a piece of shit he really was. Cally was a fool for going out with a jerk like Brad. She deserved someone better than him. David thumped the side of his head lightly with the palm of his hand. What was he thinking? Cally was supposed to be the enemy, too. Why was he finding it so difficult to hate her? Why was she being so nice? He didn't know how—but she was so different from all those other snobby girls in school.

David couldn't let Josh find out about Cally. He was glad his mom hadn't said anything about Cally stopping by when Josh was here. He knew how much Josh hated Cally especially after yesterday. David was sure if the professor found out he had a friend in the school, the whole mission would be canceled. He couldn't risk that happening.

David laid his head down on the pillow and closed his eyes. His mind slowly drifted, and he could see Cally standing on the side of the football field, the wind was blowing through her blond hair as she shouted school cheers. She looked toward David sitting in the stands and waved.

David's eyes suddenly flew open. He quickly dismissed the foolish daydream from his head. He figured his medication was causing him to hallucinate. He closed his eyes once again and started imagining himself in the cool accessories they'd bought at the mall. With this thought in mind he slowly drifted into a peaceful sleep.

***

"Poor little kitty," Charlie stroked the bloody limpness cat. He lifted the lifeless cat, laid it down on the newspaper, and wrapped it up neatly. He tucked the corners of the paper in neatly and secured it with masking tape. "Mrs. Perkins will be glad to see you again. I'm sure she has missed you terribly." Charlie leaned forward and cupped his hand around his ear. "What's that? You think she's an old snoop, too." He paused. "She really shouldn't pry into other people's business, should she?"

Mrs. Perkins had come over to Charlie's house earlier that morning to give him a piece of mail that was accidentally put into her mailbox on Saturday. She'd commented on the letter being from Wyoming and continued to quiz him. She wanted to know if that was where his family was from, where he was originally from, and what he did for a living. Charlie finally had to tell her he was extremely busy, and he didn't have time to visit.

Charlie laid the package down on his desk and examined his hands. He'd gotten blood on a couple of fingers. He stuck the two fingers in a glass of water then wiped them dry with a towel.

Charlie walked over to the window in his small kitchen and peered through the blinds. Mrs. Perkins lights were all off. He knew she habitually was in bed before nine on Sunday nights. She regularly went to town early on Monday mornings. He glanced at his watch; it was almost ten-thirty.

He picked up the wrapped package and slipped out the door quietly. He shot a quick glance up and down the street before proceeding across. Charlie opened Mrs. Perkins's mailbox and slid the package into it. He swiftly closed the box and momentary looked up at her house. The house looked almost vacant; it was solemnly dark and silent. He crossed the deserted street back to his own house. He briefly glanced up the street toward the blond hair girl's house before going in. How he would love for her to be out walking tonight. He'd had his mind on her ever since the night he ran into her on the sidewalk. He was just about ready to cover her mouth and pull her down the street to his own house when her mother opened the front door. He'd been so disappointed. He had finally driven out of town that night to satisfy his uncontrollable urge. But his mind still kept drifting back to the attractive blond girl with the striking blue eyes.

Charlie flipped his overhead light in the computer room on and poured himself a drink while booting his computer up. He read the message David had sent him and wondered why David hadn't mentioned the fight. Slug had called earlier and said he'd

115

heard David had been beat up by a hoodlum from his school. Charlie hated it when his pupils weren't honest with him.

Charlie tapped his pencil lightly on his desk as his mind raced. Damn demons, he thought! He picked up a dart and threw it toward his homemade dartboard, which was a cut out picture of a University full of college students, glued on top of plywood. The dart hit a girl right in the center of her forehead. "Bull's-eye! Take that you fiend!" Charlie jumped up and grabbed the jar of blood out of the refrigerator. He unscrewed the lid, stuck a paintbrush in it, and returned the jar back to the refrigerator. He dashed back to the dartboard and painted blood around the dart. He didn't hit a bull's eye very often, and it always excited him when he did.

He grabbed a box of doughnuts as he headed back to the computer. He needed to get his mind back on the mission. He hadn't been sleeping too well lately; the mission occupied every waking moment. Every time he thought about the catastrophe he was about to create, his adrenaline soared. He bit into a doughnut and grinned. He was satisfied with the direction he'd taken— everything was going smoothly just like he planned.

Charlie figured David and Josh didn't tell him about the fight because they were scared the mission would be delayed. But actually the fight was a good thing; it will make them even more vindictive now—even more reason to carry out the mission as planned. Charlie was going to let them slide this time, but he was going to let them know that they hadn't fooled him.

Smurf,

I am glad you got the necessary supplies for the mission. It sounds like we are on schedule so far. You didn't mention anything about your fight. Are you all right? I hope you didn't get hurt too badly. I don't want to delay the mission, but if we have to, we will.

It is very important for you to keep me posted on incidents like these. Remember that the mission is based on you trusting me, and I trusting you. You are very important to me, and I depend on you and Scooby a lot more than you will ever know.

116

You are not at fault for what this creep did to you. He should be punished, and he will be soon! He shouldn't have messed with a member of the 'Hidden Undertakers'! He'll be the first to be punished, and you'll get the honor of doing so.

When you boys get the pictures and sketches, I'll have you drop them off at the City Park in your town. You'll put them in a paper sack and drop the sack in the trashcan located next to the slide, and Slug will pick them up and get them to me.

Slug will also be the one picking you up when the mission is over and taking you somewhere safe. I will give you more information on that as we get a little closer to the mission date. I'll let you know the date soon. We are real close now!

Keep up the good work! I'm very proud of you boys! Your next job will be even better and more rewarding!

Professor Slate

Charlie proofread his letter before emailing it to David. He picked up his drink and held it up. "Cheers—to my amazing wits," he said aloud. He drank the remaining contents in one gulp. He threw his head back and laughed aloud. He couldn't believe how naive the boys actually were. They truly believed that Professor Slate would save them after the mission was completed. Little did they know that the police would have them arrested in a matter of minutes, and the TV news crew would be everywhere. By then Charlie would have succeeded because the damage would already be done. The whole world would be watching the news of the disaster that he created. Charlie laughed as he stared at the picture of the girl holding her mutt. "Thank you, Eliza, for coming into my life."

117

CHAPTER ELEVEN

Monday, April 26, 2001

Cally stepped heavily on the gas pedal causing her speed to instantly increase seven more miles. She checked her rearview mirror to make sure there weren't any police in sight. She had overslept and was running way behind schedule. She hated to start Mondays off like this. It never failed; if she had a bad Monday, the rest of the week went sour, too. At least she and Brad had made up, and she could look forward to seeing him at school.

She pulled up in front of Beth's house and blared on the horn. Beth was out the door before Cally had time to remove her hand off the steering wheel.

"It's about time. You know how much I hate to miss my first hour class," Beth giggled before slamming the door shut.

"I forgot to turn my alarm on. We'll make it; we still have ten minutes." Cally glanced at the clock and quickly pulled away from the curb.

"Hey, did you get a call yesterday? You didn't even bother to call and tell me about it!" Beth said with a playful grin.

"Boy, who has the big mouth?"

"You can't keep secrets from me, sister. Brad called Mark and told him he talked to you yesterday." She waited for Cally to respond. "Well, are you going to tell me what happened?"

"Brad said he was sorry, and I forgave him. That's all there was to it."

"You forgave him? I thought you said you weren't ever going to talk to him again!"

"Shut up! Why are you talking to Mark so much anyway?" Cally pulled into the parking lot at the school and parked in the first vacant spot available.

"He asked me out for this weekend." Beth gathered her books and jumped out of the car.

"You're kidding? I knew he liked you." Cally kicked the car door shut with her knee as she juggled her school bag. "Are you going to go?"

"I think so. He said something about seeing if you and Brad wanted to go to the drive-in on Saturday night."

Cally followed Beth through the big double doors just as the first bell was ringing, which meant they had three more minutes to get to their lockers and back to their first class. "That sounds fun! I'll talk to you later about it. See you at lunch." Cally waved and ran down the opposite hall.

She rushed to her locker, flipped through the combination, and threw her bag inside. She grabbed her Algebra book and slammed the locker shut. She spun around and jumped at the sight of Brad. "Oh! You scared me. I didn't hear you."

"Sorry, I didn't mean to." Brad nodded toward his watch. "You better hurry—you're going to be late for class."

Cally increased her speed as she hurried down the hall—Brad tagged along next to her. "Well, if I'm late, you're going to be late, too. You have further to go." She knew Brad had Biology for his first hour class, and it was a few doors down from her Algebra class.

"That's true. You're so smart," he added playfully.

The bell rang just as they reached Cally's class. Cally leaped into the classroom and called back to Brad, "You better hurry."

"No shit. See ya." Brad broke into a jog down the hall.

Cally and the rest of the students scampered toward their seats.

119

She threw her book on her desk, flopped down in her chair, and spun around toward Jessie, who sat directly behind her. "Whew, I almost didn't make it." She sighed.

"You're running later than usual. Everything okay?"

"Yeah, I just overslept."

"Okay, class," Mr. Bechtle pointed to a page number written on the chalkboard. "This assignment is due today. I will give you five minutes to go over it before I collect them."

Jessie whispered to Cally, "Did I hear that you and Brad made up?"

Cally casually leaned back in her chair and whispered over her shoulder, "This is such a gossip town!"

"Then it's true?"

"I would have called you last night and told you, but I had so much homework to do." Cally twirled around to face Jessie. "It was after eleven before I got it all done, and I figured you'd be asleep."

"I assume Miss Reeves that you have your assignment completed and ready to turn in?" Mr. Bechtle folded his arms across his chest.

Cally, blushing, spun back around toward the front of the class. She pulled her assignment out of her book. "Yes, I'm finished with it."

"Then there aren't any mistakes on it?" Mr. Bechtle asked.

"I'm not sure."

"Well, then I suggest you take this time I am giving you to look over it and not visit with the other classmates."

"Okay." Cally could feel every eye upon her as she lowered her eyes to the paper.

She tried to swallow, but her throat was sore. She hoped she didn't get sick before the upcoming weekend.

***

David had gotten up early so he could get started on his drawings. He had the details of almost every room memorized in his head, and he wanted to get them down on paper while they were fresh on his mind. His right arm was the one that was sore,

120

and unfortunately, that was the one he needed to draw with. He could only sketch for so long before he would have to stop and take a pain pill. The pain pill made him drowsy so then he would have to sleep for a while. It had been a slow process, but he finally got all the drawings done.

He was glad to be feeling better. He was now able to walk up the stairs to get food. He figured he would be back to normal in a couple of days.

He studied the sketches as he took another bite of the ham sandwich. Something was wrong with the drawing of the boy's bathroom, but he couldn't quite figure out what it was. He turned the picture around so he could look at it from a different angle while stuffing another bite of the sandwich in his mouth. Breadcrumbs fell on the sketch, and he blew them off onto the floor.

He suddenly remembered that he hadn't drawn the girl's restroom, yet because he hadn't any clue what it looked like. He wondered how Josh was going to get pictures of it. If Josh was caught in the girl's restroom, what kind of excuse would he come up with? David smiled to himself as he imagined Josh being busted in the girl's room. That would be hard to explain to a teacher.

David wished he could have gone to school to help him. Josh was supposed to take the pictures sometime after the school activities were over while the janitor took his break. David's insides stirred just thinking about it.

He glanced at the clock on his computer. It was already 4:30. Josh had said he would be by just as soon as he was done.

David had been so wrapped up in his drawings he hadn't even bothered to check his email to see if the professor had written him back. He'd been planning to write the professor again once Josh got there, and they had the pictures. He hadn't even thought about getting on the computer until now. He'd also missed talking with Eliza the last couple of days. He decided he would check to see if she was in the chat room first. She usually went there after school.

He scanned the chat room until he spotted her.

Hi, Eliza. What's going on in your life?

121

Hi, David. Where have you been? I haven't heard from you for a couple of days. David thought about telling Eliza about the fight but decided against it. He was sure she would tell Professor Slate if she knew. *I've been helping my mom lately and haven't been on the Internet.*

Does she make you do all the work around the house like my mom does?

Yeah, sometimes. How's everything going with you? Have you seen Professor Slate lately?

Yeah, I was with him all weekend. Mom and I got in fight, so I just took off and went over to his place. I only came back home, so I could go to school today.

Was your mom mad because you left?

Oh, yeah, she was hot. That's another reason I came back home—to get her off my back.

What did you and Professor Slate do? David visualized Professor Slate's enormous house, and all the maids running around serving Eliza and the professor champagne and fresh fruit. David wished the Professor lived closer.

We had a blast. We went to a movie yesterday, out to eat, and played rummy for a while. But then I decided I better get home to the bitch before she called the police on me again. Have you heard from the professor? He really thinks you're the best he has.

Really? Did he say that? David was thrilled.

Oh, yeah. He said he wishes he had met you years ago. He said you'd probably be paid more than the rest of his students once he gets you trained. He doesn't want to risk losing you. Hey, don't tell him I told you any of this.

I won't. Well, Eliza, I need to check to see if he has emailed me, so I will talk to you later.

That's cool. Later

David rubbed his hands together—he couldn't believe the professor was speaking so highly of him.

He went straight to Professor Slate's email. He read the letter from him slowly and then reread it again. He was stunned—he wondered how the professor had found out about the fight.

122

David read the letter for the third time to see if he missed a clue. He could hardly believe it. At least the professor didn't sound mad. He just sounded hurt that he hadn't been told. David wished now that he'd told him. He didn't know why he didn't tell him in the first place. So far he'd been the only person he could really trust besides Josh.

"Damn it." He banged the desk with his fist. Who was he kidding? He knew the real reason he hadn't told the professor. It wasn't because he was scared the mission would be delayed, but because he didn't want the professor to think he was weak and foolish. He didn't want the professor to doubt that he was capable of pulling off the mission. David was paranoid that Professor Slate might try to replace him with someone else if he found out about any of his ludicrous incidents.

He leaned forward in his chair and tilted his ear toward the stairs; he thought he'd heard someone knocking on the door upstairs. He listened—the knock came again. He left the email and slowly made his way up the stairs.

David assumed it was Josh and jerked the door open. He immediately stumbled backwards in surprise—Nate Meyers and his friend Rodney stood in the doorway, grinning from ear to ear. David tried to push the door shut, but Nate stuck his foot in between the door and shoved it opened. Now, he stood directly in front of David.

"That ain't no way to treat company, is it?" Nate nudged his friend. "You'd think he'd have learned some manners by now, wouldn't you?"

Rodney nodded his head in agreement as he glanced around the room.

"What do you want?" David asked dryly. He could feel the blood pumping through his veins. His heart was beating faster than he thought was possible—he briefly wondered if he was too young to have a stroke.

"Oh, we were just in the neighborhood..." Nate extended his hands in front of his body and popped his knuckles on one hand and then the other. "And we thought we would stop by and see if you've been talking to the police about the other day?"

"I haven't talk to any police."

123

"None?"

"No," David's said, trying to keep the quiver from his voice. He was scared for his life. He knew he wasn't in any shape to take another beating. Nate would probably kill him this time.

"You wouldn't lie to me now would you, Davy boy?" Nate pulled a knife case out of the inside pocket of his leather jacket and twirled it around on his fingers. "I don't like liars."

"I'm not lying!"

"Do you plan on talking to the police in the future?"

David knew what Nate was getting at. "No, I'm not going to the police about anything. Let's just forget about the other day," he said, trying to sound convincing. His whole body was trembling, and he wondered if they could actually see him shaking.

"You do catch on fast! That's just what I wanted to hear. Isn't it, Rod?" Nate poked Rodney with his elbow.

"Yes, I think those were the words you were looking for, Nate."

"Well David, remember, you don't want to get on my bad side." Nate took his leather case and thumped the palm of his other hand with it. "If I hear anything about you going to the police, you'll be sorry!" Nate yanked the knife out of the case and slid his fingers lightly down the sharp edge while glaring into David's eyes. "Do you understand me, David?"

A cold chill rippled through David's entire body as he took a step backwards. He had a terrible phobia when it came to knives, probably from watching too many horror flicks. "I understand. I won't be talking to anyone," he whispered.

"That's a good boy." Nate suddenly crammed the knife back into the case and spun on his heels. "Come on, Rod, let's get kicking before his old lady comes home."

"I wouldn't mind waiting—his mom's an eye-full." Rodney winked at David before spinning around and strutting out the door behind Nate.

David remained motionless as he watched them both climb into Rodney's Mustang. Stupid-ass jerks, he thought, how dare they come to my house and threaten me. If only he'd had a weapon.

124

He thumped the side of his head with the palm of his hand as he remembered the gun downstairs—a lot of good that would do him now. He wouldn't have had time to run and get it anyway—they would have pounced on him.

David was furious that he had coward to the creeps! He'd been scared shitless. He kicked the door shut with his foot, doubled up his fist, and slammed it into the door. "Stupid bastards!" He instantly regretted the punch and grabbed his arm in pain. He'd forgotten for a slight moment about his arm and had allowed his temper to flare out of control. He fell down on the couch holding his right arm, rocking back and forth, and trying not to cry out loud as the painful throbbing ran up the side of his body and down his arm. It hurt so badly—he didn't think he could make it downstairs to get his pain pills. He kept thinking if he would lie still the pain would ease up enough for him to get up, but after a few minutes, it still wasn't letting up.

David had been lying on the couch for over fifteen minutes, panting with each throb. Suddenly, his breath caught in his throat as the knock on the door silenced him. He glanced nervously toward the door and realized that he'd forgotten to lock the door back. Maybe, Nate and Rodney had changed their mind and decided to come back and beat him up anyway. David bolted to a sitting position as he glanced around the room, searching for a weapon. He forgot about the pain in his arm as terror set in.

He jumped to his feet and reached for the brass candleholder setting on the coffee table, knocking the candle out with one hand and grasping a hold of the brass end with the other hand. He tiptoed toward the door quietly and held the candleholder above his head. This time he was going to fight back, whether he won or not. He wasn't going to be a scared little puppy anymore—he would show Professor Slate that he could be brave.

The door creaked as the doorknob turned and the door slowing eased opened. David held his breath—he was certain he was going to die.

"David, are you home?" Josh hollered into the house.

David pulled the door opened so fast that Josh stumbled forward. He brought the candleholder down to his side with a thud. "I'm going to kill you for scaring me like that!"

125

Josh barely caught his balance. "Scaring you? What do you think you just did to me? I almost fell on my face!"

"Well, that serves you right! You shouldn't go around sneaking up on people!" David was actually more relieved than he was mad.

"The door was unlocked." Josh glanced uneasily around the room. "What's going on anyway?" Josh stared at the candleholder that David was holding. "Surely, you weren't planning on hitting me with that thing, were you?"

David picked up the candle he'd knocked on the floor and placed it back in its holder before returning it to the coffee table. "I thought you were my recent visitors returning."

"Recent visitors? Who was here?" Josh plopped down on the end of the couch.

David hurried to the door and locked it. "Nate Meyers and Rodney decided to stop by and threaten me not to go to the police." David massaged his arm—it was throbbing.

"They came here?"

"Yeah, about twenty minutes ago."

"What nerve! What did they say?"

David could hardly think—his arm was aching so badly. "Let's go downstairs, so I can take something for the pain."

"Okay." Josh followed him down the stairs. "Well, what did the losers say?"

David popped a pill in his mouth followed by a drink. "Nate took out a knife and fiddled with it while telling me I'd be sorry if I went to the police."

"You're kidding? What an ass-hole! I wouldn't hesitate to blow him away."

"No doubt—his day is coming."

"Let's waste him first." Josh pulled a bag of marijuana from his pants pocket and rolled a joint.

"You bet. I'd like to blow his damn head off." David suddenly remembered the letter from Professor Slate. "Oh, we got a letter back from the professor because I went ahead and wrote him yesterday." David walked over to the computer. "Go ahead." He motion to the chair at the computer. "Sit and read it." Josh lit the joint, sat down at the computer, and started reading the letter.

126

David continued, "I know we'd decided not to write him until today, but I thought we should let him know we got the supplies. I didn't tell him anything about the fight, but I guess I should have."

Josh finished the letter. "Well, it looks like you didn't have to. He probably knows everything we do."

"Yeah, you're probably right."

"Well, at least he's not mad," Josh added.

David snatched the brown envelope that Josh had carried down the stairs. "Hey, what about the pictures. Did you get them?" He carefully opened up the envelope.

"Sure, I did. I didn't have any problems what-so-ever." Josh took a hit off the joint. He held the smoke in his lungs briefly before releasing it.

"That's cool. There wasn't anyone in the school?"

"Just the janitor and I waited for him to leave for his dinner. He left around four like always. The track team was out of town at a meet, so there wasn't anyone else in the school."

David used his left arm to pat Josh on the back. "Good job, Scooby. Sorry, I couldn't help you."

"Don't worry about it—it was a piece of cake. Hey, how are you feeling anyway? Your face is looking better. It's healing fairly fast." Josh reached for the jar lid behind the computer.

"I feel a lot better, too. I'm just a little sore. I got all the sketches done except for the girl's rest room. I hope you took pictures of it." David didn't mind that Josh smoked weed in his house. He always sprayed air freshener before his mom came home. Every once in a while David would get high with Josh, but he didn't care to do it too often.

"I did. I got pictures of every room."

David pulled the disk out of the envelope. "Well, let's take a look."

Josh jumped out of the chair so David could sit. "I hope they turned out good. I took a lot of them."

David popped the disk into the computer. The first picture he clicked on was the octagon gym. There were at least eight different pictures of the gym alone. "Boy, these really turned out great."

Josh leaned over David's shoulder. "Yeah, they did."

David continued to view all the other pictures. Josh was right—he'd taken plenty of them. He'd even snapped some of the hallways. When he got to the boy's restroom, he studied the picture carefully. "Hand me my sketch pad on the bed, would you?"

David flipped the pages until he reached the sketch of the boy's restroom. He immediately saw the difference between the picture and the sketch he'd drawn. "Look, I forgot the big mirror over on the side wall. I knew something was missing, and I couldn't figure out what it was."

"You did a good job on the sketch. Let me see the rest."

"Okay."

Josh flipped through the pages. "These are really good."

"Thanks." David studied the girl's restroom. "They have a lot nicer one than we do. Weren't you scared you'd get caught in there?"

"I would have freaked if someone would have came in. I already decided if I got caught, I was going to say someone threw my hat in earlier today, and I was looking for it."

"That's pretty clever." David clicked on the next picture of the sinks in the restroom. "I wouldn't have thought of that. I would have just stood there in humiliation probably."

"Well, I thought of everything before I ever started taking the pictures. I didn't want anyone to get suspicious if I got caught."

"Good thinking."

"Are you going to try to go to school tomorrow?" Josh asked.

"Maybe. I haven't decided yet. I'm still sore, so I may wait until the following day. He paused. "You took plenty of pictures. I bet the professor will be glad you did."

"Well, I figured the janitor would be gone for an hour, so that gave me plenty of time." Josh closed the sketchbook and laid it back on the bed. "Should we write Professor Slate now?"

"Yeah, let me finishing looking at the rest of these real quick." David hurriedly clicked on the remaining pictures. He removed the disk and slid it back into the envelope. "You pulled it off—way to go." He held his hand out for Josh to high-five. "Not hard, please...my arm."

128

Josh gently smacked David's hand. "I think it should have been me that stayed with Nate and his low-life buddies, and you that went to the car. I would have beaten the shit out of all them!" Josh flexed his muscles.

"Yeah, whatever? Just remember the day of the mission..." David pretended he was aiming a gun. "Nate Meyers is mine."

"Okay, it's a deal."

David connected to his email and started typing.

Professor Slate,

I'm sorry I didn't inform you of my fight this past weekend. I wasn't hurt too badly, and I didn't want the mission to be delayed. I didn't think it was important. I realize now that I should have told you. Please forgive me. I will not hold any more information from you that could be vital to the mission.

We have all the sketches drawn and the pictures taken. Do you want us to take them to the park tomorrow? I am planning to go back to school on Wednesday. I'm just a little bit sore, but I should be completely back to normal in a day or two.

Let us know what to do next. We are eagerly waiting for the mission date.

Smurf and Scooby

"Does it sound okay?" David asked.

Josh quickly scanned the email. "It sounds fine"

"Okay." He sent the message and leaned back on the back legs of the chair. "Well, we ought to be getting real close to the mission date now."

"I can hardly wait. I didn't sleep too well last night just thinking about it." Josh walked over and picked up the envelope. "Should we get this ready to go?"

"Yeah, we better. Can you think of anything else we need to add?"

"No, I think that's it." Josh added the sketches and sealed the envelope shut. "What time should we take them?"

"Well, if the Professor wants them tomorrow, can you come by after school and pick me up? And then we'll drive to the park."

"That's cool with me." Josh handed the envelope to David. "I'll leave this with you. I've got to get home; ma has a list of things for me to do today. Imagine that."

"At least your mom is home. I haven't really seen mine since Saturday. She just runs in and out." David sighed. "I don't care anymore, though."

"I know what you mean. My ma might be there physically, but she'll more than likely be drunk."

"We're two lucky losers, aren't we?"

"That's for sure. Hey, call me if the professor writes back."

"Okay, if it's not too late."

Josh hurried toward the stairs. "See you tomorrow, Smurf. I'll lock up for you, so you don't get any more unexpected company."

David listened as Josh's heavy footsteps crossed the upstairs floor and the front door opened and shut.

He was glad Josh had to leave because the pill was making him drowsy. He laid his head down on the pillow and closed his eyes. It wasn't long before he started dozing off. Visions of Cally floated in his head. This time he was too tired to fight off the images.

CHAPTER TWELVE

Cally glanced down at the clock—it was 3:25 p.m. She had only five minutes to get to work. She'd gone down Main Street, not aware that they were doing roadwork. There was only one lane open. She sat impatiently, tapping her thumbs against the steering wheel while waiting for her turn to go. She fiddled with the radio, trying to find a better station. She glanced toward the clock again—it was 3:28. She impatiently watched the endless oncoming traffic.

It had already been a bad day, and now, she was going to be late for work. It didn't surprise her any. She'd been late for school, got in trouble for talking in class, scratched her arm by falling down in PE, and had tuna casserole for lunch which she hated. She might as well be late for work, too! At least she and Brad were getting along—that was the only good thing about the day. Finally, the flagman motioned her to go forward. Her clock read 3:30—she was now late.

She pulled into The Diner's parking lot. The lot was already full of cars. The kids from school must already be there.

Cally wrapped the apron around her waist as she trotted toward the entrance. "Wow," she mumbled as she entered and spotted the tables full of teenagers. Ann was rushing around frantically. Cally quickly snatched a pen and order pad. "Sorry I'm late. I didn't know they were doing road work today."

Ann lifted an order of fries off the ledge. "Don't worry about it." She nodded her head toward the back of the room. "I haven't waited on any of the kids back by the pool table yet."

"Okay. I'll get them. What time will the boss be in?"

"Virgil said he'd be here for the dinner hour."

"Good." Cally grabbed a wet rag in case Johnny hadn't got there yet. He was the after school dishwasher. She figured she might have to wipe off a few tables before she could take any orders. She was right—a group of kids had sat down at one of the empty tables that hadn't been cleaned. She quickly ran the rag over the tabletop. "Hi, guys."

"Hi, Cally," a chorus of girls said simultaneously.

"Do you all want the usual?"

"You know us too well," Amanda said.

"Not me. I want something different this time." Trisha smiled. "I don't want just french fries this time—I want french fries with ketchup." She giggled and the girls at the table joined in.

"Okay. I think I can handle that. I'll be back shortly." Cally wiped off a vacant table on her way back to the cook. The table might be vacant now, but she knew there'd be more kids coming in after track practice.

Cally had worked a good hour before the place started thinning out. She wiped her forehead with the back of her hand as the last of the school kids left. "Whew, I don't know about you, but I could use a break," she told Ann.

Ann finished filling her glass up with coke and sat down at the end of the counter. "I totally agree! That was a rush."

Cally grabbed a drink and sat down beside Ann. "We better take a break while we can. We'll have to start all over shortly for the dinner hour."

"I know what you mean."

Johnny passed by the counter with his tub full of dishes. "Hey, Cally, are there more tables in the back that need to be cleared?"

"Yeah, there's about two or three more. Sorry, I wish I could say no."

He nodded his head and hurried toward the back of the cafe.

Cally turned back toward Ann. "How's David doing?"

132

"I think he's doing better. I really haven't had too much time to spend with him since the day of the fight. He says he is feeling a lot better, though."

"Good. I'm glad to hear that. Did he report the guy to the police?"

"I don't think so. I brought it up once, and he jumped down my throat. He said that he would take care of it."

"Well, I think he should press charges against the thug."

Ann took a sip through her straw. "I started to go ahead and call the police myself but then I decided not to. I don't really want to make David mad, but if he doesn't do something soon, I think I will report it. I don't know why he's so hesitant to talk with the police."

"Maybe he will when he's feeling better."

"I hope so." Ann sat her coke on the counter and picked up the pitcher of water. "Well, I better go check my customers."

"Okay. I'll start getting things ready for dinner." Cally checked the silverware. They kept the silverware wrapped up in napkins, and she had to be sure there was enough for the rest of the evening. Poor Ann, she thought, what a nightmare she must live.

The rest of the afternoon went by rather fast. Cally made it through the dinner hour without any major mishaps. She was glad when Virgil let her take off at seven—she was exhausted.

***

Cally stood in the doorway to the kitchen. "I'm starving." Her family was already sitting at the table eating dinner.

Bob glanced up and laid down his chicken leg. He wiped his mouth off with a napkin. "Don't tell me you could smell mom's cooking from work?" He smiled lovingly at his wife and then at Cally. "How did you manage to time dinner just right?"

"I know when there is a good meal on the table. Remember, I can sense things."

"Can you sense how stupid you are?" Corey asked, grinning.

"Do you have to eat with us?" Cally stuck her tongue out.

133

Mary pointed to the empty chair. "Sit down and eat. He really does miss you when you're not around."

"Yeah, right," Corey snapped.

Bob pulled the chair out for Cally. "How was your day? Mom said you over slept this morning."

"I did. I forgot to turn on my alarm clock. The rest of the day fell in the same category. It was just a blue Monday."

Mary handed Cally the plate of chicken. "Here, this will make you feel better."

Cally picked up a chicken breast with her fork. "Your fried chicken always makes me feel better." She took the bowl of mashed potatoes from her dad. "And your mashed potatoes and gravy makes me feel great, too!"

"Well, if you clean your plate you may have a piece of apple pie." Mary smiled.

"I'll take some apple pie!" Corey beamed.

"Did you really make an apple pie? That's what I smelled when I walked in." Cally bent down to pet her cat, Diamond—he was rubbing his body up against her leg and purring softly.

Mary rose from the table to retrieve the apple pie. "Honey, are you ready for a piece, yet?" she asked Bob.

"You bet I am."

Mary sliced Corey and Bob a piece of pie. "Enjoy! Cally, let me know when you're ready."

Cally had her mouth full of potatoes and gravy so she nodded. She eagerly cleaned her plate, ate another piece of chicken, and two pieces of apple pie. "Wow, I am going to gain so much weight. I am so miserable."

"Me too!" Bob agreed. "That was very good, honey."

"Yeah, it was. Thanks, Mom. It was wonderful!" Cally gathered her dishes and carried them over to the sink. "Hey, did anyone ever find out who that man was that bought the Jones's house?"

"I saw Juanita Perkins at the store the other day, and she says his name is Charles Hains." Mary collected a few of the dishes off the table and set them on the counter.

"He likes to be called Charlie," Corey added as he headed for the living room.

Cally froze, holding her plate midair over the sink. "Hey, wait a minute! Freeze, buster. How do you know his name?"

Corey spun around and leaned against the wall of the doorway. "Because he told me so, dork."

Mary snatched the plate out of Cally's hand and set it in the sink. She glanced toward Corey. "And where did you meet him at?"

"I see him all the time in the park. He helped me put the wheel back on my skateboard"

"Mom, you better tell him to stay away from him. He's really strange," Cally said.

"What makes you say that, Cally?" Bob asked.

"Haven't you seen him? He gives me the creeps." Cally snarled up her nose and pulled her arms close to her chest. "Yuck!"

"Well, you aren't no Cinderella yourself." Corey chuckled. "A matter of fact, you're not even close." Corey's laughter slowly ceased, and he turned toward his mother. "He's a nice man."

"Cally, you shouldn't judge him by his looks. That isn't the way I raised you." Mary said.

"I'm not. He's really strange, I'm telling you." Cally glanced from her dad to her mom. She sensed that everyone in the room thought she was exaggerating. She shifted her eyes toward Corey. He always managed to find a way to piss her off. "Fine, find out the hard way, Mr. Know-it-all."

"Okay." Corey shrugged his shoulders before continuing into the living room.

Cally spun back around toward her mom. "Do I have to help clean up tonight?"

"No, honey." Mary turned the faucet on. "You can go start your homework—I'll clean up. Your father will be glad to help me." She winked at Bob. "He loves to spend quality time with me."

"Yes, dear." Bob picked up his plate and walked over to the sink. He planted a kiss on his wife's forehead. "Now, no distractions tonight," he teased.

135

Cally rolled her eyes. "I'm going." She grabbed her bag and headed toward the stairs.

She was glad her parents got along so well and that they didn't mind showing affection for each other in front of their kids. Most all of her friend's parents fought all the time. Her parents every once and awhile would have a disagreement, but they didn't argue about it all night long like most couples do. There was never any yelling in the house except for Corey and herself. She felt fortunate to have such loving parents.

She didn't have much homework to do, so she quickly finished it and ran her bath water. She decided a relaxing bath is what she needed after the day she'd had. She poured the bubble bath into the running water, letting the water fill up close to the rim. As she eased slowly into the hot water, some of the tension left her body. She leaned her head back in the water, letting the water encircle around her neck.

She closed her eyes while wondering what Brad was doing. She'd thought he might call, but he hadn't yet. Her mind drifted to David's fight—she couldn't seem to shake Brad's cruel words. If only he would have shown a little more compassion. Cally didn't know if she would ever truly forgive Brad for that day. Maybe in time, the memory of that dreadful day would fade away.

***

David suddenly woke and sat straight up in bed. It must be Tuesday, he thought, rubbing the sleep out of his eyes. It was so quiet though. He didn't hear his mom's usual prancing around upstairs as she got ready for work. His recent dreams faded as his memory cleared. He recalled falling to sleep around 7:00 Monday evening. Maybe, it's still Monday night, he decided.

His mom had bought him batteries for his clock on the wall, but he hadn't put them in yet. He hadn't bothered to wind up his alarm clock the last few days, either. The only correct time in his room was the clock on the computer. He slowly edged himself out of the bed and gradually crept toward the computer. He moaned—his body was stiff from lying in the same position. He glanced at the clock on the computer and was amazed that it was only 11:30 p.m.

David had a sudden urge to go to the restroom. He wondered if his mom had come home yet, and why she hadn't bothered to wake him.

As he washed his hands he studied his reflection in the mirror. The swelling in his face was almost gone. He had changed the bandages on his face earlier but was eager to see if there was any more improvement. He dried his hands thoroughly before carefully pulling the bandages off his stitches. David examined his face carefully, turning from side to side. He hoped there wouldn't be scars. The doctor had seemed to think the cuts would fade into thin faint lines. He'd said they would look more like natural wrinkles. David hoped he was right. He sure didn't want a bunch of scars all over his face. His face had enough problems as it was especially his unsightly pug nose. It took up half his face.

His stomach rumbled reminding him that he hadn't ate dinner. David made his way up the stairs, trying to be quiet in case his mom was sleeping. He tiptoed to her bedroom door and quietly opened it. He wasn't surprised to see Roy snuggled up next to his mom. Although a thin sheet covered them, David could tell they weren't wearing clothes underneath it. Now, he knew why she hadn't bothered to check on him. She was engaged in more important things.

He gently pulled the door shut. What a lousy mother, he thought. A sharp stab traveled through his chest. He'd experienced the same pain before...every time he expected his mother didn't love him. He swallowed; his throat was dry from the lump forming. He strained to keep the tears from falling. He knew he had to keep his shield up—he couldn't let her hurt him anymore. She wasn't worth the trouble. If she didn't care about him, why should he care about her?

David opened the freezer and was about to grab a TV dinner, but decided against it because the microwave might wake up the beauty and the beast. He studied the food in the refrigerator and decided on a ham sandwich. Lately, that was all his diet had consisted of. He made a sandwich and poured himself a glass of tea. He grabbed the bag of potato chips on the counter and made his way back down the stairs.

He turned on the TV to search for something interesting to watch. He didn't have cable, so he didn't have much to choose from. His favorite show, Cheers, was already over, so he left it on the late night news and flopped down in the chair in front of his computer. He was anxious to see if the professor had written him back.

David fired up his computer. He quickly spotted the professor's email.

Smurf and Scooby,

You boys really are the best! This has to be the smoothest mission I have had yet. Pat yourself on the backs because you guys well deserve it. You got the pictures and sketches done super fast! I need you to take them to the City Park tomorrow after school. You need to put them in the trashcan beside the slide at exactly 3:30 p.m. Pretend you are throwing the envelope away and get out of the park as fast as you can without making it obvious. I'll have Slug pick them up. I'll look at them and get back with you about the mission date. Be prepared, though, because it could be any day now.

Go over all the material I sent you when you first joined. Be sure you know all the laws of the 'Hidden Undertakers'. They are vital for a successful mission! You must follow all laws during the mission regardless of anything else! Remember that everyone is the enemy. Do not trust anyone! We must get rid of as many enemies as we can! If for any reason, you and Josh do not think you can go through with this, now is the time to tell me. You both must be 100% sure that you can do this. Remember, that I am putting my trust in you boys for a very important job, which could lead to higher supervisory jobs, depending on how well this mission is done.

Smurf, I am glad you didn't get hurt too bad. Let me know if you are having any trouble that would prevent you from completing the mission.

138

Be looking for an email from me tomorrow evening with the mission date.
Professor Slate

David smiled proudly. The professor's words were stimulating. This letter was exactly what he needed to cheer him up especially after realizing how trivial he was in his mom's life. He wondered how a man that he'd never met could respect him more than his own mother could.

He couldn't think about her now. He wasn't going to let her crush his high. To think that he was so close to the most important day of his life was unreal. He glanced at the clock on his computer—it was midnight. It was too late to call Josh and tell him the news.

David hurried and finished the rest of his sandwich and chips. He slid over to his bed and carefully lifted the mattress up to pull out the folder the Professor had sent him. David pulled the sheet up over his legs as he spread the material out over his lap. He'd gone over the material thoroughly when he'd first joined, but it had been awhile, so he thought he would refresh his memory.

He was eager to get revenge on all the kids who had been cruel to him during his life. He knew the mission would settle some of the anger that had been building up inside of him the last few years.

He studied the 'Hidden Undertakers' laws for a while, but he couldn't seem to concentrate—his mind kept wandering—some of the worst incidents in his life flashed through his head.

David recalled the episode from last year's PE class. It was still as vivid as though it happened yesterday. It was the end of the school year, and they were playing softball during PE class. David had never been very athletic—he hated PE. He was up to bat and the score was tied. It was the last inning and there were already two outs. He recalled the sly remarks from his teammates as he took his position over home plate. He heard one of them say, *'Boy, we're going to lose for sure now.'* And another one said, *'Great, the loser nerd is up.'* Although David tried to block the insulting comments out of his head—they still had hurt. He ended up striking out just like he figured he would.

139

When they returned to the shower room, all the boys teased him and called him vulgar names. David tried to ignore them by slipping into the shower. But when he returned from his shower, his clothes were missing. All the jocks stood around snickering as he searched under the benches. The bell rung and they all ran out the door, leaving David standing there in a towel.

He was so humiliated. The PE teacher had gone to the office while they were taking their showers, so David had to wait until he came back to the room to tell him what had happened. The teacher helped search for the clothes which they finally found in a toilet. The teacher called David's mom at work and had her to bring him some dry clothes. The rest of the day hadn't been any better. The word passed around fast, and he was teased all day.

However, that wasn't the only unforgettable moment David experienced—there had been many.

At the beginning of the school year Aaron Case, Kody Dorsey, and Andy Githens had shoved David into his locker and locked it. David had to beat on the locker and yell for help. Luckily, Josh passed by and heard him. He ran to the office to get help since he didn't know David's combination. By the time the secretary had finishing spinning the combination and unlatching the door handle, all the kids had gathered and were laughing as David climbed out of the locker.

Another embarrassing moment was when he entered his English class, and Clark Starke told him that the secretary had called his name on the intercom, and he was to report to the office. Class hadn't started yet, and Mr. Rowden wasn't in the room, so David went down to the office. At the time he was worried that maybe something had happened to his mom. The secretary in the office was flabbergasted—she didn't have any clue what David was talking about. She said she hadn't announced anything over the intercom.

The tardy bell rang while David was walking back to the classroom. By the time he'd reached the door, it was already pulled shut. When he entered the room, the teacher had stared at him accusingly. Mr. Rowden demanded an excuse why he was late. David heard a few snickers from the back of the room and realized Clark had set him up. He decided it wasn't worth the

140

hassle telling his teacher the truth—he probably wouldn't have believed him anyway. David had told him that his locker had been stuck. Mr. Rowden didn't think that was an adequate excuse and gave him a detention anyway.

David remembered all the lonely nights before he became one of the 'Hidden Undertakers,' and how he used to huddle under the covers and cry himself to sleep. He recalled other occasions when he'd thought about killing himself, but in the end, he'd always chicken out.

He'd always been scared of everything—he never had the courage to stand up for himself. He had always hated life for as long as he could remember.

Luckily, he found Professor Slate. He had saved him from the hell he'd been living in. The professor had made him feel important and worthy. David now felt like living, but more important, he now wanted to get even.

David glanced back down at the law he had previously been reading. It read: *'Thou shall show no mercy on the enemy once the mission is in progress under any circumstances.'* David smiled and thought there was no way in hell that he was going to show any mercy for the enemies! They could all rot in hell for all he cared!

David was proud that he was the one chosen for the mission— he and Josh would become heroes and be on national TV. He wondered where the professor planned to hide them, probably at his very own house, so they could help him with the next mission. Everyone would be searching for them. David thought they might even get on 'Americas Most Wanted' list. That would be so awesome! He imagined his mom might cry at first but would probably be happy because she wouldn't have to work as hard, and she could marry her lousy lover.

David had a hard time concentrating on the rest of the laws because his mind kept drifting to the day of the mission. The waiting was getting tougher and tougher—David could hardly wait for the world to see who got the last laugh in the halls!

CHAPTER THIRTEEN

Tuesday, April 27, 2001

Cally made it to school on time, but she felt horrible. She'd coughed continuously throughout her first and second hour classes. Her throat was so sore she could hardly swallow. Her mom had tried to persuade her to stay home, but Cally had insisted on going. She didn't like to get behind in her schoolwork. Now, she wished she'd listened to her mom and stayed in bed.

Jessie approached her from behind. "Are you feeling any better?" she asked. "You don't look so hot."

"I feel absolutely terrible."

"Maybe you better go on home."

"I'm considering it." Cally reached her classroom and stopped outside the doorway.

"I could bring your homework by to you after school."

"Thanks, I appreciate that. But, I think I'll go ask all my teachers for it before I check out."

"So, you're going to go home?"

"Yeah, I think so."

"Does Brad know you're sick?"

"Yeah, he offered to bring my homework by, too." Cally reached in her pocket for a Kleenex and blew her nose. "Oh, I can't handle this. I should have known yesterday when I was having a bad Monday that the rest of the week would be a disaster, also."

Most of the kids in the hall had already gone into the classroom. Jessie glanced at her watch. "Hey, I got to go before the bell rings. I hope you start feeling better soon. Call me tonight."

"Okay." Cally slowly made her way to the front of her History class to let Mrs. Hawkins know she was checking out. Her teacher was sympathetic and gave her the assignment for the following day.

She also collected assignments from the rest of her teachers. She didn't know if she would actually get them done, though. Maybe she would feel better by evening. She sure hoped so.

Cally immediately thought of David and wondered if he was getting behind in his schoolwork. She wondered if Ann had thought to come and pick up his homework, or maybe that punk-looking rude friend of his had picked it up. She doubted that Josh would get it—he hadn't even wanted him to go to the hospital. Some kind of friend he was.

Cally pulled the rest of the books out of her locker and stuck them in her bag. She was debating whether to call David to see if he needed her to pick up any homework. She really didn't feel like driving over to his house in that creepy neighborhood. She just wanted to go home and go to bed. She quickly discarded the idea.

She needed to call her boss to let him know she wouldn't be at work. She couldn't remember what time Ann was scheduled to come in but was sure Virgil would want her to come in early. Cally decided to call Ann's house, and leave a message with David. She didn't want Ann to be overwhelmed when she showed up for work and realized she didn't have any help. Maybe David could catch her at the factory before she went to lunch. She found Ann's number and went down to the office to sign out.

The secretary, Miss Ray, quit typing and glanced up at Cally. "Are you checking out for the day?"

"Yes, I don't feel good." Cally leaned against the counter.

143

Miss Ray stood, picked up a pen off her desk, and walked toward Cally. "Do you want to see the nurse?"

"No, I don't think so."

Miss Ray placed the back of her hand on Cally's forehead. "You are warm." She handed Cally the sign out book and pointed to a blank line. "Sign here, please."

Cally took the pen and signed her name. "Anything else?"

"That's all. I hope you feel better."

"Thank you." Cally gathered her purse off the counter and went to use the phone outside the office.

She dialed a few of the numbers while digging a Kleenex out of her purse. "Damn," she mumbled. She blew her nose and finished dialing the number. She let the phone ring several times. She was just about ready to hang up when the ringing stopped.

"Hello." David said in a raspy voice.

"David? I'm sorry. Were you sleeping?"

"Yes. Who is this?"

"I'm so sorry. I didn't mean to wake you. This is Cally Reeves." Cally paused and dabbed at her nose. "I was wondering if you could get a hold of your mother and let her know I won't be working at The Diner today—I'm sick."

"Sure," David said softly.

Cally hesitated. She wondered if she should ask about his homework. She quickly decided against it—she was just too tired to make a trip to his house. "Are you feeling better?"

"Yeah. I'll be going to school tomorrow."

"Well, I'm glad you're doing better. Maybe I'll see you tomorrow."

"Okay."

Cally hung up the phone. She felt bad that David had been beat up. He seemed like he could be a nice guy if given a chance. She dug her car keys out. She couldn't wait to get home. All she could think about was climbing in her warm cozy bed. This is going to be a lousy week, she thought, as she started the car and pulled out of the parking lot.

***

David sat dazed after he hung up the phone. His mind was still a blur from his previous dream. He shook his head, trying to recall why the hell she'd called him. He couldn't quite figure her out. Did she call just to have him tell his mom she wouldn't be at work? She'd said she was sick. Her voice did sound a little hoarse, like she might have a cold, which was why he probably hadn't recognized her.

A little voice tugged at the back of his mind—maybe, she really was a nice person. David quickly tossed that thought out of his head. He wouldn't allow himself to have any sort of feelings toward her or anyone else in that crappy school. It was too close to the mission date, and she was supposed to be the enemy. The last thing he needed right now was for her to be nice to him.

David only had one thing on his mind and that was the success of the mission. He sure wasn't going to let her stand in the way. He made a glass of tea before making his way back down the stairs. He was wide-awake—he was certain he wouldn't be able to go back to sleep. He'd ended staying up until 3:00 a.m. and was hoping to sleep in later.

He glanced at his clock on the computer—10:10 a.m. He glanced toward the silent clock on the wall and decided it was time to get it running. He placed the new batteries in the clock and set it to the correct time. David glanced around the room, debating what to do next. The heap of clothes piled in the corner of the room needed washed but that didn't sound too appealing. He eyed the 'Hidden Undertakers' material spread out all over the floor. He gathered it up neatly and stacked it on the bed. He'd have Josh go over it when he got there.

David's pain had diminished almost completely. He was relieved because he wouldn't be able to take any more pain pills when he returned to school.

He slipped his Kid Rock CD into the player and slipped into the bathroom to change his bandages.

145

David decided to play war games on the computer to pass the time. He hadn't played for months—it used to be his favorite past time before he started going to chat rooms.

Once David started the games—time slipped away. He got up only once to make something to eat. He immediately returned to the computer, and before he knew it, it was 2:45 p.m. He turned off the computer and anxiously got dressed, so he would be ready to go to the City Park when Josh arrived.

David doubled checked the package and hurried upstairs to wait for Josh. He'd only been waiting a few minutes when he spotted Josh pulling up in front of his house. He dashed out the door before Josh had time to get out of the car.

Josh flipped the switch to unlock the door, and David climbed in.

"What's up? You must have been waiting by the door."

"Well, I knew we had to get to the park as soon as we could. We got an email from the professor last night, but it was too late for me to call you."

"Really? What did it say?" Josh peeled away from the curb.

"He said we needed to get this," David held up the envelope, "to the City Park by 3:30 today. We're suppose to pretend we're throwing it away in the trashcan by the slide and then get the hell out of the park, so Slug can pick it up. He also said he would email us tonight and give us the mission date."

"No way! Really?"

"Yeah. Can you believe we're this close?" David held up two fingers indicating an inch.

"No, I can't, but I'm thrilled."

"Me, too! Oh, he also said for us to go over the laws again which I did last night."

"I still remember them, but I'll look over them anyway when we get back to your house."

"I woke up around 11:00 last night and couldn't go back to sleep, so I stayed up until 3:00 this morning. Then early this morning the phone rang and..." David caught himself before he blurted out that Cally had called. "And woke me up."

"Who would call you so early? Surely, it wasn't your buddy, Roy, was it?" Josh grinned.

146

"I hardly think so. No, they had the wrong number. Anyway, I just stayed up the rest of the day." David pointed to an empty parking space at the park.

Josh whipped his car into the parking space and flipped off the ignition. "Do we both need to go?"

David anxiously looked up and down the sidewalks. "We better both go, so it doesn't look suspicious. We'll walk by the slide, and I'll toss it in. Just keep talking to me, so we don't draw any attention then we'll walk around the slide and admire the flowers before we hurry back to the car. It's not quite 3:30—let's wait a few minutes to see if that lady pushing that kid on the swing leaves." David popped his knuckles nervously. "I don't see anyone other than her, do you?"

"No." Josh turned the key back on the ignition and turned on the radio. He fumbled with the radio knob until he found a station.

***

"Mom?" Cally called out as she slowly moped down the stairs. She'd slept most the afternoon away.

Mary hurried through the kitchen doorway. "Are you feeling any better?"

"I feel horrible." Cally coughed.

Mary placed her hand on Cally's forehead. "You still have a bit of a fever." Mary opened the front door and glanced out across the yard. "Well, I've got a problem. Diamond slipped outside when I went to get the newspaper, and I can't find him now." Mary glanced at her watch. "I'm supposed to be at the beauty parlor in ten minutes."

"Go ahead—I'll look for him," Cally knew Diamond couldn't survive out in the real world. He had no claws and was kept inside. Every now and again, he would slip out the door, and they'd have to search for him. However, he never wandered too far away.

"You sure you feel up to it?" Mary asked as she lifted Cally's chin and kissed her forehead.

147

"I'll be fine. I'll find him. You better get going." Cally slipped on her slippers.

"Thanks, honey. He hasn't been out too long. I'll be back as soon as I can. You want me to pick you up anything?" Mary reached for her purse.

"No, I just need more sleep. I'm going back to bed as soon as I find him."

"Take some more cold medicine first, sweetie. I will see you after while." Mary slipped out the door.

"Diamond, why did you have to pick today to go out and play," Cally muttered as she crept toward the back door. She figured she would check out back first since that is where they found him last time.

"Diamond...here kitty kitty." Cally scanned the yard past the swing set and into the next-door neighbor's yard. The warm breeze was causing the growing grass to sway. It wouldn't be too much longer it would need mowed. Cally thought it looked plush enough to lie down and sleep. She was glad it was finally warm, and she didn't need a jacket. She didn't see Diamond, so she moved toward the side of the house and immediately noticed that the yellow tulips had already started to bloom. She hadn't noticed them before which didn't surprise her. Her life was so hectic. She usually took nice days for granted. No wonder Diamond wanted out today. It was absolutely beautiful.

Her eyes shifted toward the front of the house. However, two familiar figures across the street caused her to freeze. It was David and his friend Josh. She quickly squatted behind a bush on the side of the house. The park was still completely visible to her. It usually wasn't her nature to spy on people, but she was curious why David was out. He seemed to be walking okay. Josh and him seemed to be in deep conversation. Cally watched as the boys stop at the slide, and David threw something in the trash. They both quickly walked around to the other side of the slide and bent down to smell a row of daisies at the edge of the park before walking back to their car.

How bizarre, Cally thought. She waited for Josh's car to pull off before she stood. But she instantly crouched back down as a bearded bald headed man hurried toward the trashcan. He reached down, pulled a large envelope out of the trash, and slipped it inside his jacket. Cally was sure it was the same envelope David and Josh had just thrown away. The man hurried up the sidewalk.

Cally rose up slowly, tiptoed around to the front of the house, and peaked around the corner. The man stopped in front of the Jones's old house, where the vile man now lived, slid the envelope into the mailbox, and then continued onward up the street.

"What the heck was that all about," Cally mumbled under her breath. Surely, David and his friend aren't doing drugs. But it did look like a drug transaction. And the pencil-thin middleman that picked up the package looked shabby enough to be on drugs. Cally was shocked—she knew how disappointed Ann would be.

Something suddenly brushed up against the back of her leg. She glanced down and saw Diamond's piercing green eyes staring up at her. She'd completely forgotten why she was outside. The cat purred, and Cally bent down and swept the black fur ball up in her arms. "Where have you been?" she whispered, as she nestled him up close to her cheek. She turned toward the back of the house.

She didn't want to be outside when Charles or Charlie, whatever his name was, came out to his mailbox. If they all wanted to do drugs—that was their business. Cally didn't intend to tell Ann or anyone else what she'd just witnessed. She just hated to see David throw his life away life that. Poor Ann, she thought. She definitely had her hands full.

Cally pulled the door shut and locked it. She lowered Diamond down to the floor and quickly dismissed the incident as she stumbled up the stairs. All she could think about was crawling under the covers and sleeping.

CHAPTER FOURTEEN

Josh parked the car in front of David's house. "Well, that's done. What do we do now? Just wait?"

"Yep. You can go over that material while I make you one of my famous TV dinners." David smacked his lips together.

"Just what I wanted." Josh rolled his eyes and grinned. "Hey, I'm not picky! I'll eat just about anything when I'm hungry, and I'm starving."

David stayed upstairs to cook while Josh stayed downstairs to go over the laws. After they ate the dinners, they watched TV and listened to music while they waited for the professor's email. It was after 6:30 when they finally got the email.

David clicked on it and turned to Josh. "It's here."

Josh jumped up and rushed over to stand behind David. "Finally, I can't stand the waiting any longer."

"I'll read it out loud," David said.

Smurf and Scooby,

What a marvelous job you boys have done on the sketches and the pictures! There were plenty of pictures, and the sketches were very detailed. Well, it is time for the mission! The date is this Friday, April 30, three days from today. I'll have Slug leave you a package back in the trashcan at the park. You need to pick it up right at 3:30 p.m. tomorrow. In the package you will see diagrams of the school. You'll have complete instructions on how the mission will operate. You're to follow the instructions exactly the way I instruct you. Follow the X's on the diagram in the order that I have them. As you will see on the plan, your first stop will be in the boy's bathroom where the guns will be hidden in the vent.

You'll also notice in the plan that I want you to take the guns to school on Thursday night and hide them in the vent. The mission's package will describe everything in detail. It would look odd for you to wear big coats to hide the guns in, so I want you to take your school bags into the restroom with you on Friday morning.

I will wait and let you read the rest tomorrow when you get the package. We are so close to a successful mission by the 'Hidden Undertakers and your names will go down in history because of it!

I'm very proud of you boys! You're the best I have! I'll have Slug pick you up after the mission and bring you to me. You will be staying with me from now on out. I'll finally get to meet the heroes of this mission! The escape plan after the mission will also be explained in your package.

I want you to email me tomorrow night as soon as you both go over all the material in the package thoroughly and let me know if either one of you have any questions. Good Job! I'll see both of you real soon!

Professor Slate

David spun around to catch the expression on Josh's face—his mouth was hanging opened. He looked as stunned as David felt. "Can you believe it? I knew it was close, but not this close."

"Wow! Do you think we'll be ready?"

"We don't have much choice, do we?" David nervously chewed on his thumbnail.

"I guess not. Well, I think we're ready."

"I know I am, especially after the fight with Nate Meyers. He's going to wish he never had touched me." David reread the email again.

"No joke! You're not even a little bit scared?" Josh asked.

151

"No, of course not." David yanked his thumbnail out of his mouth. He didn't want Josh to see how nervous he really was. "Are you?"

"Not at all. I'm excited, though."

"Me too! I'm anxious to meet the professor. I can't believe he wants us to stay with him!" David disconnected from the Internet.

"I know. That's way too cool. You think your mom will be upset?"

"Maybe at first but then she can spend more time with Roy. What about your mom?"

Josh rolled his eyes. "My ma? If she could stay sober long enough to hear the news, she might be upset. But then that would just give her another reason to drink."

"Yeah, you're probably right." David knew Josh's mom always had excuses for her drinking. "What are you going to wear with the stuff we bought?"

"I'm not sure. What about you?"

"I don't know." David strolled over to his closet and skimmed through his shirts. He found a solid black pocket T-shirt and held it up. "What about something like this with blue jeans?"

"Yeah, I think I have a solid black shirt, but it doesn't have a pocket on it."

David laid his shirt over the back of his computer chair. "That's alright. I think with our bandanas, gloves, and shades, we will look tight.

"That will look sweet! Hey, I better get home. I've work to do, like always." Josh grabbed his keys off the bed and headed for the stairs.

"Okay. I'll see you tomorrow. We're real close now."

"Don't chicken out on me, Smurf," Josh said.

"No way! See ya, Scooby."

Josh went up the stairs, skipping every other one. He turned at the top and yelled back down. "I'll lock up."

"Thanks." David turned his stereo off and lay down on his bed. He folded his arms under his head and stared up at the ceiling. This was too good to be true—he was so close now. He cogitated over everything the professor had said. David was

152

thrilled that the Professor was happy with the sketches and pictures. He wondered what his next mission would be.

However, he still couldn't shake the nagging sensation seeping through the excitement. He couldn't help but wonder what if they were caught, or what if things didn't go as planned—they would be in a world of trouble.

He ignored the questions popping up in his head and tried to think of the positive things that would happen after the mission. David smiled up at the ceiling—he knew this was going to be the best Friday he ever had.

***

Josh was full of doubts as he drove home. For some reason, he was worried whether David could carry out the mission. Although they were best friends, they still came from different worlds. Josh sympathized that David thought his life was horrible, but it was nothing compared to the life Josh had lived.

He switched on the radio, hit the steering wheel with his fist, and mumbled, "Shit Smurf, you haven't a clue how rough life can be out there." David had never had to go without food, or stolen food from grocery stores just to eat.

Josh loved David as a brother, but he wasn't sure if David could go through with the mission. He feared that David would back out at the last minute. Josh hadn't slept well last night because he couldn't quit thinking about David and the mission. He didn't have the nerve to tell David he had doubts.

Josh had also seen that Cally chic wave at David when they'd passed the cafe at the mall. He'd pretended he hadn't seen it but he had. He wondered how well David knew her before the fight. He should've confronted David about it then; especially since they weren't allowed to have any other friends. But he'd ignored it.

"Damn it," Josh swore. He'd had one hell of a bad life and this was his only chance for something good to happen—his only opportunity to escape his abusive ma. He knew he wouldn't have any trouble completing the mission. He didn't care who he had

153

to waste to get to the top. People were just robots to him, anyway.

How could he have compassion toward people he didn't even know? He would do whatever it took to survive, and he didn't care who he had to kill to do it either. No one would notice if the tables were turned, and he was the one killed. So why should he care about anyone else?

He wanted so much for the mission to be successful. However, he realized that there was a possibility that it might not go as planned, but he was willing to take that risk. Josh needed the professor now more than he ever needed anything in his life.

Professor Slate had given Josh something no one else had ever given him—hope. If it weren't for the professor, Josh knew he would probably be lying dead in some street somewhere.

He'd been doing drugs frequently when he first met Professor Slate on the Internet. A girl from a chat room, Eliza, introduced him to the professor and David. After a while, Josh trusted Professor Slate more than he trusted anyone. He spilled his guts to him, confessing his destructive lifestyle. The professor comforted him and told him that many kids wouldn't have survived the life he'd lived and that he was a strong-willed and courageous guy. It wasn't long before he and the professor became the best of friends, despite the fact that Josh had never actually met the professor.

And then one day the bombshell hit—Professor Slate offered them the vital job. Josh had been thrilled that the professor had considered him and David for the mission.

He now had a chance to prove his worthiness and make Professor Slate proud of him.

Josh was furious that his computer wasn't working, and he was no longer able to communicate with the professor one on one. Although David filled him in on everything, it wasn't the same as getting his own emails from Professor Slate.

Josh pulled up behind an unfamiliar car in front of his house and flipped the ignition off. He hoped his ma didn't have male company like she sometimes did.

He slowly opened the front door of the house and immediately heard the laughing coming from his ma's bedroom.

He silently slipped into the kitchen and started cleaning up the mess. There was a half-empty whiskey bottle sitting on the counter. Josh quickly picked up the trash, finished sweeping the floor, and carried the garbage out. He was anxious to get to his own room and lock the door. One other time when his ma was entertaining, she'd accused him of listening in on her lovemaking, and she'd thrown her shoes at him. He didn't want to risk the same scenario happening again.

Josh quietly sneaked into the restroom to use the toilet. He tiptoed back to the kitchen, grabbed a bag of cookies off the counter, filled a glass with water, and hurried to his own room. He would have to skip his shower tonight. He locked the door—there was no way he was coming out until morning. He sat down on his bed and stared at the bleak wall—the mission was right around the corner—it was his last chance to get out of this hellhole.

***

Wednesday, April 28, 2001

Charlie leaned back in his computer chair and lifted his feet upon his desk. He folded his arms behind his head and closed his eyes. He'd been working on the material for the mission's plans all night. It was nearly 4:00 a.m., and he was beginning to wear down. He had almost everything ready to go except for a few minor details.

He still needed to write up an escape plan, which he knew wouldn't amount to anything anyway. He knew there was no way the boys would get away, and he had no intention of sending Slug anywhere near that place. He was much too valuable to Charlie—he'd been working for him for several years and was the key ingredient to the huge success he'd had. Slug wasn't from Shelby, but from Bronx, New York—he enjoyed traveling around to the different cities to do the assignments. Charlie had brought him to Shelby to be the middleman. He paid him well, and Slug had plenty of time off to enjoy the things he liked to do, such as partying. Most of the work that he had Slug

155

to do was simple, but every now and again, he would have him get rid of someone who was standing in the way of a mission. However, Slug would never do anything unless Charlie told him to—he was very obedient. Charlie grinned—there wasn't a dog more trained than Slug.

He opened his eyes, placed his feet back on the floor, and extended his hands over his head and stretched. He quickly turned to the computer and typed up a simple escape plan that would satisfy the boys. He knew it wouldn't take much to please them.

Charlie didn't think there would be any complications with this mission because David and Josh were too eager to prove their heroism to him. He finished typing the rest of the procedures.

He reread his work, and satisfied, he printed the material out. He gathered all the papers off his desk, arranged them in order, and stuck them neatly into a vanilla envelope. Before he sealed the envelope, Charlie hurried to his file cabinet to retrieve a folder. He pulled out two small round medals from the folder that read 'Hidden Undertakers'.

Charlie smiled—he was well aware of what it took to motivate his pupils. They all liked compliments, any kind of praise, and most of all—rewards. He attached a small note to the material explaining the medals were just a small token of what would lie at the other end when they arrived to meet him. Charlie informed them that he would give them a medal five times that size once the mission was completed.

Charlie figured if he gave the boys an incentive to strive for, they would be less likely to chicken out. He didn't expect them to bail out. But a little extra shove for more motivation couldn't hurt any.

He picked up the pen and added to the note that he would be fixing them a gourmet dinner when they arrived.

Charlie tapped the pen in a steady rhythm as he sung '*We Don't Need no Education*'. He laughed silently at the thought of him preparing a gourmet dinner.

He was just about ready to seal the envelope when he realized he'd forgotten to tell the boys to burn the package of all the materials before they actually carry out the mission. He quickly typed up another sheet, printed it out, and stuck it in the envelope. Charlie had to make sure there were no links to connect him back to the mission. He'd already informed the boys in the plan that on Thursday night they were to delete all the emails and get rid of any links to the 'Hidden Undertakers'. One of his laws was to keep the 'Hidden Undertakers' confidential— no matter what.

He thought for a moment longer and then sealed the envelope. He left the front blank.

Charlie smiled. He was so close to another successful mission without even a trace leading back to him. There wouldn't be anyone in the town of Shelby, Idaho who would ever know who Professor Slate was. He was sure the boys would never mention his name or their organization after they were caught because he had purposely brainwashed them not to. Charlie threw back his head and laughed shrewdly. Suddenly he stood and spread his arms out as if he were addressing an audience. "Watch out world because there's no stopping me now!"

CHAPTER FIFTEEN

Cally had a sore throat all night long and crawled out of bed several times through the night for a drink. By the time her alarm clock had gone off, she was totally exhausted. She'd told her mom that she would stay home from school if she weren't feeling any better. She didn't hesitate to turn her alarm off and pull the covers up over her shoulders. She knew there wasn't any way she could sit through any of her classes. She quickly drifted back to sleep.

The next time Cally flipped over; it was 1:10 p.m. She couldn't believe she'd actually slept through the morning. She thought about going back to sleep but the urge to go to the restroom changed her mind. She was surprised her mother hadn't been up to check on her.

After finishing Cally slipped into her robe and headed down the stairs.

Her mother was at the sink, washing dishes. She turned as Cally entered the kitchen. "Good morning, sleepy head. Are you feeling any better?"

Cally pulled out a kitchen chair and sat. "No, I had a really bad night. I was up all night with a sore throat."

Mary retrieved the milk out of the refrigerator and the box of cereal off the counter, and set it in front of Cally. "I came upstairs earlier to check on you. You were sleeping—so I figured you needed it." She hurried over to get a bowl and a spoon, and placed them in front of Cally.

"Thanks." Cally poured the cereal in a bowl and covered it with milk. "My throat is still sore."

"I think if you're not any better by tomorrow we need to go see Dr. Hall."

"I was hoping I could go back to school tomorrow."

"Well, don't get your hopes up. Soon as you're done eating, I want to take your temperature."

"Mom, there's no need to baby me. I can take my own temperature," She mumbled through a mouthful of cereal.

Mary placed a glass of orange juice down in front of Cally. "Here, drink this. You need juices to get better." She leaned over and kissed her daughter on the cheek. "You might think you're all grown up, but you're still my baby girl, you know?"

"You'll probably be saying the same thing twenty years from now." Cally laughed and immediately regretted it—she covered her throat with her hand.

"You're probably right, and I'll probably still have to drag you to the doctor when you need to go, too." Mary set some cold tablets down on the table. "Take these when you're done eating."

"Yes, mother dear." Cally finished her cereal and juice, and swallowed the cold tablets. "I think I'm going to go lie back down for a few minutes before I try to do my homework."

"Not yet…open up." Mary held out a thermometer.

"Oh, Mom." Cally decided it would be much easier to give in to her mother than to argue with her. She opened her mouth.

"Under the tongue." Mary placed the thermometer under Cally's tongue and strolled back to the kitchen sink to finish the dishes. "Now, don't take it out until I tell you to."

"Okay," Cally mumbled.

"No talking either."

Cally rolled her eyes and sat still as she waited for the time to pass.

Mary finished the dishes and took the thermometer out of Cally's mouth. "Just what I thought! It's a hundred and one. You're not going to school tomorrow unless your fever breaks."

"Okay, I won't. May I be excused now?"

159

"Okay. But I want you to get some more rest. I'll bring you some more juice after while."

"Yes, Mommy," Cally said playfully before trampling up the stairs.

Cally wasn't at all surprised by how her mother was treating her. Her mother had always been over-protective; especially when it came to her children being sick. She really didn't mind. She usually liked all the attention but sometimes her mother could get carried away. She knew that she meant well, though.

She laid her head down on the pillow. She couldn't believe she was still tired after sleeping all morning. She blamed it on the fever. Cally thought briefly of all the homework that she had. However, the thought didn't linger with her long. She massaged her temples and closed her eyes. She turned on her side and cuddled up under the blanket. It was only a matter of minutes before she fell into a deep sleep.

***

Finally, the last bell of the day rung—David thought it had been the longest day that he'd ever had. He was anxious to get to the City Park and get the remaining material for the mission.

He was feeling like his old self again. His pain was completely gone and most of his energy was back. A few jerks had made comments about him getting beat up. However, David had chosen to ignore them and finally the comments diminished.

David jammed his books into his locker and forced the door shut. He had homework for tomorrow but decided he didn't need to do it because he was only going to be here two more days anyway. He smiled as he realized he wouldn't have to ever go to school again after Friday.

He glanced up and down the hall, searching for Josh. He was supposed to meet him after school. David casually glanced down the opposite hallway toward Cally's locker. He hadn't seen her all day and wondered if she was still ill. He glanced once more up the hallway to see if Josh was coming and then strolled over toward the office door. They always posted the absentee list on the door. It didn't take him long to locate Cally's name.

"What are you looking for?" Josh asked over his shoulder.

David jumped, startled. "What? Oh, I was just killing time waiting for you."

"Well, you sure seemed to be in another world. Is anything wrong? You looking for some particular name on that list?"

"No, of course not. C'mon let's get out of this dump!" David moved toward the double doors.

"I'm right behind you."

Josh unlocked the car door for David. "Well, how did you get along today? Any problems?" Josh peeled out of the parking lot, laughing at the circle of dust he created.

"None, whatsoever. I'm not in any pain at all. The day just dragged by."

"I know what you mean. It did for me, too. Tomorrow will probably be even worse."

"Yeah, I know. I'm getting impatient."

"Me too," Josh said.

The boys drove the rest of the way to the City Park in silence. David had Josh to wait in the car. He hurried over to the trashcan and nervously glanced around before reaching down to grab the package. He quickly slipped it into his school bag and rushed toward the car.

He glanced around the surrounding area before climbing into the car. He pulled the fat vanilla envelope out of the bag. "Look how thick this is. We'll be up all night." David looked up and down the street, trying to catch sight of Slug. "I don't mind, though."

"Me, neither!" Josh pulled away from the curb.

After several minutes, Josh pulled up in front of David's house. David bounded out of the car and into the house with Josh right on his heels. Once inside they ran downstairs and plopped down on the bed.

A gold medal fell out as David tossed it on the bed. The package must have come unsealed. He picked up the medal and read it silently. He held it up for Josh to see. "Wow, this is sweet!"

"Awesome!" Josh took the medal from David and examined it. "Where's mine?"

161

David shook the envelope but nothing else fell out. "It must have fallen out somewhere. Here, you go ahead and take this one. I'm sure he has more. He pulled out the rest of the material and spread it out in sequence across his bed. "Here's the first sheet. I'll start reading and pass it to you."

"Okay."

David and Josh read in silence for a good hour.

David finished the last sheet and sat in silence while he waited for Josh to finish reading. He nervously chewed on his fingernails until Josh had finished. "Well, what do you think?"

Josh looked stunned. "I'm impressed! He sure is thorough, isn't he?"

"I thought so, too."

David picked up one of the diagrams and pointed to the X on the sheet. "Did you see here? He wants us to stand with our backs together when we start firing the shots."

"Yeah, and he said it had to be in front of the trophy case, too. I wonder why." Josh pulled a joint out of an empty cigarette package and lit it.

"Probably because we'll be able to see both hallways from there and the lunchroom."

"That's true," Josh agreed. "And the part about how we're supposed to shoot without any hesitation. He said to show no mercy toward anyone."

David picked up a small bottle that contained two tablets in it. "He said to take these before we go to school and it will relax us. What do you think they are?"

Josh passed the joint to David, took the bottle, and popped off the cap. He dumped the pills into the palm of his hands. "I'm not sure. I've popped a few pills before, but I've never seen anything like these. But I'm game to try anything. Besides, I'm sure Professor Slate knows what he's talking about."

David inhaled the weed, holding the smoke in briefly before exhaling. "Yeah, you're probably right." David passed the joint back to Josh and picked up a different sheet. "How about this page—the gourmet dinner?" David smacked his lips while rubbing the palm of his hand over his stomach. "Along with the larger medals we'll be getting?"

162

Josh ran his hand though his hair. "That's my favorite page of all! Did you read where we are supposed to go out the double doors when we're finished, and Slug will be waiting for us?"

"This is going to be a piece of cake."

Josh stubbed the joint out in the jar lid. His face turned serious. "Can you do this, David?"

"Sure I can. Why? Can't you?"

"I know I can. I'm just worried about you?"

"What do you mean—worried about me? You think I don't have any balls or what?" David couldn't believe that Josh doubted him.

"I'm sorry. I didn't mean anything by it. I just want to make sure we can do this before we go any further."

David's anger didn't cease. "Well, you don't have to worry about me. I could shoot anyone in that school and feel no remorse about it. Remember, blood don't bother me as much as it does you."

"Hey, chill out. We don't need to get into a disagreement right before the mission. You're right, blood does bother me, but it's only my blood that freaks me out. If it's someone else's blood, I could care less."

David instantly wished he could take his words back. He softened his tone. "Hey, I'm sorry. I'm just stressed." He threw the pill bottle up and caught it with his left hand. "Maybe I need to take my pill now," he said as he rolled his eyes.

"Don't worry about it. I know we'll both do a good job." Josh stood. "Well, I better be getting home, I still have chores to do." He paused then added, "But just for two more days."

David walked over to his computer. "I'm supposed to write the professor. Do you have any questions to ask him?"

"No, I think he nailed it right on the head." Josh headed toward the stairs and then turned back. "What time should we take the guns to the school tomorrow night? The professor said it should be after the custodian has cleaned the restrooms."

"Yeah, but we have to get there before he locks up the school, too."

163

"He cleans the boys' bathroom toward the first of the evening. Maybe we can sneak in while he is on the other side of the building," Josh said.

David nodded. "That would be best. You think somewhere around seven?"

"Sounds good to me. I'll talk to you more about it tomorrow." Josh glanced toward the clock on the wall. "I hope that's not right."

David spun and looked toward the clock. "Yeah, it's right."

"Shit! I have to get out of here. I'll see you tomorrow." Josh dashed up the stairs.

David decided not to write the professor right away. He spent the rest of the evening going back over the material. He waited until he was sure he understood every detail before he wrote the professor.

Professor Slate,
We got the material for the mission. We have thoroughly read it and went over it twice now. We understand all the details, and we are totally committed to the mission. We are set and ready to fulfill all the plans. As of now, we don't have any questions. You explained everything in great detail.

We are ready to carry out the mission on Friday, April 30. We won't let you down. We look forward to meeting you, too.

Smurf and Scooby

It was already after 10:00, and he hadn't even eaten his supper yet. He grabbed some clothes to take upstairs with him, so he could take a shower as soon as he finished eating. David looked in the refrigerator and didn't see anything good to eat. He was getting tired of TV dinners. The telephone rang, interrupting his thoughts. "Hello."

"Hi, honey. It's your mom. I haven't seen much of you, so I thought I would call and see how you got along in school today."

"Where you at?"

"I'm with Roy. I'll be home soon, but I figured you'll probably be asleep."

164

"Yeah, I probably will be." David was beginning to wonder if he even had a mother. She was seldom home anymore.

"Well, are you feeling okay?"

"I feel fine."

"Did you find the lunch money this morning that I left for you?"

"Yeah, thanks. Hey, I got to go. I have homework to do," David lied.

"Okay, honey. I'll talk to you tomorrow. Maybe, you can come by and eat dinner at The Diner."

"I'm not sure; I'll let you know."

"All right. Bye, honey."

"Bye, Mom." David hung up the phone. He couldn't help but mock his mother aloud, *"Bye, honey."* The only honey she cares about is the loser she's with, David thought. Why couldn't she come home like a normal mother when she got off work? Maybe, she could even cook supper every once in awhile. David grabbed a TV dinner, ripped the lid open, and popped it in the microwave. He slammed the microwave door shut. He blamed his mother for his bad mood! He wished she hadn't called! David fixed a glass of tea and sat down at the table as he waited for his dinner to finish cooking.

He suddenly felt lonely and wished he had a father he could talk to. He got tired of eating supper alone every night. David wondered what it would be like to have a normal family with a mom and a dad—one that he could come home to every night and have supper with. Cally's life was probably like that. He secretly hoped she was still sick on Friday. She was the only person in that school who had ever been kind to him. Although he tried to hate her, he couldn't bring himself to do it.

David's eyes watered as he stared at the picture hanging on the wall of him and his mother. It was taken when he was seven years old. She had her arm wrapped around his shoulders, and she looked so happy. David wondered if her mind was really on him that day or was she smiling because she'd had a good time the night before. All his life, all he ever wanted was for his mother to love him more than she did her boyfriends, but she never had. She always seemed to put her male friends first and

165

him second. He used to try everything to get his mother's attention. David even brought home straight A's a couple years ago. She merely patted him on the back and told him he'd done a good job. David didn't know what he'd expected, but he'd wanted her to show more enthusiasm or something. After that year, David didn't care anymore, and he quit trying to make good grades. He finally gave up on trying to please his mom at all. She just didn't seem to care.

He often wondered if he ruined his mother's life by being born, and if that was the reason that she didn't acknowledge him. Slowly, his love for his mother had faded. Maybe, deep down, he still loved her but only because she was his mom. Now, he wanted her to pay for not loving him more. David wanted her to suffer the way he'd suffered. He wanted her to feel the pain of losing someone that she cared about.

A broad grin slowly spread across his face as he thought about the mission. After Friday he probably would never see her again. David was finally going to get revenge after all these years.

CHAPTER SIXTEEN

Thursday, April 29, 2001

Cally didn't know if she was dreaming or if the phone was actually ringing. She rolled over and focused on the blurred numbers on the clock—7:08 a.m. The phone rang again as she wondered who would be calling so early. The ringing stopped, and Cally figured someone must have answered it downstairs.

A few seconds later her mom called up the stairs, "Cally, are you awake? Beth's on the phone."

"Okay." She forgot to call Beth last night. She jumped out of bed and grabbed the receiver. "Hey, Sweet Potato?"

"You forgot to call last night?"

"I know—I'm sorry. I didn't feel good, and I just forgot all about it. Sorry."

"That's okay. It's no big deal. Are you going to school?"

"No, my mom won't let me. I've been running a fever." Cally shivered and snatched the blanket off her bed.

"Bummer! Would you like me to see if your teachers have any more assignments for you?"

"That'd be great. Sorry, I can't give you a ride."

"Oh, that's not a problem. I was calling to let you know Mark was coming by to pick me up, and I wouldn't need a ride."

"Why didn't you say so in the first place?"

"You didn't ask." Beth giggled.

167

"Very funny. Are you and Mark a hot item now?

"Maybe, we'll see." Beth paused. "Hey, are you coming to school tomorrow? We're supposed to have a cheerleading meeting after school."

"I plan on it if my mom will let me. You know how she can be?"

"What's wrong with you anyway?"

"I think I just caught a bug. I've had a sore throat, runny nose, and a fever, but I don't feel so bad now."

"Well, that's good. You don't want to be sick for the weekend."

"I think I'll be okay by then. I better be!" Cally dug her cold toes into the plush carpet. "I actually feel like going to school today, but I know that there's no way my mom will let me."

"Did Brad call you last night?"

"Yeah, he did." We didn't talk very long because I wasn't feeling good. He did mention something about us all going out on Saturday night, though."

"You did say yes, didn't you?"

"No, I said that didn't sound fun at all." Cally giggled. "Of course, I said yes, silly."

"Well, I'm glad you haven't lost your sense of humor."

"Don't you have to get ready for school?"

"Oh, I'm just about ready. All I got to do is slip my shoes on, but I guess I better go do that before he gets here."

"Okay. Will you be by after school then?"

"Sure. I'll see you then."

Cally hung up the phone and pulled the blanket tighter around her, while she debated whether to go back to bed. She didn't feel sleepy any more. She couldn't believe how good she felt compared to the night before when she'd gone to bed. She'd felt awful. Her mother had taken her temperature, and it had been one hundred degrees. She'd taken some nighttime medication which helped her fall asleep and sleep throughout the night. Cally figured the medicine must have broken the fever.

After a few minutes, she tossed the blanket on the bed and threw her robe on. She strolled over to the window that overlooked the park and stared out at the numerous children walking through it. Some of them were wearing backpacks while others were carrying bags or lunch boxes. Cally knew from experience that it was shorter to go through the park to get to the elementary school.

Her eyes shifted to the trashcan by the slide. She reached into her jacket pocket that was hanging on the back of her desk chair and pulled out a small round gold medal. She studied the insignia 'Hidden Undertakers' and wondered what it meant.

She'd been sitting at her desk yesterday afternoon when she'd witness David and his friend pulling up at the park. She'd watched curiously as David strolled up to the trashcan, reached down, and pulled out a package. She'd seen a small object fall out of the package as he was rushing back to the car. Although she'd felt like hell, her curiosity outweighed her frailness. While her mother was in the kitchen baking, she'd slipped out the front door and over to the park to retrieve the mysterious piece. She'd expected to find something that would confirm her suspicious that David was doing drugs. But instead, she'd found the silly gold medal.

Cally flipped the gold piece over again, thinking she might see some faded writing that she'd missed yesterday. But the back was as smooth as her desktop.

"Cally, how are you feeling this morning?" Mary called up from the bottom of the stairs.

Cally stuck the medal back into her coat pocket and rushed toward the top of the stairs. "Good morning, Mom. I feel better. Is there any chance I can go to school?" Cally knew what the answer would be but decided to try anyway.

Mary stared at her daughter. "I hardly think so. I'll keep an eye on your temperature today. And if you don't run a fever today, I might let you go back to school tomorrow. We'll just have to wait and see."

"Okay, but I think I'm well." Cally hesitated. "I guess I can start that homework that I never got done yesterday."

"Don't you want some breakfast?"

"I'm not hungry right now."

"Well, you need to eat something. At least get some juice down."

Cally realized her mother wouldn't give up. "All right. I'll be down in a bit. I want to do some homework first."

"Okay, but don't be too long."

"I won't." Cally got her assignments out and spread the papers out on her desk. She laid her Algebra sheet on top. She always did her math before she did anything else since that was her easiest assignment. She wanted to get all her homework out of the way, so she could have the afternoon to catch up on some of her soaps that she hadn't seen for awhile. Besides, Beth might bring her more homework to do later, and she would have to spend the evening doing that.

Cally had called her boss yesterday to let him know she wouldn't be able to work for a few days. He was very understanding and told her not to worry about it. She hoped they didn't overwork Ann.

She reached for a rubber band and twisted it around her hair. After she finished with her homework, she was going to eat and soak in a hot tub of water. By then it should be time for her soaps. She felt renewed, and if she couldn't go to school or to work, she might as well enjoy the day. Cally flipped the page in her textbook. She was so glad she was feeling better. It was perfect timing just in time for the weekend. She was looking forward to an outing with Brad, Beth, and Mark. She knew it would be a good time!

***

David was in his last class of the day—German. He was glad the day was almost over. Mrs. Stosberg was writing sentences in German on the chalkboard when the secretary spoke over the intercom.

"Mrs. Stosberg?"

"Yes?" She laid down the piece of chalk and turned toward the voice.

"Could you please send David Clemons to the office?" The voice boomed over the intercom.

"Yes, I will." Mrs. Stosberg glanced toward David. "David, you're excused."

David couldn't imagine why he was being called into the office. He closed his textbook and grabbed his bag on the back of his chair; just in case he didn't make it back before the bell rung. David wondered if something might have happened to his mother. He sure hoped not—that would be bad timing. David could hardly sleep last night because he was worried something would go wrong before the day of the mission. Now, he was really concerned.

David glanced through the glass windows surrounding the office as he approached the door. His eyes darted to the gray room in the back of the office. It was the room detentions were usually served in. He saw Josh sitting in a chair and a police officer standing nearby. David's heart skipped a beat. He was certain that the police had found out about the mission. He couldn't imagine how they could have found out, though. David quickly decided he would lie about knowing anything about it—and he could only hope that Josh hadn't told the officer anything either.

David jerked the office door opened and approached the front counter.

The secretary quit typing and gazed up at him. "Are you David Clemons?" she asked.

"Yes." He was trying not to look nervous, but he could feel his hands starting to tremble.

The secretary pointed to the back room where he'd seen Josh and the police officer. "Go straight back. They're waiting for you in there." The secretary didn't wait for a response; she bowed her head back over the typewriter.

David entered the room and uneasily glanced at Josh for some sort of sign. Josh's face didn't reveal any information. He looked scared shitless.

Chief Brady pointed to a seat for David to sit. "Good afternoon, boys. My name is Chief Brady."

"Hello." David and Josh said simultaneously.

"I have you both here because your mother, David, spoke to me this morning about a fight last Saturday, and I'd like to hear both of your stories before we continue on." Chief Brady glanced toward David. "Which one of you would like to start?"

171

David and Josh exchanged glances and remained silent.

"Well?" Chief Brady asked.

Finally, David spoke, "There was a disagreement and a little bit of shoving but nothing more than that."

"Are you sure it was just a little shoving? It looks like you've had some stitches in your face."

David had forgotten about the visible stitches. "It was no big deal," he said, flustered.

Chief Brady examined David's face more closely. "Are you sure about that? It looks to me like you got worked over pretty good."

Josh was quick to reply. "There was a minor disagreement, but no one got hurt that bad. We didn't think anything of it."

Chief Brady looked from one boy to the other. "I've already heard more to this story than you boys are telling me. I've even got the names of the boys that were harassing you two." Chief Brady's voice grew louder. "One of the same boys was in a fight, earlier this morning, down in the locker room. That is another reason I'm here. I know who did it, but for some reason, everyone is covering up for this creep. I would like to nail him, but I need some names, and the truth from both of you. My hands are tied unless someone starts talking."

David wasn't going to give in—he wanted Nate at school tomorrow. "I'm sorry, sir, but that's all that happened."

"You know if those kids threaten you in any way they can get in a lot of trouble." Chief Brady locked eyes with David. "I don't want you boys to be scared of doing the right thing." He glanced toward Josh, waited a few seconds, and then continued, "And the right thing to do would be telling me exactly what happened on Saturday."

"That's all that happened," Josh added.

David nodded his head in agreement. "Yeah, that's all."

Chief Brady shook his head. He reached in his back pocket and pulled out his wallet. "Okay. I can't help you boys any more until you agree to cooperate. Here is my card." He handed one of his business cards to David. "If you boys change your mind and decide you want to talk, we can continue on with the charges but

172

until then there's nothing more I can do. Think about it and then give me a call."

"Yes, sir." David glanced toward Josh then back at Chief Brady. "We have no reason to change our minds. We're telling the truth."

"All right. You boys may leave now." Chief Brady shook his head as if he was disappointed in the boys' decision.

The final bell of the day had already rung, so David and Josh didn't have to return to their classes.

Josh waited until he was outside the office door to speak. He kept his voice low so others couldn't hear. "That was close. Boy, I'm glad you didn't break."

"No kidding. I was scared to death."

"Hey, I need to run to my locker. Do you want to go with me or wait here?"

"I'll just wait here."

"I'll be right back." Josh spun and jogged down the opposite hall.

David waited until he saw Josh rounding the corner and then hurriedly looked at the absentee list hanging on the office door. He was glad to see Cally's name still on the list. She must really be sick, he thought. Hopefully, she'll be sick tomorrow, too. David quickly turned away from the list, not wanting Josh to catch him reading it again.

A few minutes later, Josh returned carrying his school bag. "Okay, I'm ready. You don't need anything out of your locker?"

"No." He held up his German book. "I think I'll throw this book away when I get home." David lowered his voice to a whisper, "I won't need it any longer."

Josh didn't respond but smiled secretively.

David waited until they were in the car and driving toward his house before he brought up the earlier episode. "Did you know why you were being called in the office before I showed up?"

"No. The chief said he would wait and explain it to me when you got there. I had no clue what was going on."

"My first thought was that he knew about the mission. Did you think that?"

"I did at first." Josh turned down David's street. "But then I realized there wasn't any way he could have found out."

"Man, I was really worried."

Josh pulled in front of David's house. "Well, I won't stay today. I'll be back over after while to pick you up to go to the school. I need to get my clothes and all ready for tomorrow."

David jumped out of the car, grabbed his bag and German book, and slammed the car door shut. He leaned back in the car's window. "Well, tomorrow's the day. Can you believe it?"

"Not hardly. I'm glad, though."

"Later," David called out.

David hurried up the sidewalk, turned back, and waved before going into the house.

He was relieved that Chief Brady's concern was only about the fight. He chuckled and thought this time tomorrow the chief would have a lot more to be concerned about.

***

David and Josh arrived at the school five minutes before seven. Josh parked in the farthest space in the parking lot. It wasn't unusual for kids to park their cars in the school's parking lot while they rode around with other kids. David was sure that no one would suspect anything unusual.

Josh flipped off the ignition. "Well, what do you think? Should we both go in or should one of us go check to see where the janitor is?"

"I'll go check. If he sees me, I'll just say I forgot one of my books and was coming back to get it. As soon as I think it's clear for you to come in, I'll wave to you from the door. And then you bring the bag in when you come." David gnawed nervously on his thumbnail.

"Okay, that sounds cool. You did remember the screwdriver, didn't you?" Josh flipped the key backwards so the radio would come on.

"Yeah—it's in the bag." David climbed out of the car and quickly scanned the parking lot, making sure it was empty. "I'll see you shortly." He closed the door gently.

174

David's stomach churned nervously as he entered the building. He stopped for a second and inhaled a deep breath, trying to relax. His hands were trembling, and he wondered how he would ever get through tomorrow.

He slowly crept up and down the lengthy halls of the school until he spotted the janitor in the Biology room at the end of the building. The guy had just started mopping the floor, so David assumed he'd be in the room for a while. His back was toward David, so he didn't see him walk by.

David quietly jogged back down the hallway until he reached the double doors that led outside. He opened one of the doors wide enough for Josh to see him and motioned for him to come in.

They both quickly entered the boy's restroom in silence and flipped on the overhead light. They didn't waste any time getting right to work. They'd already discussed the tasks they were each to do when they reached the restroom. They'd agreed to do as little talking as possible.

David unscrewed the vent rapidly as Josh carefully pulled the guns and magazines out of the bag. David eagerly pulled the vent off the wall, making a louder noise than he had anticipated.

Josh froze as he waited to make sure the janitor didn't hear the noise. He glanced toward David before gently placing the guns inside the vent. Josh stood to make sure the guns weren't visible and then gave David the thumbs up signal to go ahead and screw the vent back on. David pushed the magazines back behind the guns and hurriedly started screwing the vent back on.

He had the last screw in and had just finished tightening it when a loud racket down the hall made him jump. Sudden footsteps approaching was enough warning for David. He quickly pointed to the empty stall next to him, indicating Josh to go inside. David backed up in the stall where the vent was, quietly picked up the empty bag, and climbed carefully onto the toilet seat, keeping his feet straddled. He could only hope that Josh was doing the same thing in the next stall.

The footsteps suddenly stopped right inside the restroom doorway. David held his breath for what seemed like an eternity.

175

Finally, the light flickered off, and the footsteps moved out of the restroom and back down the hallway.

David waited until the footsteps had faded away. He then climbed down off the toilet and quickly stuffed the screwdriver in the bag. He didn't have time to zip up the bag because Josh was already at the door motioning him to follow.

Josh stuck his head out of the doorway, glanced up and down the hallway, and jogged toward the double doors. David was right on his heels. He turned only once to make sure no one was following them.

They both quickly inspected the parking lot before jogging across to the car.

Josh immediately started the ignition as David slammed his door. He floored the gas pedal. "Let's get the hell out of here before someone sees us."

"No kidding!" David pressed his hand against his chest. "My heart is still pounding. I thought we'd been caught for sure."

"I wonder if he heard you when you pulled the vent off. I'm sure it was the janitor."

"There wasn't anyone else in the school. It had to be him," David added.

"Well, he scared the shit out of me. I couldn't think straight. When I saw you backing into the stall and pointing for me to do the same, it suddenly dawned on me what you were doing."

"Did you stand on the stool seat, too?" David asked.

"Yeah. I didn't think he was going to leave. Didn't it seem like he was in there forever."

"It seemed like it, but it was probably only a few seconds. I think we were just freaking out."

Josh frowned. "You don't think he suspected anything, do you? He probably wonders why the light was on."

"Nah, he probably figured he just forgot to turn it off."

"I hope so. I hope he don't start snooping around in there."

"Now, Scooby, you're stretching that imagination of yours."

"You're right. I just don't want anyone to screw up our plans for tomorrow." Josh pulled up to David's house. "Well, I guess this is your last night in your house."

"Hooray! I couldn't be more thrilled."

176

"I'll be by around 7:30 in the morning, so we can take the pills and get to school early. Be sure to delete all the emails and get rid of all the material about the mission." Josh rubbed the sweat off his forehead with the back of his hand. "Oh, don't you think we should carry our sunglasses, gloves, and bandana in our bags."

David climbed out of the car. "Yeah, that would be alright and then we could put them on in the bathroom right before the mission starts." His gaze met Josh's. "Don't worry; I'll take care of everything I'm supposed to."

"Are you getting nervous, Smurf?" Josh asked running his hand through his hair as he glanced in the mirror.

"Oh, I got a few butterflies, but I'll be okay. How about you?

"Yeah I am, but I'm more anxious than anything."

"Well, I'll see you bright and early in the morning. Get some rest," David said.

David waited until Josh had pulled away from the curb before he moseyed up the sidewalk toward the silent house. There was a slight chill in the air, but it felt good. He glared at the dark, empty house and realized there wasn't any rush to get inside. He wasn't on any schedule to eat dinner alone.

David sat down on the wobbly stair and gazed up into the sky. It was just starting to grow dark and only a few stars were twinkling. He was glad the days were starting to get longer. He preferred them to the long nights. He inhaled a deep breath of fresh air, exhaled, and closed his eyes. He slowly opened his eyes and glanced up and down the street. There were a few kids at the end of the block playing kickball. Other than that, it was a quiet night, which was unusual for the rowdy neighborhood.

David looked down at the ragged stairs and realized he would probably never sit here again. It didn't bother him, though. He'd always hated the run down house and the neighborhood, but his mother had told him they didn't have any other choice.

David thought about the mission and what his life would be like after it was completed. He would be of great importance to the professor if the mission were a success. He knew the professor lived in a nice house because Eliza had told him so. He imagined that it was a roomy white plantation house with several

177

servants. It probably had a huge swimming pool in the back yard, and red roses growing all around the patio. David wondered if servants would be cooking his gourmet dinner tomorrow night. His stomach growled at the thought of food. He visualized sitting at a large table, eating lobster and steak with a big bowl of fruit all cut into precise cubes, sitting in the center of the table, including his favorite, seedless watermelon. On each side of the fruit he imagined fresh baked cakes, hot apple pie, and hot rolls. David would feast like a king. He'd probably have his own room with a hot tub in it. His sheets would be made of silk, and fresh cut flowers in expensive vases would freshen his room. Life would finally be worth living.

Suddenly, another vision slipped into view. He couldn't fight the image. David could clearly see Cally smiling warmly at him and asking how he felt. He closed his eyes, hoping she would disappear, but her face was etched into his mind. Damn, why does she have to be so beautiful? As much as he wanted the mission to be a success, he wanted Cally to be absent tomorrow even more. He'd fought the feelings he had for Cally for some time now. David didn't think it was love he felt, but he admired her and respected her as a person. She was a bright, beautiful, and popular girl who didn't think she was better than other people. Cally was for real and not a fake bimbo like the other girls in the school.

David knew he'd go through with the mission, regardless of anything, but he truly hoped Cally wasn't there to witness any of it. He normally wouldn't wish sickness on her except for this one time. He hoped she was so ill that she couldn't get out of bed tomorrow.

David shook his head—he was trying his best not to think of Cally. He was feeling terribly crummy inside—he felt like he was dishonoring Professor Slate by having these feelings. She was supposed to be the enemy after all.

David sat silently. Finally, after several moments he accepted the fact that he had to hate Cally to succeed in this mission. He couldn't have even one more enjoyable thought about her, or it would only cause him pain in the end. He rested his elbows on his knees and leaned his forehead down on his doubled-up fists.

He made a silent pact that he would toss all feelings of Cally out of his head and heart. He would feel nothing for her ever again.

He somehow convinced himself that he didn't care what happened to Cally if she showed up at school tomorrow. He wouldn't let her get in the way of the most important challenge he ever had to complete.

He straightened as calmness settled through his body. He realized he'd just overcome the emotions he'd been struggling with. He felt an unknown power that he'd never experienced before. He suddenly felt stronger, and he had no doubt about his obligation to the mission. David knew he would show no mercy toward anyone.

***

Cally flipped through the channels on the TV and settled for a rerun of the Brady Bunch. She set the timer for the TV to go off at 10:00 p.m. It was already after nine, and she wanted to go to sleep early. She'd felt so good all day that she'd done more than she should have, and now she was pooped.

She propped the pillows so she could see the TV and crawled under the covers. She never had a problem drifting off to sleep while the TV was playing and assumed tonight wouldn't be any different. She tucked the end of the covers under her feet and pulled the blanket up under her chin.

Cally's mother had told her she could go back to school tomorrow. She'd finished all of the homework that Beth brought over earlier. Jessie had come with Beth, and they'd visited for a couple of hours. They had discussed the weekend plans. Cally felt bad for Jessie because she didn't have a date. She wished Jessie could find a boyfriend. For some reason, she'd always had trouble getting dates. Jessie said she had to help her mom with a garage sale anyway and would probably be too tired to do anything on Saturday night.

Before Jessie and Beth left the girls had all agreed to do something together tomorrow night after Cally got off work.

Cally had just closed her eyes when the phone rang, sending her back to the present. She extended her arms above her head

179

and stretched. The phone rang again. She figured it was probably for her and climbed out of bed to answer it. "Hello."

"Cally? Were you busy?

She immediately recognized Brad's voice. "Hi. No, not at all."

"I just called to see how you were feeling?"

"Oh, I'm much better since I talked to you last night." Cally sat down at the desk. "I'm going back to school tomorrow."

"I'm glad to hear that. I've been worried about you."

"Thanks, but I'm fine now." Cally was impressed that he'd cared enough to call and check on her.

"Do you remember me asking you about Saturday night? I know you weren't feeling too good last night. You sounded kind of groggy."

"I didn't feel well, but I remember."

"Are we still on?"

"Sure."

"Great!" Brad hesitated as if he wasn't sure what to say next. "Have you talked to Beth or Jessie today?"

"Yeah, they were here earlier. Why?" Cally reached for a pen and drew a funny face on a note pad that was lying beside the phone.

"Did they happen to say if they were called into the office today about that fight last weekend?"

"You mean with David Clemons?" Cally scribbled through her drawing.

"Yes."

"Yeah, they were questioned, and Chief Brady stopped by earlier today to ask me questions about it, too."

"Well, for some reason they called me to the office, too. I have no clue how they got my name," Brad said.

"What did they ask you?" Cally started sketching a new face.

"The chief just wanted to know if I saw anything at the mall Saturday."

"What did you say?" Cally traced the pen around the eyes to add glasses to her funny face.

"I said I'd been at the mall, but I couldn't recall anything unusual happening."

Cally stopped doodling. "Why would you say that?"

"What do you mean?" Brad asked.

"Why would you say you didn't see anything after what that creep did to David?"

"I don't know—I just didn't think it was any of my business."

"But it was your business." Cally tightened her grip on the pen and scribbled heavy circles on the pad. "And mine. It was everyone's business that witnessed that horrible incident."

"Oh well, the kid's okay, isn't he?" Brad said flatly.

"Maybe this time he is, but what about next time? What if there's no one around to break up the fight next time."

"Cally, I'm sorry. I shouldn't have even brought it up."

"No, I'm glad you did. If Nate Meyers thinks he can get away with this, he's going to keep on beating up kids and possibly killing someone."

"I didn't think it was that big of deal."

"You didn't? Well, I do." Cally threw the pen down on the desk and stood.

Brad chuckled. "That's silly."

"Well, obviously Brad, we don't have much in common at all," Cally snapped.

"What do you mean by that?"

"I just think it is best that we cancel the plans for this weekend!"

"You can't be serious! You're going to let that little punk come between you and me?"

"He's not a punk. David happens to be a good friend of mine," Cally lied. She was so mad—she didn't care what he thought of her anymore. "I've got to go. I have things to do before I go to bed."

"Well, if this is the way you want it. I guess I'll see you around." Brad hung up the phone before she could reply.

Cally held the receiver in her hand for a few seconds before she realized Brad had just hung up on her. "You jerk." She screamed into the silent phone and then slammed it down into the cradle.

The reality of the conversation suddenly hit. Tears were rolling down her cheeks before she even realized it. She grabbed

181

some tissues off her desk and carried them over to her bed. She blew her nose and wiped her eyes before crawling back into bed. All of a sudden, she wasn't tired at all anymore. Cally laid her head down on the pillow and stared at the TV, not actually watching anything. She couldn't get the conversation with Brad out of her head. Everything had happened so fast.

Cally couldn't believe she'd liked such an unsympathetic guy. He'd seemed so kind at first. She wished she wouldn't have fallen for him so fast.

She knew Beth would be disappointed that they weren't going on the double date this weekend. Nevertheless, there was no way she could go out with Brad ever again.

She wiped her eyes with a tissue and thought about Jessie—she wouldn't have to spend her Saturday night alone after all. She thought about calling Beth but decided she wasn't really in the mood to talk to anyone. She would just wait until in the morning to tell her the latest scoop.

Cally's tears finally ceased after what seemed like hours. She tossed, turned, and finally drifted into a restless sleep.

CHAPTER SEVENTEEN

Friday, April 30, 2001

David rolled over on his side to glance at the alarm clock. Surprisingly, it read 7:15 a.m. He quickly leaped out of bed and squinted at the clock on the wall. Sure enough—it was 7:15 a.m. He'd set his alarm for 6:00 a.m. and it hadn't gone off. He checked his alarm to see if he'd turned it on and realized he'd set it for 6:00 p.m. This couldn't have happened at a worse time.

He speedily threw on the clothes that he'd laid out to wear. He was glad he'd already packed his bag. He dashed to the restroom, brushed his teeth, and ran a comb through his hair.

It was exactly 7:25 when he heard Josh knocking on the front door. He took one quick look around the room, grabbed his bag, and ran up the stairs—almost tripping on the last stair. He saw his lunch money lying on the table, scooped it up, and tucked it into his jean pocket, not realizing he wouldn't even need it. He wished his mother had woke him up before she'd left for work, but she seldom did that. Besides, she might have suspected something if she noticed how nervous he was.

David jerked the front door opened. "Good morning. Would you believe I overslept?"

Josh entered the living room. "Did you really?" He shook his head in disbelief. "Hey, we better take those pills now so we'll have some water."

"Oh yeah, I almost forgot. I'll be right back." David disappeared down the stairs and returned a few seconds later. "Here they are." He popped the cap off the bottle and handed Josh one of the pills.

David got them each a glass of water and they both popped a pill in their mouth. David placed the glasses in the sink. "You ready to go?"

"Yeah, I think so. I couldn't sleep last night," Josh said.

"I did. I fell right to sleep." David picked up his bag and followed Josh out the front door. "But I'm getting nervous now."

"I am, too. Maybe these pills will start working soon."

"I hope so. Do you understand everything we're supposed to do?"

"Yeah, I'm fired up and ready to rock and roll. I just have to try to remember there are only ten shots in each of those magazines. I'll have to fire skillfully and not get carried away just shooting the gun."

"Yeah, we'll have to be careful." David climbed anxiously into the car. He couldn't believe the day was actually here.

***

Josh pulled away from the curb. He was so excited he could hardly stand it. His mother had told him to come straight home after school to do his chores. He wanted to tell her to kiss his ass but had decided against it. He didn't want a big fight to break out and something happening to prevent him from going to school. He'd just shrugged his shoulders as he slammed the screen door. He was glad that he would never have to look at her face again.

"The professor said to try to save at least one shot in each gun just in case we need it for our escape. But it's going to be hard to keep track of the shots," David said.

"I know what you mean." Josh flipped the volume down on the radio.

"I'll meet you in the restroom right after first hour class. Don't forget your bag."

"I won't." Josh glanced at the image in the rearview mirror. He was satisfied with what he saw. He thought he looked exceptionally tough today. He'd taken extra time with his hair so it was tousled just right. He wanted to look bad as hell just in case someone snapped a picture.

David continued, "We'll each go into a separate stall—I'll go in the back one where the vent is."

Josh interrupted, "We'll only have a few minutes. We'll have to hurry."

"I know. I'm going to go in and loosen the screws as soon as we get to school."

"We should just throw on our bandannas, gloves, and shades as soon as we get into the stall." Josh glanced toward David and noticed his hands were trembling.

"Okay. You get in the stall right next to mine, and I'll pass your gun under the stall. I'll make sure I don't see any feet outside the stall before I do. And then stick the gun in your bag, and we will go out together. Everyone will be staring at us, so don't hesitate—go straight to the trophy case. It should only take a few seconds to get there. We'll stand back to back, and I will signal you with a thumb up sign and we'll drop the bags, pull out the guns, and start firing?"

"That sounds simple enough. But what if everyone has already gone to their classes?" Josh asked.

"That's why we're going to have to hurry. Be sure you take your bag to your first hour class, so you won't need to go to your locker."

Josh pulled into the school parking lot. "Boy, you did think this through." He hoped David would settle down some—he was trying to see too far into the mission instead of just going with the flow.

"Yes, I did my homework." David cocked his head sideways. "Well, any more questions before we go in?"

"No. I think you covered everything."

"Well, my friend, good luck." David extended his hand for Josh to shake.

Josh accepted his hand with a firm grip and shook it. "Good luck to you, too. We'll be together forever as soon as the mission is over."

185

"I better get going, so I can get to the restroom and loosen the screws. I'll see you shortly." David opened the car door and attempted to get out. He tried to stand but had to grasp the car door for support. "Whoa. I feel dizzy."

"Are you okay?"

"I think so. I'm just dizzy and feeling funny."

"I'm feeling a little funny myself," Josh rubbed the sweat off his forehead with the back of his hand. "Oh, I bet it's the pills because I'm a lot more relaxed than what I was earlier."

"Oh, yeah, I bet it is. I'm not as nervous as I was either." David giggled. "Well, I'll see you later." He sniggered again before closing the car door and heading inside the school.

Josh wasn't sure what David said that was so funny, but he had to laugh, too. He glanced one last time in the mirror and then he giggled aloud again for no reason. This time he couldn't seem to stop laughing. He glanced around to see if any of the other kids were watching him. He hoped the pill didn't make him laugh all through his first hour class.

Josh finally sobered up and crawled out of the car. He didn't feel dizzy but more like he was floating. He felt so peaceful—he would definitely have to get some more of these pills from the professor.

***

David had been sitting in Mrs. Denton's Speech class for only thirty minutes, but it seemed like hours. He had a hard time concentrating on anything except the way Mrs. Denton looked. The longer David stared at her, the more she reminded him of a donkey. He had to bite his lips several times to keep from laughing. She always wore her hair in a bun; with it pulled slicked back behind her ears. Her ears were gigantic, and she had a long protruding nose like a donkey.

Mrs. Denton turned to write on the chalkboard. David's immediate thought was how big her butt was, too—just like a jackass. He chuckled loud enough that the kid in front of him turned around and glared at him. David stuck his tongue out at

186

the boy and then giggled at his own gesture. The boy rolled his eyes before turning back toward the front of the room.

David had never felt this mellow before. He wasn't even the slightest bit nervous about the mission. He couldn't wait to blow some jock's head off. He thought it would be so cool to watch someone's head fall off their body. David laughed to himself as he imagined kids lying around without heads. Then he imagined police officers walking up and down the halls, trying to figure out what heads went to what bodies. David bit down hard on his lower lip, trying drastically not to laugh aloud. The pill that Professor Slate had given him was the best. He couldn't imagine anything more fun right now than killing people, especially all of the creeps in this classroom. If only he had his gun right now, he wouldn't hesitate to blow away anyone in the room. David could easily comprehend why people on drugs liked killing people. He wondered if he would remember anything about the day's events after the effects of the pill wore off. He sure hoped so.

The sound of the bell made David jump. He'd lost track of time. He looked toward the louder than usual ticking clock and realized he needed to hurry. He quickly gathered his book off the desk before realizing he would never need it again. He dropped it back on the desk. David grabbed his bag, pushed his way through the kids in the hall, and headed for the boy's restroom.

Josh had just entered the restroom as David approached the door. They both glanced secretively at each other. There was only one other kid, who was washing his hands. David and Josh quickly slipped into separate stalls.

David hurriedly tied the bandanna around his head, slipped on the gloves, and slid the sunglasses on. He looked under the stall to see if he saw any other feet. Luckily, the restroom was now empty. He pulled off the vent, grabbed the two guns and the magazines. David handed Josh a gun underneath the stall and one of the magazines. He quickly pushed his magazine into his own gun. He whispered loudly to Josh, "You ready? Let's go."

David pushed open the stall door—Josh was right at his heels. One boy was coming in the restroom as they were going out the door. The boy stared for a brief second, shrugged, and hurried into a stall.

187

David ignored all the stares in the hallway as they advanced the trophy case. His mind was at ease, and he felt nothing but power. He still felt a little dizzy but in complete control. There was no way he was going to screw up this shooting. He turned sideways so Josh could see his thumb up sign.

They both rapidly pulled out their guns and dropped their bags to the floor.

The hallways were still full of students, rushing to their next class. A few of the kids had stopped to stare at Josh and David. But David was sure that none of them were prepared for what was about to happen.

The first shot came from David's gun, and it hit a guy right in the center of his back. He instantly fell to the floor, blood spilling from the wound. Josh fired next, hitting a guy in the arm. The guy screamed in pain, grabbed his wounded arm, and continued to run down the hall.

The remaining kids in the halls suddenly panicked. David could hear screams and hollering from every direction. Most of them dropped their books and broke into a run. The girl who'd seen her boyfriend shot in the back fell beside him, crying frantically.

Josh and David simultaneously shot again. This time David found the creep he'd been looking for. He'd seen Nate starting to run, and David shot him right in the chest. He started to shoot him again but decided not to waste two shots on him. Nate's blood spilled down the front of his shirt as he fell against the wall. He slapped both his hands up against the wall as he tried to keep himself balanced. Nate gradually slid down, the side of his face smashing against the wall, and David noticed his eyes were rolled up in his head.

David spun around just as a lady teacher came sprinting toward him, aiming to pounce on him. He jumped backwards and fired a shot. He knew her as the gym teacher and cheerleading coach, Patsy Allen. She instantly fell to the floor. David quickly removed his sunglasses as blood splattered on them. He looked down at the blood spilled around his feet. Patsy Allen had tried to be a hero, and now she was dead, David thought with amusement.

188

He turned just as Josh shot two more guys; one in the chest and the other guy in the leg.

David's eyes darted back to his prized possession, Nate Meyers. His body had crumbled to the ground. Nate's chest became incredibly still as he took his last breath.

David heard a muffled scream and turned to see Josh shooting a girl in the stomach. She doubled over and fell to the floor, blood gushing out of her mouth. David immediately recognized her as Jessie, the girl that hung around with Cally. She'd been with Cally the day they'd driven him to the hospital.

The more blood David witnessed, the more ferocious he became. He was sure the professor hadn't given them enough ammunition for the damage he would like to do. David shot again toward a guy running toward the girl's restroom. He barely missed him, and the boy made it through the restroom door safely. "You bastard," David swore under his breath. He was pissed for missing the kid and wasting a shot.

David saw Brad Taylor, frantically, trying to push his way through the panic-stricken kids to the side exit. Brad's eyes darted wildly toward David. Their eyes locked, and David saw a look of terror.

David hesitated long enough to witness Brad's fear and then he fired the shot. He'd been aiming for the center of his chest, but Brad had sensed the shot coming and had jumped at the last second. David hit him in the shoulder. Brad squealed in pain before grabbing his shoulder and falling forward on his knees. David knew he'd injured him but didn't think he would die.

David's mind raced back to that evening Brad had almost run over him with his car and the way he'd yelled at him. He remembered most of all, though, the beautiful girl standing beside the loser. Although David didn't want to waste another shot on him, he didn't want him to live either. He fired again— this time hitting him square in the chest. Blood splattered all over Brad's face, and he immediately fell forward onto the floor with a heavy thud.

David witnessed teachers holding the classroom doors open and screaming at the students to hurry in. He could hear sirens coming from a distance and was well aware they would have to hurry if they wanted to escape.

Out of the corner of his eye, he saw Josh fire a shot at a teacher, who was trying to help some of the students out the door. The shot hit the teacher in the back of the head. The man fell straight forward onto a girl, knocking her down. The girl was screaming and trying to push the body off her.

David realized he hadn't shot any girl students just the lady teacher. He didn't want Josh to tease him later for not shooting a girl. He swiftly scanned the crowd until he caught sight of the back of a redhead girl. She was holding onto a guy's hand while running down the hall. David didn't hesitate—he fired a shot. It hit the girl in the back of the leg. The girl grabbed her leg, moaning in pain. David then aimed the pistol at the guy's back and pulled the trigger. The girl jerked around to find her boyfriend, who had immediately collapsed to the floor. She abruptly fell to the side of him, screaming hysterically.

David recognized her at once—it was Cally's other friend. He thought he'd heard Cally call her Beth. He wouldn't have chosen to shoot her if he'd known it was her. David didn't feel any remorse but probably would have selected someone else that he didn't recognize as one of Cally's friends.

David momentarily thought about the two he'd just shot and then eagerly turned his gun toward another terrified guy. He aimed his gun to fire—but suddenly froze. He didn't know where she'd come from, but Cally was standing near the redhead girl, with a look of horror and disbelief on her face. Her eyes met David's—her mouth dropped open as if she was about to scream. However, she didn't—it was as if she was frozen. David's heart pounded loudly as he tried to swallow; he could only stare at her.

The sirens in the distance grew closer, but his only thought was how beautiful Cally looked. He regretted she'd come to school and witnessed this bloody massacre. David glanced toward her redhead friend, who was frantically screaming while hovering over the dead boy. He looked back at Cally's face—tears were streaming down her cheeks. She continued to stare at David helplessly, refusing to move. David wanted so badly to tell her to run and get out of the school. He also wanted to tell her how sorry he truly was. Since the moment he'd begun the mission he'd felt nothing but power until now. He was torn between the power, and the pain he felt for Cally.

David knew the mission's rule was to feel no mercy toward anyone, but he couldn't help the way he felt about Cally. Drugs may make a person's mind think oddly, but they couldn't change the way he felt about her.

***

Josh had fired two more shots and hadn't heard David's gun for a couple of minutes. He was half scared to turn around in fear David might not be behind him.

He quickly glanced over his shoulder and followed David's gaze toward the blond girl who had taken him to the hospital. He stared at David. Josh suddenly went numb—he instantly sensed that David had feelings for the girl. "Damn!" He should have cued in on all the clues David had left.

Josh's main concern about the success of the mission was that something like this would cause David to bail out on him. He knew he had to act fast. "David, shoot the bitch. Remember, no mercy."

David didn't respond—his gaze didn't falter.

"David, remember you're a member of the Hidden Undertakers—make the professor proud of you."

Still there was no response from David. His eyes were glued on Cally. Josh glanced from David to Cally. He assumed she was in shock because she remained stationary.

It sounded like the sirens were now right outside the school. Most of the kids had cleared the hallways with the exception of a few of the slower moving students still running for cover. Josh screamed at David, "Kill her! We've got to go. The professor is waiting for us!"

Josh knew he could easily waste her, but he knew David had to do it. If he did it himself, he would feel obligated to tell the professor the truth that David had bailed out on him. Josh loved David as a brother, but he needed the professor more. And in his warped life, love didn't mean anything anyway. The professor

191

was his leader, and he wasn't going to do anything to disappoint him. Even if he had to turn against David, his obligation was to the mission and the professor first.

**

David's heart suddenly filled with compassion for Cally—he could never hate her. He wasn't sure if the pill was making him feel this way, or if he'd always felt this way and just didn't want to admit it. Tears oozed down his cheeks as he realized he had failed the mission. He couldn't go through with it—he could never shoot Cally.

David wondered what would happen to him now. The professor would never want him, Josh would never forgive him, and Cally would hate him forever. He had so much wanted to be important to someone, and again, he'd been a major disappointment to everyone. David wished he'd never been born and then maybe he wouldn't have screwed up everyone's life.

"David, we've got to go! Kill her or I will," Josh yelled.

David realized the next few seconds were critical. He had to make a fast decision that would impact the rest of his life. From the top of his lungs, he screamed, "Cally, I'm sorry! Run! Get out of here!" David immediately twisted around to face Josh. "I'm so sorry, Scooby. Please, don't hurt her!" David suddenly pointed his gun to his own head and pulled the trigger.

**

Josh watched in horror as David's blood splattered across the trophy case as his body hit the floor. He'd tried to scream for David to stop, but he'd pulled the trigger too fast.

Josh fought the tears that were stinging behind his eyelids. He'd just witnessed his best friend killing himself because of the enemy. He felt pain for losing David, but mostly he was angry with David for screwing up the mission. He could hear the police shouting on megaphones for him to come out with his hands up.

192

Josh assumed Slug had already left—he wouldn't have stuck around this long. He tried to swallow, but his throat was too dry. Josh knew he'd never escape now.

He instantly thought of Professor Slate, realizing how disappointed he'd be. Now Josh knew he'd never amount to anything and would have to stay with his horrible mother, or even worse—jail for the rest his life.

Josh looked down at his best friend's sprawling body, lying in a pool of blood. He looked toward the blond girl who was screaming hysterically. Josh was getting angrier by the second. She was the reason the mission had failed. She was the reason David had killed himself. "Why did you have to screw everything up," he shouted at her. All he wanted was to make this girl pay for destroying his last hope!

***

In the last few minutes, Cally had witnessed more bloodshed than she'd ever seen in her life. She'd gone to the restroom right after her first hour class and was searching through her purse as she exited, when suddenly, there was chaos everywhere. At first she thought maybe they were having a fire drill. But abruptly, screaming students ran into her, knocking her to the floor. It was from that position she witnessed Brad being shot twice. Still confused, she'd pulled her body up against the wall, keeping flat on her stomach while praying the students wouldn't trample over her.

A couple of times she tried to stand only to see someone else being shot down. The reality of what was taking place terrified her. She remained on the floor, thinking she'd be safer than trying to run. She'd considered crawling but didn't want to bring any sort of attention to herself. She hadn't seen who was doing the shooting or how many there were.

Cally saw Beth and Mark running down the hall and decided to catch up with them. She'd just stood when Beth was shot in the leg and Mark in the back. Cally gasped and flattened her back against the wall. She couldn't believe this was happening in her own school. She'd wanted desperately to run and help Beth,

193

but her own fear had stopped her. She couldn't imagine anyone in the world wanting to hurt Beth—she was the friendliest person in the school.

Cally feared if she moved she too would be shot. She remained plastered to the wall as kids rushed by her in terror. She wanted to see where the shooters were standing before she tried to escape. She finally got up enough courage to cautiously curve her body in the direction the shots had come. She was scared to make any sudden movements in fear she would also be shot. She glanced toward Beth who was cradling over Mark and crying uncontrollably. She noticed the huge gash in Beth's leg, and the blood that was gushing out. She wanted to scream for Beth to run, but again, her own fear silenced her.

Cally slowly lifted her head up toward the shooters and what she saw numbed her! It was David holding the gun. The guy she'd helped, the guy she'd felt sorry for, and the guy she'd defended when no one else had. He'd purposely shot her friends, Beth, Mark, Brad, and many other innocent students. Out of the corner of her eye she saw a body lying near David's feet—she glanced down and saw Patsy, her cheerleading sponsor, covered in blood. She instantly shifted her gaze and covered her mouth, trying not to puke. The other shooter had sunglasses on, but Cally still recognized him—it was David's friend, Josh.

David pointed the gun toward a guy who had stumbled to the ground. Cally wanted to scream at David but nothing escaped from her dry lips.

Suddenly, his eyes were on her.

Her legs grew limp as her heart raced—it was as if he were staring right through her. She knew she should turn and run, but she couldn't move a muscle.

She held her breath—she was certain that any moment he'd turn the gun on her and shoot.

However, he just stood there, motionless, staring at her.

Cally's face remained solemn except for the tears escaping down her cheeks. She knew she was going to die at any moment, but she remained stationary. Her head was spinning. In the whirl of panic, Cally heard Josh's voice yelling at David to shoot her.

194

And just when Cally thought David was going to aim the gun at her, he unexpectedly screamed for her to run. She was stunned, but even more so, when David turned to his friend to say he was sorry and then turned the gun to his own head and pulled the trigger.

Cally freaked—she screamed at the top of her lungs as blood gushed out of David's head. His body hit the floor with a solid thud. As much as she wanted to turn her head away from the bloody scene, all she could do was scream and stare at David's blood-covered body on the floor.

The shock finally ceased as Cally slowly looked up to meet Josh's eyes. Her screaming suddenly stopped as she saw the rage in his eyes. She cringed and took a step backwards. She knew he was going to kill her any second.

He pointed the pistol toward her. "You bitch. This is your fault. You've ruined everything."

Fear engulfed Cally in a way she'd never experience before. She always wondered what people thought about right before they died. Her immediate thought was of her parents and of her little brother. She could imagine how broken hearted they would be without her. Her stomach knotted as her body trembled—she couldn't imagine leaving her family.

Josh slowly marched toward Cally. "Now, it's your turn."

Cally glanced toward the spot where Beth had been and noticed that she'd pulled herself away from Mark and was dragging her body toward the end of the hall.

Cally winced as Josh took another step toward her. She didn't want to die! Suddenly, he stopped, as someone outside warned him to come out. Cally glanced nervously around the halls. She had to find a way to get away from him—fast!

Josh glanced toward the doors where the loud speaker voice had come.

Cally didn't dither—she immediately dove into the boy's restroom. A shot rang out just as she reached inside the doorway. He'd just missed her head. She ran to the back stall and squeezed in the corner beside the stool. She squatted down as low as she could and bit down on her lower lip, hoping to keep her teeth from chattering.

She listened frantically as Josh's footsteps entered the restroom. She couldn't control her shallow breathing or the small sobs escaping from her throat. She knew it was only a matter of seconds before her life would be over. She saw Josh's feet approaching outside of the stall. She sucked in her breath and held it.

Josh swung the stall door open with such force it startled her; she screamed fiercely with all her might. She covered her face and sobbed hysterically, "Please don't kill me!"

"You're the reason the mission failed—you're the reason David is dead. You teased him and pretended that you liked him." Josh aimed the gun at Cally's head. "And now I'm going to make you pay."

"I did like David," Cally uttered in between tearful sobs. Please God, hurry, let this be over with—please don't let me suffer, she prayed silently.

***

"Drop the gun, Josh," Chief Brady's voice boomed like thunder as he entered the restroom and pointed his pistol toward Josh.

Josh, startled, glanced toward the Chief. He hadn't heard him come in. "Shit," he mumbled. He glanced back toward Cally, keeping the gun aimed at her head. "You better leave, or I'll kill her."

"No you won't, son," Chief Brady roared. "I can shoot a hell of a lot better than you, and I am going to hit you right between the eyes before a shot is ever fired from your gun."

Josh's mind raced—he wasn't sure if the Chief was bluffing or not. He looked toward Cally—her sobs were increasing. He couldn't believe what a mess this had turned into. All he'd wanted was a new chance at a different life. He had wanted desperately to be a part of the professor's team. Now it would never happen.

"Throw your gun on the ground, Josh," Chief Brady ordered.

Josh glanced one last time toward Cally. As much as he wanted her dead, he wasn't quite ready to die himself. He hesitated a few seconds longer before throwing his gun on the floor and holding up his hands.

Chief Brady motioned to the policemen positioned outside the restroom. The chief quickly approached Josh, pushing him up against the wall while snatching the gun off the floor. The other policemen handcuffed him and took him out to the patrol car.

Josh scanned the hysterical crowd as he was pushed into the back seat of the patrol car. He hadn't seen Slug anywhere and hadn't really expected to. Too much time had elapsed, and Slug was probably long gone. Josh felt no remorse for what he'd done only sadness because he'd disappointed the professor.

***

Chief Brady helped Cally out of the corner of the stall. Her eyes were swollen and tears streaked her face. "It's going to be all right. You're okay now," he assured her.

Cally clung to the chief. "He was going to kill me!"

"You're safe now. Come on, your family is waiting outside." Chief Brady wrapped his arm around Cally's shoulder and guided her though the opposite end of the school, so she wouldn't have to pass any more bodies. He was certain she'd just experienced the worst nightmare in her life.

He released Cally to her parents and the doctor standing by.

He glanced awkwardly around at the other distraught parents and students. Some parents were hugging their teenager, while others mourned for the loss of their son or daughter. T.V reporters were scattered, trying to get comments from the students. The chief was fortunate that his own daughter hadn't been harmed. She'd been at the opposite end of the building and had gotten out safely.

The chief flicked a single tear off his cheek and cleared his throat. He couldn't believe the brutal hostility that had taken place today. He'd heard of school shootings in other towns, but he never imagined that it would happen here.

He glanced toward the patrol car that was transporting Josh and wondered what could have possessed the two youngsters to act so violently. He shook his head in disbelief. He stared at David's mom, who was crying hysterically and trying to slide closer to the stretcher that was carrying her lifeless son.

Chief Brady wondered why David had turned the gun on himself. He realized it was going to take this town a long time to get over this horrible crime. He didn't have the answers to the day's events, but he was determined to find out one way or another.

CHAPTER EIGHTEEN

"Mom, I just want to go home." Cally's parents wanted her to go to the hospital for a thorough examination. "I'm fine." She reached for the door handle on her car. She was devastated—she'd just been told that Jessie had been killed and that Beth had been transferred to the hospital.

"I'll drive your car home, sweetie, and you ride with your mother," Bob volunteered.

"No, really—I just want to be alone. I'll meet you at home." Cally noticed the crowd was thinning down except for the police officers.

"Are you sure you're okay?" Mary ran her hand over the top of Cally's head.

"I'm ready to go, too. Just leave her," Corey grunted. He walked toward his dad's vehicle.

"I'm fine. I just want to get away from this place." Cally grabbed her jacket out of the back seat and slipped it on. She climbed behind the steering wheel. "I'll be home shortly."

Cally pulled the door shut before her parents could protest. She knew they were concerned, but she desperately needed to get away from all the horrible memories.

As soon as she pulled out of the parking lot, the tears started again. She couldn't believe that Jessie and Brad were dead. Cally hit the steering wheel with her fist. "Damn, why did this have to happen?"

She was still shocked that she wasn't also on the deceased list. Josh had been so close to pulling the trigger. She could still feel his warm breath against her face as he screamed he was going to kill her through his clinched teeth, and she could still visualize the rod of the gun just inches from her head. That was the closest she'd ever been to death, and it was the worst thing she'd ever experienced in her life. She had never been so frightened.

But now the fear was subsiding and the anger was settling in. How could they kill sweet Jessie? She'd grown up with Jessie. She'd been her long life friend for as long as Cally could remember. Cherished memories filled Cally's head—she recalled all of the slumber parties at Jessie's house, the birthday parties at the City Park, the time they went to Girl Scout camp together, and all the summers at the swimming pool.

Cally sobs increased, and she slowed the car. She pulled over to the side of the road and reached for a Kleenex in the glove compartment—empty. "Damn it! Where are they?" She slammed the compartment door and wiped at her nose with her jacket sleeve.

She folded her arms across her steering wheel and bowed her head. She bawled as the earlier episodes crept back in her mind. She couldn't seem to shake the inexcusable images. She kept going over every detail and every word that was said. She was dumbfounded! She couldn't believe that David and Josh could do such a thing.

Cally reached for her purse and rummaged through it, searching for a tissue. Not finding any, she stuck her hand in her jacket pocket—she stiffened as she touched the cold medal. She'd totally forgotten about the gold medal. She slowly pulled it out of her pocket and stared at the words 'Hidden Undertakers'. She remembered Josh shouting something about the Hidden Undertakers. What was it? He'd been shouting at David about something. Then it hit her—Josh had told David that as a member of the Hidden Undertakers he had to shoot her.

Cally traced her finger over the letters on the medal as the pieces started fitting together. "Oh my God, that vile man must know something," she said aloud.

200

She'd thought David and Josh were into drugs with her neighbor, but now she was certain it had something to do with the medal. She was sure that the creepy neighbor had to be involved in the shootings somehow or at least know more about it. After all, the package that the boys had picked up from the trashcan was from Charlie Hains. It had to be. Because the day before, when the boys had dropped the large envelope into the trashcan, and the scrawny guy had picked it up, he'd stuck it into Charlie's mailbox. She was certain they all had to be connected somehow.

Cally slipped the shiny medal back in her pocket, shifted the gear in drive, and pulled away from the curb. And to think, no one believed me when I said the man was crazy, she thought.

She'd been furious with David and Josh, and now she was equally enraged at this Charlie creep. She'd known from the very beginning something was peculiar about the man, and it wasn't just his looks either. She had known that he couldn't be trusted.

Cally turned down her street. She scanned the front lawn of Charlie's house, searching for a sign of him. She slowly approached the front of his house. Suddenly, she knew what she had to do. She whirled the car into the driveway, slamming on the brakes. Her best friend was dead, and she wanted answers.

Cally didn't bother to turn the ignition off. She slammed the gear in park, jumped out of the car, and stormed up to the front door. She pushed the doorbell several times and waited. After a few minutes and no response, she strolled around to the side of the house. She proceeded to the back yard, prepared to confront the strange man. The yard was large; two oak trees stood on each side of a newly plowed garden spot. The lawn mower was sitting toward the back of the yard as though it had recently been used. But it didn't look like any of the lawn had been mowed. She glanced toward the screened-in back porch but still didn't see a sign of him.

She jogged back to the front of the house and peeped through the garage door window. It was completely empty with the exception of a few rakes and shovels leaning against the wall. She figured he'd gone somewhere in his car.

She glanced uneasily around at her surroundings and then kicked the garage with her foot, swearing under her breath. She instantly regretted it—she was sure she'd jammed her big toe. She wished she wasn't always so quick-tempered. Her dad always said that was why Corey and her fought so much. He used to tell her to just walk away from him when he teased her. But she never could—she always had to blow up.

Cally limped back up to the front door and rang the doorbell again. She pulled the screen opened to beat on the wooden door. But just as she hit the door with her fist, the door eased slowly opened. He must not have got it shut all the way, she thought. She leaned forward and peered into the long hallway. "Hello," she called out.

The urge to go inside was so tempting. She didn't think twice about it. She quickly glanced up and down the street before slipping through the door and shutting it softly behind her. "Anyone here?" She paused as the eerie silence surrounded her.

Cally was sure he wasn't home. She just wanted to take a quick look around before she called the police. She wanted to be sure her intuition was right before she contacted Chief Brady. The chief would want details, and right now, all she had to go by was a gold medal and her gut feeling.

She tiptoed softly into the front room while chewing nervously on her bottom lip. She scanned the cluttered room, searching for some kind of proof of Charlie's involvement. The couch and loveseat was the only thing that didn't have papers or books scattered across them. There were stacks of newspapers on the coffee table and end table. She quickly flipped through them. Not finding anything of interest, she moved on toward the computer desk.

She hesitated—the poster on the wall caught her attention. It was a group of college kids coming out of a university. There were pinholes all through the picture. A red blotch was in the center of one of the girl's forehead with a big pinhole in the middle of it. Cally couldn't seem to pull her eyes away from the poster. It was disturbing somehow, and she didn't know why. She edged closer to the picture and immediately noticed that the red blotch was not part of the picture—someone had added it on. What a sick man!

She turned her attention back toward the desk full of papers. She hurriedly sorted through the loose pages and spotted some snapshots—the first few were of a young dark hair girl holding a black poodle. Cally didn't recognize her. She moved on to the next ones which were David and Josh's school pictures. Her perception of this man was growing stronger every second. She hurriedly flipped to the next picture. Her jaw dropped as she stared in disbelief at the photo. It was herself—at the park—leaning forward to pick up the gold medal. "Oh my God!" she mumbled.

Suddenly fear paralyzed Cally as her eyes darted madly around the room. She leaned forward and listened—making sure she didn't hear any unusual noises. The terror she'd felt earlier while in the restroom with Josh was returning. Her head was full of disturbing questions. What was she thinking coming into this weirdo's house by herself? What if he walked through the front door right now? She crammed her hand in her jacket pocket, her trembling fingers clasping around the gold piece. She knew she needed to get out of there fast—something didn't feel right.

She glanced toward the front door as she debated whether to go to the police station. But the situation seemed too urgent, and she felt the need to tell someone immediately. She caught sight of the phone on the end table and clumsily reached for it, knocking it off onto the floor. She nervously fumbled with the long cord, trying to pull it up. Finally, shifting the mouthpiece up to her mouth, she quickly dialed 911 while keeping her eyes fixed on the front door.

Suddenly, the cord jerked out of her hand and the phone flew to the ground. She spun around and screamed as she came face to face with the dreadful man.

"Breaking into someone's house is against the law, young lady." Charlie inched slowly toward Cally.

She took a step backwards. "The door was open—I was just looking for something," she said with a quivering voice. She thrust her hand into her pocket and pulled out the gold medal. "I was looking for the owner of this. I thought you lost it." She dropped the gold medal on the end table and took another step backwards as Charlie took another step toward her. "I didn't mean to intrude. I'll be going now." Cally quickly spun around and dashed toward the door.

But Charlie was too quick. He grabbed her by the arm and slammed her up against the wall. "Where do you think you're running off to?"

The back of Cally's head throbbed. "Please let me go."

He pinned her arms up against the wall, pressing his weight against her. She struggled to get free, but his hold was too tight. His face was inches from hers. She could see the crazed look in his piercing eyes, and the mixture of alcohol and body odor made her nauseous.

He suddenly released her arms and slid his hands around her neck. She felt his grip tightening, and she tugged wildly on his arms—but he was too strong. She gasped for air as he squeezed her throat tighter. Her eyes locked with his—he was smiling. She swung at his chest but that only provoked him to compress more.

Cally knew he was going to kill her. She tried to suck in air—nothing. She glanced wildly around the room as she searched for something to hit him with. Black dots were slowly forming in front of her eyes—she needed air—she gasped again. Her head was spinning.

With all her strength, she flung her knee up between his legs. Charlie grunted and fell to the floor moaning. Cally wheezed and coughed as she sucked the needed air into her lungs.

All of a sudden, his hand was wrapped around her ankle as he tried to pull her down to the floor. She screamed and kicked like mad until she pulled her foot out of his hold. She ran toward the front door, stumbling over the phone cord and falling down on her hands and knees. She glanced back—he was coming toward her. She didn't think she could make it to the front door. She quickly jumped to her feet and dived toward the door, yanking the coat rack down behind her. She heard Charlie cursing as he tripped over it. Her heart raced and her hand shook as she pulled on the doorknob. She was too frightened to even look to see if he was behind her. The door flew open, and she ran outside screaming.

204

The sirens were already sounding as patrol cars pulled up in front of the house.

She fell to her hands and knees and sobbed uncontrollably as officers ran to her. "He tried to kill me!" She gasped, pointing toward the front door.

The officers ran inside the house as the chief assisted Cally.

"Are you okay, Cally?" Chief Brady reached down and pulled Cally to a standing position.

"I think so." She buried her head into the chief's shoulder and sobbed.

"We got a 911 call from this address, but we were disconnected. I knew you lived on this street. What happened?" Chief Brady stared toward the front of the house.

Cally glared at Charlie as the policemen brought him out of the house in handcuffs. She shivered as his protruding eyes met hers. Oh my God, he's still smiling. She shifted her eyes toward the ground so she wouldn't have to look at him.

She spun toward the chief. "He was involved in the school shooting. He knew that I knew about him, and he tried to kill me." She glanced up just as the officer was pushing Charlie into the back seat of the patrol car.

"Are you sure?" Chief Brady asked with raised eyebrows.

"I'm sure." She accepted the handkerchief the chief handed her and dabbed at her eyes. She saw her parents climbing out of their car and rushing toward her. "May I go home now?"

"I know this has been an awful experience for you today, two horrifying incidences in one day are more than anyone should have to go through." Chief Brady wrapped his arm around Cally's shoulders. "However, we're going to need you down at the station. Go meet with your parents, while I do some searching inside. I'll meet you down at the station in about an hour."

"Sure." She turned back toward the patrol car as it was pulling off. Charlie was still staring at her with those bulging eyes. A wicked grin slowly spread across his face. He lifted his cuffed hands and pressed them flat against the window. In the center of his left palm was the gold medal—'Hidden Undertakers'.

205

CHAPTER NINETEEN

Five Years later- April 30, 2006

Cally placed the fresh cut flowers in the vase that was attached to Jessie's tombstone. She dabbed at her eyes gently with a tissue. She remembered how devastated she had been when she'd heard Jessie had been killed.

She kneeled down beside the grave and said a silent prayer. She let the tears slide freely down her cheeks.

Cally couldn't believe it had already been five years since the horrible shooting. She stood and listened to the wind blowing peacefully through the trees. The air still had a slight chill to it. She crossed her arms and hugged them tight against her body, being careful not to smash the remaining flowers she was holding. The graveyard was empty except for an elderly man near the entrance gate. He was bent over a newly dug grave, crying. Cally assumed he'd just buried his wife.

She strolled over to Brad's grave and stuck the remaining flowers in his vase. She had often, in the last five years, gone over their last conversation. She regretted terribly the fight they'd had the night before the shooting. Cally had no right to judge Brad's motivations. She wished she could take back everything she'd said that evening. She had defended David, and in return David and his friend had shot the people she'd cared about.

Cally blew her nose before kneeling to say a silent prayer for Brad. She stood and mumbled softly, "I'm so sorry, Brad."

She casually walked around the graveyard, visiting the different gravestones of the victims from the shooting. She'd been coming here every year on the date of the shooting for the last five years. This was the first year she'd come alone. Beth had always come with her in the past. However, this year Beth had to travel out of town for business reasons.

Cally was fortunate that Beth had lived. She'd had trouble with her leg at first but after a few surgeries—she was fine now. Beth had to see a counselor for awhile to help her cope with losing Mark and Jessie. She'd had a difficult time adjusting at first.

The whole town had suffered from the tragedies.

Cally slowly ventured over to David's grave. There was a newly decorated wreath with the word 'Son' inscribed in the center of it. She was sure Ann had come by earlier in the day and left it on the grave. Cally felt sorry for her—she'd lost her only child in a horrible, tragic way. The media wouldn't leave Ann alone after the shooting. She finally moved away to a small town over sixty miles away.

Cally never saw Ann again after the incident. She'd sent Cally an apologetic card right after the shooting. For a while, she'd kept contact with her through letters. Cally could tell by Ann's letters that she felt a lot of guilt for not spending more time with David. She'd blamed herself for David's involvement with Charles Hains.

Cally had spent many days sitting inside Chief Brady's office after the killing-spree. She had to repeatedly go over all the details of the shootings and the occurrences at Charlie's house.

Charlie, also known as Professor Slate on the Internet, received life in prison without parole. He was found guilty and was linked to five other school shootings. He apparently had started a group called the 'Hidden Undertakers.' He would brainwash young students to raid a school and shoot whoever they could.

Because of Josh's age, he only had to serve three years in a correctional facility for young boys. He ended up moving to

207

Wisconsin with his father after he got out. Cally had heard that he never would talk about that day to anyone. Even in court, Josh had refused to comment on why they'd done the crime, or why David had killed himself. He denied Professors Slate's involvement. The court ended up blaming Charlie for brainwashing Josh into doing the things he did.

Cally graduated from Shelby High School and continued her schooling at ISU, a nearby college. She got a degree in teaching and now taught high school Algebra at the very same school from which she graduated.

In her spare time, Cally managed a club for teenagers after school. She dedicated the club to Jessie, 'Friends and Fun'. Anyone is welcome to join. They kept the club running by donations and fund raising events. They mostly did social things where they could interact with each other such as bowling, skating, or making art projects when funds were low. Her objective was to keep students involved rather than staying at home alone. She also has professional people every once in a while come and talk to them about peer pressure and youth crime. Cally's main goal in life was to make certain that nothing like she experienced ever happened at Shelby High again.

She'd just recently in the past year moved out of her parents' home into her own little apartment. Her new family now consisted of two adorable kittens.

Cally still had nightmares of the horrible day, and she knew it would linger her in head for many years.

She'd survived the tribulation of the school shooting, but she'd never forget it. There wasn't a day that went by that she didn't think about that day.

The healing had been a slow process. She now takes each day of her life as a blessing.

208

CHAPTER TWENTY

Delta, Wisconsin, April 30, 2006

Chad patiently waited for Shawn outside the school in his run down 1986 Ford truck. The black paint was faded and there was a big dent in the side, but he was still proud of it. He'd worked all summer carrying out groceries at the local supermarket in order to buy the truck for five hundred dollars from his uncle.

Chad impatiently flipped through the radio stations as he waited. He couldn't understand why it took Shawn so long to get out to the truck after the last bell of the day.

Chad and Shawn had been best friends for a little over two months now. They were both sophomores at the Delta High School in Delta, Wisconsin.

He found a station he liked and drummed his thumbs on the steering wheel as he scanned the crowd of kids coming out the school exit. He finally spotted Shawn walking slowly behind some jocks. Chad noticed that the guys kept spinning around and making comments to Shawn, and then they would all laugh. But Chad couldn't hear what they were saying.

Shawn kept his head bowed until he was far away from the jocks. He finally lifted his head and waved at Chad. He broke into a jog across the parking lot. He opened the door and crawled inside. "Hey, sorry it took me so long."

Chad jerked the truck in drive and peeled out of the parking lot. "What do you do in there anyway that takes so long?"

"I was trying to wait until those damn preps left. But I think they wait for me on purpose."

Chad glanced over at Shawn and then back toward the road. The jocks had been picking on Shawn for a long time now. Shawn was a nice guy but because of his severe acne problem, the kids were always teasing him. Chad used to try to defend him. He'd even got in a few fights for him; but after a couple of bloody noses and a black eye, Chad realized they weren't going to stop taunting Shawn. Chad and Shawn both agreed it was easier just to ignore them.

Chad pulled up in front of his grandma's apartment. It wasn't much of a home, but he didn't complain. It was a small two bedroom, run-down dump, full of cockroaches. The landlord was always drunk and never available when you needed him.

Chad's parents had died a little over two years ago in a car accident, and he'd been living with his grandmother ever since. His grandma and his dad's brother were the only two living relatives he had left.

Chad's grandma was sitting in her rocking chair, knitting while watching a soap opera. She casually glanced away from the TV. "Hello, boys."

Chad bent over and kissed his grandma's cheek. "Hi, Grandma." He nodded his head toward the TV and grinned. "You know, Grandma, that junk isn't good for you."

"Don't you worry about me. You just go get some fresh baked cookies on the stove and leave me be." She smiled at the boys as they scurried into the kitchen.

Chad loved his grandma and feared she would die soon, leaving him all alone. She was over seventy years old and didn't get around too well anymore. She had to use a cane to walk and wasn't able to go out too often. She only went out to get groceries once a month when her check came—if she was feeling up to it. Sometimes she would make a list, and Chad would pick up the groceries after school.

Chad and Shawn both grabbed a handful of cookies and two sodas out of the refrigerator, and hurried into Chad's tiny room.

Chad stuffed a cookie in his mouth as he closed his bedroom door and threw his bag on the bed. "Do you want to eat dinner here?"

"I've eaten here every night this week. Your grandma can't afford to keep feeding me."

"She doesn't mind. Besides, I give her money for groceries when I get paid."

Shawn hesitated. "Well, if you really don't think she'll mind."

"Hey, maybe you can even stay all night." Chad figured Shawn's mom would probably be working anyway. His mother was a single mom that worked at a nightclub as a bartender and usually didn't get home until late. Shawn spent most of his evenings at Chad's house. Chad still had the computer, TV, and stereo that his mom and dad had bought him before they were killed.

"Sure! Mom won't care if I stay. I'll have to run home and get some clothes later." Shawn plopped down on the bed as his eyes wandered toward the computer. "Do you think he has emailed us back yet?"

"I hope so." Chad connected to the Internet.

"I hope he was satisfied with our report," Shawn added.

"Me, too! I hope he accepts us. That would be so awesome." Chad scanned his email. "There it is." He highlighted the email so Shawn could see what he was talking about.

"Hurry, open it," Shawn said impatiently.

"Okay. Keep your fingers cross." Chad opened the attachment to the email and the boys read silently.

Casper and Popeye,
You boys are marvelous! I was truly impressed with your report. I most definitely need you in my unique group.
You both have been accepted! You boys are now official members of the 'Hidden Followers'. You both should be very proud. I haven't been able to find anyone that I was this pleased with for quite some time now. You both seem exceptionally bright.
I've been saving a special assignment, and I think you two would be perfect for the job. It's a special operation that will

211

take a lot of commitment. If you succeed then you will move up the ladder to even bigger assignments. I will definitely give you both a big cash bonus when the operation is completed.

You boys don't realize how much you have made my day! I think one day you two will be the top two leaders in my group.

Go to my web page and click on the star on the page and type in the word 'operation', which will take you to a page of all the rules of my organization.

I'll write again tomorrow night to see if either of you have any questions. Both of you boys are going to be heroes when this operation is complete!

Your Friend,
Dr. Scooby

THE END